WORLD OF LOST SOULS

JASMINE SIDHU

WORLD OF LOST SOULS

JASMINE SIDHU

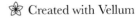

To my mom, who has always been my number one supporter.

1

I JUST MESSED UP.

That's all that runs through my head as I stare at the wall, at where my finger scanner was, waiting to be pricked—until it vanished into nothing. For the following seconds, I'm motionless, the same thought running through my head.

Somehow, I manage to feel the blood racing through my veins again. Running my fingers through my long, dark brown hair, I lean against the wall of my cell and exhale slowly. There's nothing I can do except wait.

Minutes pass while the others around me leave their rooms. A few screams deafen my ears. I assume they're from the ones who also forgot. But I'm used to the cries. What I'm not used to is the silence that comes after everyone else is gone, trapped in this metal box.

I swallow down a lump in my throat, trying to stay upright. My back aches from my stone bed, sharp pains slicing through my body like a knife. I wonder what they will do to me and to the many others who didn't give their blood.

My hands run down the steel walls, and I struggle to keep my eyes open as footsteps echo down the hall. I ignore the fire burning in my body, the urge to scratch my skin off, the temptation to end it all. I don't even know how I'm still going, how I'm still living my life like this.

"Three-nine-seven," someone says from outside my room. I think it's Gavril. He's usually the one who gets me. "Where is your blood sample?"

"I woke up late," I say.

"Speak up!"

"I slept in!" I say louder. "I didn't do it on purpose, I promise—"

"You know the punishment for ignoring the rules."

"But I didn't ignore them."

"It doesn't matter."

Of course, it doesn't. The demons create as many rules as possible, so they have a reason to torture us. I don't understand the point. Why not just torture us whenever they want?

My door opens, and I stare at the demon in front of me. It *is* Gavril. The corners of my lips twitch up. He's my favorite, but only because he fakes being nice.

His human vessel's strikingly blue eyes vanish as darkness pools inside them, the black horns growing from his blond hair are longer than I remember. My chest tightens, my teeth gritting together. He steps forward and he grabs me by the arms, shoving me outside. I try to hold my breath, but a gasp escapes my mouth.

I don't remember exactly what they did to me the last

time I was punished. That was when I first got here, around two years ago. When I was an idiot and thought by disobeying, I was making a difference. I wasn't afraid of them like everyone else was, but I learned quickly that I was doing nothing because I *am* nothing. That's what I tell myself every day to make myself stay in place.

"What are you going to do to me?" I ask. My legs are stiff while we walk down the hall. The lights flicker, on purpose, I assume, and the steel walls seem to close in on me. There are multiple doors on both sides, small pools of crimson in front of those who also forgot to give their blood today. I shudder. It doesn't matter how many times I walk down this hall, with or without my fellow inmates, it will always feel abandoned. And this is just one of the many female cell blocks.

"Nothing," he says, his grip tightening on my skin, fingers digging into my collarbone.

My heart stops. "What?"

"I figure when I need it, you can repay me in other ways. You are my favorite, you know." His words are the barest of whispers. As if he's telling me a secret that no one should ever know. "Even if you look like all the blood's been drained from your body."

My skin turns cold. I have to bite my tongue to prevent myself from saying something I'll regret. I would rather be tortured to death than help Gavril.

"What other ways?"

He sighs. "Don't make me say them, Three-nine-seven."

My eyes widen, and suddenly I don't even know what's happening. I kick his shin, step on his foot, scream at the top of my lungs—anything to get me in more trouble. I would rather take lashes or cuts than owe him a favor. He lets go of me for a second after pulling out some of my hair, but then he grabs my waist and lifts my small body.

He laughs. A warm laugh that makes it seem like we are friends. Hot breath against my skin, I shudder when a chilling whisper enters my ear.

"I know what you're trying to do. Save it."

My lungs ache. He puts me down and pulls my arms to my back. The rest of the walk blurs as he grabs my wrists to the point where I think the blood stops flowing to my hands. As we turn a familiar corner toward the outdoors, I realize that he's going to act as if nothing happened. And I'm right. Soon enough, we're passing steel doors which lead outside in the courtyard. The sun blinds me, my hands scrape against the pavement after Gavril pushes me forward.

A small cry escapes my mouth before I can stop myself. No one runs to help me. If they did, they'd die.

I get up, brushing at the brown rags I wear. The demons on watch glare at me with intense gazes, and I make sure I don't stare at any of them too long.

The courtyard is small, with demons circling around the inmates. Most people sit on the ground and socialize with people they've managed to get to know. But most of the time, they sit alone, frozen as they try to stay invisible.

"Mahi! Thank goodness you're alive," Laurel, my best friend, says once I approach the bench she's sitting on. "I thought you missed checking in, but others who did were let off today. My guts have been killing me while waiting for you. I thought—never mind what I thought."

"I accidentally stepped on a demon's toe," I lie.

"They pretended I assaulted them. It took me a while to get up after."

She gives me a reassuring smile, but I notice the water pooling in her eyes before a single tear strolls down her cheek. "It could've been worse, way worse."

It *is* worse. Now I can only wait until Gavril comes to claim what he wants. I try to make the frozen expression on my face vanish by looking up at the sun to warm my skin. I also take the time to sniff the dewy morning air.

"You're going to go blind," Laurel says. I give her a crooked smile. At least the demons haven't gone after her yet. I'm surprised they haven't. Her dark skin glows under the light, and her long black hair sits in a braid on her shoulder. Her baby hairs form small, frizzy curls that only make her stand out more. Somehow, she's managed to look healthy after all this time.

She and I grew up together. We *came* here together two years ago. I don't know what I'd do if I lost her.

"How was it? Sitting out here alone?" I ask.

She frowns. "I know we always talk about how we wished we got more than one hour, but I felt so alone without you here. And right at the beginning, someone walked out of line and bumped into a demon. They gave him two public lashings before taking him away. I've been shaking since. I really wanted to go back inside."

"I'd probably feel the same." I gaze at the fence that traps us here. The fence that separates us from the rest of the world. I would do anything to go back out there, even if the only thing I can see behind it is nothing but empty land covered in grass. I *know* there's more out there. My dad used to tell me all the time before I ended up in containment. And if he was lying, at least I know that my hidden home is outside that fence. I miss the place. Still, it's not like I could go back to the hideout Laurel and I lived in without risking everyone's life there. The demons might follow us.

Yet, the unknown must be better than what's here, in containment. Even if Lucifer owns it now.

"Damn," I whisper. A truck comes in from the second fence. "Looks like they got some new people."

"There'll be space for them since I'm going to be taken to The Lab next week."

I don't care about the truck anymore. A knot forms in my stomach. "What? Why you?"

She sighs slowly, leaning in toward me. "I don't know. They just told me today, so I can torture myself thinking about it. It'll probably give them more pain to feed on."

I breathe out heavily. Everyone had heard the rumors about The Lab, which is what the demons called it. Whenever someone went there, they never came back. I always assumed that they took the poor soul down to Hell and turned them into one of the many deformed demons that I'd heard roam the earth outside this place. I never worried because Laurel and I didn't mess up that badly. There was *always* someone who did something worse. But maybe no one had done anything in a while, and now the demons were desperate.

I shake my head and I look into Laurel's watering eyes, turning to stone as I think of her bones twisting into a soulless beast.

"They're kidding. Maybe they just want you to worry for no reason," I say, keeping my voice low.

"I don't doubt they'd do that," Laurel says with a

weak smile. "But you know they always go through with their punishments."

"But what did you do to get punished?" I raise my voice a little, looking around to see if I have gained anyone's attention. "I don't get why they chose you. You did nothing. You're the perfect prisoner."

"That's far from true." Laurel sniffs and continues, "we get away with some things because they like us. You know they don't punish without reason. I did something stupid yesterday."

"What?"

"I talked back," she whispers, her voice cracking as she wipes away a tear. I regret asking. "I-I just heard them saying things about how I'm nothing, and I'm used to it. But then I started thinking about home and how they don't have to do this and—why did I—I'm so stupid—"

"Calm down!" I say in a harsh whisper, placing my hand on her shoulder. I can't see people like this. I never know how to make them feel better. "They said in a week, right? Someone will probably mess up by then. Do something way worse than you. Then you won't be the one going."

Talking back isn't even a big deal. All those other times Laurel talked back, all she got were some lashings. I do it often, but maybe that's because Gavril lets me. A chill runs through my body.

Laurel looks at me with hurt eyes, a tear strolling down her cheek. The demons are probably enjoying this. "I know this is bad, but I really hope so. I just—oh, man. What if they cut me open? What if they inject me with some disease?"

Small gasps come from Laurel, drawing people's stares. Soon enough, some demon will start to feed on her pain, and she'll be drained for the rest of the day.

I rub her arm. "Remember when you lost your mom's dinner rations? And you thought she was going to kill you, but she didn't. Just like that, this will be okay. It's going to be okay," I tell her, although I don't believe the words coming out of my mouth. I wish I did. Because if they take Laurel, they'll be taking the last piece of my sanity away.

2

AFTER OUR TIME OUTSIDE, we're taken back to our rooms. The demons usually separate us into random groups for whatever they've planned. Although, sometimes, I've spent the entire day confined in my room.

After two years, though, I've kind of started to predict what I'm going to be doing for the day.

As expected, I stand in line in the cafeteria. My stomach backflips when I notice Laurel walking over to a table. It's been a while since we've been together for lunch. Simply her presence brings my tense shoulders down.

I look away quickly. The demons know we're friends, everyone does since we came here together, but I don't need to give them any reason to hurt us.

My stomach growls as the line moves. Once we get in, the food is served on the very opposite side of the room. Not everyone gets sent here since the room is so cramped. The heat is already starting to hit me, thanks to the number of people crowding the area.

It's as if we're inside an oven. I always wonder if the demons built this entire building out of steel, or if it was already here before Lucifer took the world nineteen years ago. There are five rows of silver tables, six in each, all bolted into the floor. Demons line the walls, but most of them talk to each other instead of keeping watch. Sometimes, I feel as though they are just as miserable as the rest of us.

I try to hide my smile when food finally plops onto my tray from the auto dispenser, turning only to come face to face with a demon. This one doesn't have horns or veins yet.

She grabs my jaw, and I quiver at the cold touch. "You're nothing but a flesh bag."

Nails dig into my skin, and I can't help the tears that form in my eyes. Luckily, I blink them away before the demon lets go of me. I almost drop my tray, yet somehow I regain my composure. Sitting across from Laurel at one of the many silver tables bolted into the floor, I give her a nod. She eyes the nail marks, but I shake my head. Frowning, she bites a piece of hard bread. It's best not to think about what happens and move on. That's the only way to survive.

Unlike the courtyard, the cafeteria is silent. No human talks to anyone. Like me, they try to eat up all that they can from their tray. I've never timed it, and they've never told us, but we need all the time we can get to finish.

And that's all I focus on, shoving my face with food like I'm a wild animal.

Eat.

Hurry!

The munching coming from around me stops when a tray slams into the floor. I flinch before dropping the mashed potatoes in my hand. For five seconds, there is piercing silence. No one breathes, no one moves. My stomach is rock hard when I turn around.

A girl stares at a giant demon, frozen in fear. Food layers his clothes. He's gigantic next to her, rubbing his large black horns while dark veins pulse from his grey face.

Say nothing. I bite my lip, mentally yelling at her as I watch her open her mouth.

"I-I'm sorry," she whimpers. "I didn't mean—I didn't see you and—"

"You didn't see me?" he asks casually, wiping at his white shirt. My chest starts to pain from my racing heartbeat. This isn't good. Something like this is never good.

"I—" She looks at all of us, her wide eyes pleading for help. "Please, please, I didn't—"

Her cries are cut off when he grabs her jaw, and I turn around before his fingers meet her eye. "You won't see now."

Demons love their sick sense of humor.

I stare straight ahead, everything starting to blur. I don't breathe. My hands turn into tight fists at the girl's screams, and I don't dare move another muscle. I've seen worse, but I'll never get used to it.

Blinking away tears, Laurel grabs my fist. Her lips are curved downwards, her eyes hiding her fear. She doesn't say anything. She can't. Not now. And even though my stomach growls, it takes me a few seconds before I bring food to my mouth. Maybe I can still finish three quarters if I stop my hand from shaking.

Just as I relax, everything gets worse.

Something large stomps into the room. Everyone stops eating once again, tensing in their seats. Laurel's hand shakes on top of mine, all the hairs rising on my body.

The warden.

I zone out, staring but not seeing. My heart skips a beat at his every step. At least I think it's a he. Unlike the other demons, who possess humans, the warden looks as if he came from a whole different world. He's at least eight feet tall, with giant claws and reptilian feet. White and black scales cover his body, and his broad shoulders make him look larger than he already is.

His long tongue slithers out as he strolls around. My legs tense when he looks at me with his tiny, blue eyes. His eyes shift to Laurel, and a grin spreads across his face. I look away. Those teeth could bite off my head if they wanted to.

I don't know what kind of demon the warden is. He's the only one I've seen that isn't like the others. He looks more like the demons I've heard about that roam outside containment—the ones I never want to see. Some people think he's one of the experiments from The Lab, only here to intimidate us. Others believe he's a higher-up demon from Hell.

The warden walks around the room, probably just patrolling to see what's going on. Maybe he sensed all the delicious fear radiating from everyone, but I can't move while he's in here. My dry tongue licks my chapped lips, my appetite gone.

A hand squeezes my shoulder. *No. No, please, no.*

My eyes widen, locking with Laurel's as her face pales. And then the slouching begins, and the dizziness increases. My limbs go limp. Tingles grow against the back of my neck as the hand disappears, and the warden drains my energy.

I blink, trying to refocus. He walks behind Laurel and does the same thing. He looks even bigger up close, and for a second, I'm grateful he fed on me. Because I would've been shitting my pants right now if he hadn't. That's probably the only good thing about being fed on. I'm not scared anymore. My mind almost feels completely empty.

But my forehead sweats, chills running through me. I squeeze my eyes shut just as the buzzer goes off, looking down at all the food I didn't eat. I yawn while my eyelids droop. I have to get up, but I'm so *tired*.

It's going to be one of those days.

3

GAVRIL HASN'T COME for me yet. I haven't seen him for three days. I find it harder to sleep at night as I anticipate the day he'll come. Will it be in the morning when everyone's outside? Or the middle of the night when everyone's asleep? I'll never know.

No one else has messed up bad enough to take Laurel's place. It's like they know the demons are searching for another test subject. I mean, I did worse than her. I should've been the one chosen, but Gavril messed that all up.

The sun is blazing today. It's mocking us. High in a cloudless sky, free from everything, while we remain in a cage. My dad told me the angels used to live up there, along with the sun, before the demons killed them all and won the war.

"I feel like they're shortening our time," I tell Laurel, leaning against the fence. She looks back at everyone, and I follow her gaze to an old man with his ears cut off. He's been here since before we came.

No one usually speaks to Laurel and me. Everyone keeps to their own business. One hour isn't enough time to socialize with everyone, but sometimes I want to ask the others how they ended up here.

"You're right," Laurel whispers. "Time is slipping from my fingers."

"Maybe someone else will go to The Lab and not you," I say quickly, my face heating up.

"You've been saying that for as long as I can remember! Nothing is going to stop them from taking me."

My eyes narrow, heart thumping. I scan the yard. I might lose a tongue for this. I might even end up taking Laurel's place.

I grab her wrist and force her up, heading straight for one of the demons. She's a redhead, standing by the steel doors of the building, and her skin is grey with long black horns on her forehead. I think she's about thirty years old, but that's the human vessel. Inside, who knows how ancient the demon is.

"What are you doing!" Laurel cries out.

Just act casual. "I'm fixing your problem," I say. My brain screams at me to back away, to go back and be invisible. Instead, I wave at the demon. "Hey! Have you seen Gavril?"

Her head slowly turns toward me, her eyes flashing black as her thin lips scowl.

"You might want to close your mouth before I sew it shut—"

"He said he needed a favor from me," I say, trying to hide my disgust. "I'm just wondering when he's going to come collect."

She studies me for what feels like hours. I can't help but look down. My cheeks burn, and I gulp when I face her again. Eventually, her lips press together in a thin line, a single finger beckoning me over. I let go of Laurel's wrist. The demon's going to hit me, or worse. I don't care. Laurel won't be the one experimented on.

I approach slowly, shivers traveling up my spine when the demon's lips come to my ear. "I admire your false bravery. You're not going to be able to save her," she says. My blood turns cold. "Gavril made you off-limits because he wants you in perfect condition. Or as perfect as you can get. But after he has his fun with you, I'm going to rip your throat out of your neck."

My legs can't move. She backs away, a small smirk on her face. She mouths a few words, but I have no idea what they are.

Slowly, I go back to Laurel. She's back in our original spot, by the fence, but I desperately need to sit on one of the overcrowded benches.

"Are you okay? What did she say?"

"She said I can't help you," I whisper. My eyes are glued to the pavement, my head throbbing, and my chest aching. I repeatedly flex my fingers and make fists, needing to control *something* in my life. "She said that there's nothing I can do."

Laurel places her hand on my wrist. I look up at her. "It's not your fault. It's just how things are."

Laurel is going to die.

My eyes begin to water. I don't want to give the demons a show, but I can't help it.

"Mahi, don't cry. It's going to be—jeez, now I sound like you. Just, don't worry—"

She's interrupted by the sound of yelling. Both our heads turn to watch what's going on. The courtyard is huge, but everyone begins to walk toward the middle.

I catch a glimpse of a pale, tall, middle-aged man with crazy wide eyes, shouting at a teenage boy half his size. Everyone else stares at them, not knowing what to do. Gulping, I glance at the demons who now have joy spread across their faces.

"I'm going to kill you," says the man as I walk closer, past the others who start to pretend nothing is happening. Sometimes, someone dangerous ends up here. Someone other than the demons who want to hurt us.

The boy straightens his back, but his face holds an expression of fear. Bruises paint his dark body, and he has no hair anywhere. "What did I do?" his voice croaks out like he hasn't spoken in days.

The man yells loudly, raising his hand and going in for a punch. The boy barely dodges the reoccurring jabs, having nowhere to run, until the man finally catches him. The boy covers his head, but the man grabs one of his hands, twisting it away and landing four hits on the boy's face. He screams in agony. My stomach flips, and my heart begins to stab at my chest as I watch the scene unfold.

As the crowd disperses, my heart races. The fight's over. The boy lost. But that's when the man meets my eyes. A gasp shoots out of my mouth when he runs toward me with what seems like super speed.

When he hits me, it doesn't hurt as much as I expected it to. What makes tears form in my eyes is the flesh from my bare arms scraping against the pavement. I lie there. My ears ring, and a groan runs past my lips.

"Hey!" My eyes shoot open.

No. Oh, hell no.

I sit up, my mouth forming a circle as Laurel shoves the man. He pushed me farther than I thought. They're at least a few feet away from me.

"Stop!" I cry out, but Laurel shoves him again. It all happens too fast. The man jumps onto her, and a deafening scream fills the courtyard. My eyes widen as something gleams in the man's hand. For half a second, the most important rule flashes in my mind.

Do nothing.

We both ended up here because of me, because of *my* carelessness. I ignore my racing heartbeat, getting up just as the man raises his arm, and run the fastest I ever have.

I push the man off Laurel before he can kill her. The knife falls onto the ground. All the air in my lungs escapes me. My vision turns fuzzy. I'm not a tall girl. I haven't had a proper meal in months, the veins under my skin were visible because of all the weight I've lost. And shit, my arms burn like hell. Yet somehow, I managed to knock this man off—this man who is a giant compared to me. I've known I was different for a long time. I've kept it hidden since I got here, but I had no idea I could do that.

I don't move. I stare at the pavement as I sit up.

"Mahi—" Laurel's voice is cut off. The demons are bringing everyone inside; our one hour of sunlight is shortened.

"Get up!" a demon yells at me. I'm surprised that they don't force me up. Then I remember that Gavril wants me in perfect condition.

Slowly, I rise to see no one else here. No one who isn't a monster. Three demons are staring at me. Their eyes are as black as ever, and dark veins pulse out of their skin, engulfing their faces. One of them grips my left hand.

"Let's go, Three-nine-seven!" My eyes squeeze shut at their voices, morphed and deep. I've heard this voice only two times before, when a demon would become consumed with rage. A sound from a different, dark world.

Slowly I relax, staring at the sky. A smile comes to my face. They are giving me death glares, all of their hands in fists. I shouldn't have stopped the fight. I'm going to be punished now.

Maybe now, instead of Laurel, I will be the one experimented on.

4

I DIDN'T LEAVE my room today. No one came to get me. So, I simply sat on my stone-hard bed while my thoughts ran wild.

Growing up, Laurel and I were the youngest in our community. I was born in 2011, a year after Lucifer took the world. She was only a one-year-old when it happened. We'd grown up like sisters.

My dad and her mom were good friends. They'd escaped the city together and created a hideout with other people in a dense forest. Somehow, the adults had really managed to create a home. I realized that now, guilt seeping into my chest. For sixteen years, Laurel and I grew up with freedom of some sort. She never complained. I was always the ungrateful one. Despite miraculously building an entire small town in the middle of a forest, I wanted to see what the rest of the earth looked like. Stories about the old world didn't help. I'd frequently climb to the top of the tallest tree and gaze up at the clouds.

A wooden fence surrounded the entire community as a border. I can't remember how many times I was warned not to go past it. About how humanity as they once knew it, didn't exist anymore; that there were human containment prisons to feed demons our emotions and monsters that would take any chance to kill us. And so, we weren't allowed to go over the border. More importantly, because if we did, we'd never be able to come back. I never understood how that exactly worked. Especially since when I was a small kid, a couple of monsters had encountered the camp.

Now *that* was a blurry memory.

Eventually, they stopped coming after my dad somehow reinforced the fence. He was always the hero. I miss his silly jokes, warm hugs, and even his overprotectiveness. If only I'd listened to his rules.

"We should head back," Laurel told me the day I ruined our lives.

I was standing by the border, leaning against that annoying fence. A squirrel running around a tree. It was so small with a cute nose. I wondered if it could see me. But before I could call out to it, it ran off. In the very direction, I desperately wanted to go.

"I wonder where it's going," I said, staring wide-eyed at the grass. The forest was denser where the little critter had gone, with thick trees and long grass.

"Where what went?" Laurel asked. A groan left her mouth. "Don't tell me you're daydreaming again. Come on, we're on building duty today."

"I'm not daydreaming, Laurel." I spun around, scowling.

She was as beautiful as ever. A deep frown sat on her

face. She tugged on her full sleeve, red sweater. It was her favorite. "Yes, you are," she murmured.

"I'm sick of being holed up here. I'm sick of the scary stories my dad tells me every night—"

Laurel scoffed. "You make it sound like they aren't true."

"You know I just want to see the rest of the world," I said. "I want to see these amazing cities. To see if they actually are as great as the grown-ups constantly talk about. Or India, my dad's home country. There's so much to learn."

"You're *already* learning," Laurel said. "Did you lose your memory? Remember your nursing apprenticeship!"

"I'm not saying I want to leave that." I turned to face the fence again. "I just want to see where that squirrel went."

"You can't go past the line."

"Because I'll never return?" I laughed. "That's just bullshit they feed us, so we'll listen. Can you think of any way that would be possible?"

Laurel didn't answer. I'd asked her that question a thousand times, but I was never daring enough to pass the border. Yet something had come over me that day. So, I climbed over that wooden fence. She gasped.

"Live a little," I told her.

Laurel was a little more of a rule follower. I wasn't a rule breaker necessarily, but I had snuck out at night plenty of times before. I stared at her shocked expression and took five steps from the fence. She waved at me, and I waved back.

"See, nothing happened."

"I can't believe it." With a childish grin, she followed my lead.

We giggled like little girls. Butterflies danced in my stomach the further we walked from the fence. We kept glancing back, letting out screams with huge smiles on our faces at the chance of being caught.

And I remember the moment the fence vanished as sharply as ever. The very second my heart stopped, and all the air escaped from my lungs. Because of my careless decision, my best friend and I were stuck here as a food source for fucking demons.

Because of my need to explore, my dad is now probably *dead*.

I squeeze my eyes shut at the thought. Why am I thinking of such a horrible memory now? I push it away, trying to fall asleep. But ignoring that memory made it impossible for me not to think about what had happened yesterday.

I barely got one meal a day. I had no strength, yet I knocked that guy off like he was nothing. It wasn't *impossible*. I live in a world full of demons. And that wasn't the only thing I could do.

Sometimes the demons would hurt us just for the sake of doing so. They claimed it was *testing*, not punishment, but their sinister smile told another story. I was the one they used to pick on the most.

The first time they'd done it, I'd come back with a small scar. It was stupid, but when I used my power to heal it, I realized I wouldn't be able to do it again, not as long as I was in here. I don't know why I can heal others or how to control it, but after a different demon picked me from everyone else here since I had no scars, I never healed myself again. I glance at my inner left wrist, where the number 397 is burned onto my flesh. I rub it and blink away tears. A painful laugh leaves my mouth.

I had always been a naturally tough person. I helped my dad build a lot of things, lifting things that usually would need two people. Yet, I didn't know I had the strength to push a giant. And I had no idea what the demons thought of it. I would be the perfect person to experiment on now. I'd hidden my power for so long, before I'd even ended up in this prison. Laurel didn't even know about it, but maybe now she'd be safe. I'd stopped someone from dying, did something, broken a huge rule.

My eyes shoot open when someone knocks on my door. I didn't even realize I was sleeping, and a knot forms in my stomach. I rub the scars on my arms. Demons don't knock.

"Three-nine-seven." I don't recognize the voice, but at least it isn't the warden. "I hope you enjoyed your time."

"Thank you," I say, my voice shaking. "I did."

"I'm glad."

My door opens and a demon I don't know walks in. His eyes are completely red and his hair is a dark chestnut brown, brushed away from his face. The demon's skin is light grey, his jawline sharp with black veins, and his muscles are hardly contained in the tight black shirt he wears. He looks young, maybe early twenties. Although born into this awful world, he is beautiful. At least the human vessel he's inside is beautiful. But I've never seen entirely *red* eyes before.

"How are you?" he asks, seeming genuine. His eyes are staring through me like I'm a meal he's about to eat. He touches his curved horns. They're different from the others, pointing back. "Must've taken a lot of force to stop that boy from dying."

"Yeah. I needed more sleep than usual," I say. I know he doesn't actually care. "But you're not here to check on me. Why are you really here?"

He smirks. "They told me you hadn't broken yet. Maybe that's why some of them like and hate you so much. I still don't know why they needed to call a royal."

His eyes gleam brighter, and I hold in a gasp as I realize who's in front of me. They have to be taking me to get experimented on if they sent a prince of Hell.

Which means this is his real body. He actually looks like that. I can't believe it.

"I'm not going to hurt you if you cooperate." He signals for me to get up. I obey. I don't know what he expects.

He comes up behind me, grabbing my wrists and taking me out of my room. We walk through the hall, and it doesn't surprise me when we take a turn into a darker corridor I don't know.

"Look down," he whispers in my ear. His breath brings shivers down my spine. I resist the urge to pull away and look at the floor. I'm not sure if it's because he doesn't want me to know the way or not. If that's the case, I'll be coming back alive.

We go down some stairs and walk some more. A cool breath escapes my mouth. I wish I could rub my arms and hug myself, but this demon, this prince of Hell, won't let me go. Judging by how cold it is, I'm guessing we're somewhere no one regularly visits.

We stop abruptly. I look up despite not being given permission, staring at a steel door.

"You're going to experiment on me?" my voice trembles.

"Not exactly," the prince says. He opens the door, moving to the side. He beckons me to go. I gulp as I pass him. He doesn't push me. He doesn't do anything remotely related to what demons do. All he does is smirk, his red eyes glowing.

The door closes once I step inside. A gasp shoots from my throat before I can stop myself.

Laurel lies on a metal table, her eyes wide open as she stares at the ceiling. Around her are nothing except a red box on the ground and a different, human looking demon standing by her. He has a knife in his hand, which he holds out toward me.

I have no time to do anything before he stabs her in the stomach, slicing downwards and leaving the blade there.

"No!" A scream erupts from my throat. I sprint forward. The demon flashes his black eyes and moves away, tilting his head.

"You can try to save her," he says casually. "But you'll get no help."

"What kind of punishment is this?" I cry out.

He shrugs, taking in a deep breath through his nose. I feel myself draining, staring at him with watering eyes as he leaves through a door at the back of the room. Being fed on was a bitch.

Laurel clutches her stomach, puffing air repeatedly. I

snap out of my anger, grabbing the red box by the table. My eyes go fuzzy when the only thing in there is a long bandage, a needle, and a thread.

"You're going to be okay," I say to Laurel. I don't tell her the truth. That I always say that, and it's never true. "It's going to be fine."

"Mahi," she weakly mumbles. Her eyes are beginning to close, blood staining her hands.

I won't be able to help her unless I use my powers, and there are no cameras or windows in here. But the demons will find out about me when they see her alive. They'll *kill* me. I raise my hands to hold my head. This is my punishment—watching my only friend die, while I stand here helplessly.

They've taken everything from this world. I won't allow it.

Tears stain Laurel's cheeks. I move her hands and watch her eyes widen in fear. They'll know, but at least they won't know exactly.

"Trust me," I tell her. Even though she doesn't give me a look of encouragement, I pull out the knife and ignore her screams. I place both my hands on top of her injury just so they are barely touching her blood-stained clothes.

Closing my eyes, I begin to feel the sensation go through me. Energy pulses through my whole body, radiating into Laurel. A breeze passes by even though we're inside. For a moment, I think I'm floating, but it fades quickly and pain floods my insides for the last moment. In just seconds, I had healed her. I rub my hands together, taking in the leftover high and shudder.

Laurel sits up almost immediately. I look away, my face heating up. My arms go limp.

"Mahi." My heart stops at the fear in her voice, my eyes shifting to her tight fists. My eyebrows furrow. Is she angry at me?

"Yes," I say, my voice coming out too soft.

"You're a demon?"

What else could I be?

"No," I quickly say, shaking my head. She was going to keep asking questions, and I wouldn't have the answers. I didn't even know what I was. I grab her shoulders and she flinches. "Listen, Laurel. You can't tell anyone about this."

"How did you do that?" she asks, her voice cracking.

"I don't know." I back up and stare at the ceiling. "I've been able to do it since before we were captured. Even when we were hidden in the forest."

"What are you?"

"I don't know," I raise my voice, and frown when Laurel stares at me like she's seen a ghost.

"Your skin—your eyes—they're—your eyes are glowing!" she screams.

I turn around and grab the box, pulling out the needle and thread.

"Laurel, you have to let me make it look believable," I say, swallowing the lump in my throat. "You have to let me try."

"No," she says, staring at me in disbelief. "No. That's going to hurt and it won't look real."

"Perfect skin after getting stabbed isn't real! And I won't let it hurt you."

"How?"

"I just healed you. I can make it painless."

I don't really know if I can, but to save both our skins, I need to do this. The first thing they'll do is kill me if they see Laurel with perfect skin. And any chance of her not being experimented on will be gone. This way, at least we might have a chance.

She shakes her head. "No. I don't want you to do that again."

I groan. "Laurel, please. This is the least you can do!"

Her eyes are full of the same fear, but slowly she nods her head. "Okay. But if it hurts, you have to stop."

"I will."

Once I thread the needle, I place my left hand on Laurel's arm and my right by her stomach. The knife is in my hand.

"I'm not going to lie, this part is going to hurt," I say. I don't give her a chance to do anything. I slice at her skin. She screams out and guilt seeps into my stomach. This is a scream of death. I grab the needle as quickly as I can, projecting my energy into her while I begin to stitch her up.

She gasps. "I can't feel anything."

I smile, but it vanishes as I continue to work. I've never used my powers this long, sweat dripping down my chin. "That's good. That means it's working."

She doesn't say anything as I continue. She doesn't say anything when I'm done.

"Are you okay?" I grab her arm, but she pulls it away.

Nothing. We sit there in silence for a few minutes. The demons probably wanted me to spend time with her dead body so they'd have an emotion feast to feed on. This pain is almost just as bad. Laurel doesn't utter a single word. Not even when a demon opens the door, shocked to see her alive and well.

My heart feels empty.

I just lost my best friend.

5

_____

I DON'T KNOW what time of day it is when someone opens my door. All I know is that it isn't morning. If it were, I would've been ready by the finger scanner.

I turn around in my bed, sitting up, when I see Gavril in front of me. He grabs my arm. His nails dig into my flesh. His horns flash before my eyes, and I catch a scream before it can come out.

"Come on!" he growls at me. I don't have a choice to listen or not. I'm already out of my room. Not like I had an opportunity anyway.

"What's going on?"

"Nothing," he says, his voice shaking. My chest tightens.

"Gavril—"

"Three-nine-seven, shut up!" His voice is monstrous. Something isn't right. Something is going to happen to me, and Gavril is going to do whatever he wants before that happens.

I have to get away. My eyes frantically look around to find an exit, but there isn't any close by.

"Quit moving—"

I pull away, breaking free from Gavril's grip and falling onto the floor in the process. I don't even have a chance to run when he grabs me again. He binds my hands with cold metal. It clicks in place. My energy slowly fades, but I can feel it lingering inside. I grimace and try to move away, but nothing works.

"Stop!" he whispers in my ear, holding my arms as we start walking. My eyes widen. He almost sounds scared. "This is the last thing you'll get to enjoy before you're taken."

"Taken where?" I ask, pulling at my handcuffs. Gavril sighs. "Come on. I won't resist if you tell me."

I feel sick after saying those words.

"You won't?" He's really desperate if he believes me.

"I won't."

A nervous laugh leaves his mouth, and it vibrates against my skin. "Lucifer," he says. "They are taking you to Lucifer."

My heart starts to race. I can feel my skin burning up while the metal cuffs dig into my flesh. "Why?"

"I don't know."

Did they figure out my power? "What—no—you can't let them!"

"Do you think I care about that?"

"Then why are you so nervous?"

"Because I want to fuck you, *Mahi*," he says my name like filth, and shocks momentarily run throughout my body at someone besides Laurel saying my name. "Is that what you wanted to hear?"

Biting my lip, I quiver in pain. The air is getting warmer, and oxygen refuses to enter my lungs. With as much strength as I can conjure, I try to pull away again, but Gavril is too strong. My entire body burns the longer we walk, like a violent fever. Sweat drenches my hair, and I try to let out deep breaths of air. It's like I'm surrounded by fire all of a sudden, and I shake uncontrollably. I have to get out of here. I pull at my cuffs.

"Three-nine-seven," Gavril says aggressively. I don't know if it's my imagination, but my cuffs feel looser and looser. "What are you doing? Stop resisting. You said you wouldn't."

"I can't go to him." I don't want to say his name. "And I won't let you take me either!"

"Three-nine-seven, stop right now—" his demonic voice breaks off as he yells. At the same time, my hands pull away and I notice the grey goo around my wrists. My mouth falls open, and I stare at Gavril's smoking hand and the burning floor. He groans in pain, and before he can stop me, I kick his leg and run toward the courtyard. That's the only place I know where to go.

I turn many corners, no other demons in my way. I slam open the doors and run into the night. I haven't seen the dark sky since the day I was captured two years ago. I haven't felt the cold, night air on my face.

My legs move straight to the large fence and my hands clamber to climb it somehow. I don't care if there are spikes on the top. My soul is Lucifer's either way, but I think it's better to die trying to get away than go to him alive. The icy wind slices at my skin, but I'm already at the top of the fence when an alarm goes off, and demons emerge from the building.

"Three-nine-seven!" they yell in unison. Glancing back, I gasp at a knife coming my way. Without thinking, I jump down the fence, crying out due to the stinging in my shin.

Groaning, I pull out a knife without thinking about the blood trailing down my leg. I suck in a breath, wincing at the pain. Staring at the wet liquid on the knife, I push forward and run as fast as I can. My stomach pinches the faster I go and my legs tire quickly. There's another fence I have to pass. This one has a gate, making it much easier.

It feels weird to be in such an open space but I don't have time to take it all in. My heart skips a beat when I see a red laser pointing at me from one of the many towers I hadn't thought about, and I scream when a bullet wounds the ground instead of me. One almost hits my leg.

They want me alive. Or my head would've been blown to bits by now.

Somehow, I finally manage to reach the large metal gate. The gate they brought both me and Laurel past when they captured us. It's different from the other fence, which was some kind of chain material, but I can still see the road behind this one through the gaps it has.

Two demons run to stand in front of it with guns pointed right at me. I freeze.

"Hands in the air!" both shout. "Drop the knife."

I do as they say, a lump forming in the back of my throat as they walk over to me. One puts his gun away and grabs both my arms, dragging them to my back. I kick the one directly in front of me and duck just in time for him to shoot the other.

My heart pounds with every bullet the demon shoots at me while I cover my head and run in a circle around him. He stops for a second and I grab onto his shoulder, pulling myself onto his back and gripping one of his horns. He claws at my throat and face, but I place all my energy on pulling his horn. Searing pain sizzles under my skin and I scream as if my lungs are on fire. It feels like I've been straining myself for days when I finally land with a thud as his horn dislodges and blood spurts from his head. An inhuman cry comes from the demon, and I scramble toward the knife, stabbing him in the stomach before he can reach for his gun.

Air escapes from my lungs while I rest my hands on my thighs, and I pant heavily. *It's okay*, I tell myself, *the human was gone.*

I know there are more monsters behind me, and they'll do whatever they can to take me to their master. And I don't even know what's waiting for me out there. I've heard stories of other kinds of demons, ones that are even more mindless and sadistic. Maybe I'm just prolonging everything.

I open the gate slowly, my teeth gritting against each other at how difficult it is. It's heavy, even for me but I manage to create a small enough gap.

"Mahi."

I freeze. My eyes feel as if they are going to pop out of my skull, and I shake as I finally manage to turn around. It feels as though it takes hours to face the prince of Hell I had seen earlier. Of course, he would still be here. His bright red eyes are striking in the dark, his body a picture of health. It only angers me, but it's not as strong as the fear coursing through my body.

"You have a chance to make things better," he says, his voice oddly quiet. The distance is far enough between us that I can run away, assuming that he doesn't have super speed or a gun. "The chance to have a better life. Just come with me."

"No, I don't." I know he's trying to psych me out, so whatever he says isn't going to make sense. "I would rather die than go with you."

He places his hand on his chest, frowning. "Ouch. That hurt."

"Wow." My voice quivers as I try to seem strong. "Didn't know you could feel."

He smirks at me, moving closer. "Oh, I can feel a lot of things."

My hands form fists, my jaw tensing. I desperately wish I could decapitate him right now and spit his name out like acid, but that dream will never come true. My eyes shift to the demons running toward us.

"If you wanted," he says, tilting his head as if he's amused, "you could destroy everything. You would have the power to do *anything*. It's astonishing what you are."

My heart skips a beat. What does he mean by that? "I don't want to destroy anything."

"But you do." His smirk grows into a smile, his eyes slowly brightening. "I can feel every desire in your body. I know you better than you know yourself."

I shake my head. "No, you don't."

He laughs. "Oh, really?"

"Really."

The warden is standing beside him now, on all fours

like he's a wild animal. There are even a few demons behind them, weapons of all sorts in hand. Unlike the prince, they all look furious. I jump when one of them shoots the knife out of my hand. My only defense, *gone.* The prince yells at them to stop, and I glance away. I think of their horns digging into my chest. That's a painful way to go.

Locking eyes with the prince again, I step outside the gate. My legs itch to run off, but I have a feeling I'll be shot the second I do. His mouth opens, eyes widening as he dramatically throws his hands up. "Damn, I am so rude. You know, I never actually introduced myself."

"I don't ca—"

"It's Israkiel. But I'll let you call me Isra. It's the least I can do."

I don't know why he's telling me his name. I don't want to believe it's because he *does* know what I'm thinking, so I don't say anything. Taking a few more steps backward, I begin to think this is all an illusion. They aren't closing in on me.

"I'm going to let you go," he tells me.

Demons scream from all around him. I didn't think it was possible, but his red eyes gleam even brighter.

I'd be pretty mad too if I didn't know this was a trick.

"Does anyone want to oppose me?" Isra asks, his voice echoing. The demons quiet down immediately, and even I feel like the entire ground just shook. If a prince of Hell is like this, I can't imagine what Lucifer is like.

"Funny joke." I fake a laugh, glancing around to find any demons who might be waiting to jump on me.

"It's not a joke." Isra shrugs. "It's simply an act of kindness."

It's nothing like that, but I don't wait for Isra to say anything else. Turning around, I run down the long road ahead of me. There's nowhere I can go. I could try to find the hideout in the forest. My entire old life was there.

As if I'd actually be able to find it.

But I can't risk the demons discovering it. I wouldn't be able to live with myself if my other friends ended up here because of me.

I'm on my own now.

6

AFTER HEALING my ankle and walking for hours, I end up
sleeping in an abandoned, broken-down building in the
middle of nowhere. I have no idea what it is. I've never
seen anything like it. It's small, but there are stands
outside under a roof. Next to each stand is some weird-
looking machine. A car leans against one. Inside the
building, there are a bunch of empty shelves. But I wasn't
really picky with where I ended up. My heart raced the
entire night at the thought of some monstrous demon
tearing it out.

I'm surprised to see I'm still all by myself when I
wake up. However impossible I think it is, maybe Isra *was*
telling the truth. This isn't some prank he's playing. Or
he's just waiting for me to have a little more taste of
freedom, so the impact hurts more when it's gone.

The sun is again high in the clear sky. For once, I
wish it wasn't there. The heat is exhausting. I feel like I
could fall at any moment.

I have no idea if the demons are following me. The

only thing I can do is keep following this road (if I can even call it that, with the layers of grass growing within it) and hopefully come across some kind of city. Maybe I will be able to hide there. Even though I had never seen one, Dad told me it was a place with hundreds and hundreds of buildings.

He'd also told me that most of the time, the savage demons only came out at night. That would give me enough time, I hope, to discover someplace to stay. And maybe I'd find some more survivors too. The demons can't keep *all* the humans in containment. I remember learning that before, there were too many humans on the earth.

A perfect reason for Lucifer to kill them all.

I can't imagine waking up one day to thousands of demons descending on my home. Sometimes, I'm grateful that I wasn't alive to experience the war. Other times, I wish I was there so I could've helped fight back.

I continue to walk. There is nothing else I can do. I run my fingers through my tangled, dark hair, sighing. If Lucifer wants me as bad as I think, then I'll have to hide my identity. Cutting my long hair is the first thing. But I don't have anything that can do that. And I honestly don't want to.

"Damn," I breathe out heavily, pressing my palm against my forehead. The wide road starts to elevate. My eyes shift to the concrete and a single tear rolls down my cheek. My body is ready to stop moving, but I have to keep going. Despite my legs feeling like heavyweights, I continue on.

I have no idea how much time has passed when I finally see something on my right side. Dozens of broken buildings, altogether looking like some kind of demolished community. Despite Lucifer destroying the world, the road hadn't been that bad. But this entire view, on a huge amount of land with structures torn in half and the roads between them reduced to rubble, makes my stomach feel sick. My eyes follow the destruction, all of it leading up to something that looks like a giant wall. It's grey, and whatever is on the inside is hidden. It's the tallest, widest thing I've ever seen, and even though the distance doesn't make it seem that big, I know that I'm an ant next to it.

I hiss as my brain drums against my skull. If this giant wall is anything like the containment center I was just in, there will be demons protecting it, which means I need to figure out a way around it.

I look down at my hands. My abilities are still unknown to me. I always thought that the only thing I could do was heal. But after my escape, that isn't the case.

I pull out a strand of hair and bring it in front of my face. How am I supposed to burn it like I did to Gavril? I take in deep breaths, shaking my arm in an attempt to burn the strand, but I'm not even sure what to do.

"Come on," I murmur, narrowing my eyes at my tense fingers but nothing happens. A groan leaves my mouth, and I drop my hands to my side. Until I figure out how to control it, this new power is useless. Rubbing my face, I continue on.

Grass surrounds both sides of the wide road, and my eyes widen when I see that it elevates into a broken dead end in the distance. I really had no idea where I was going.

I give in to my pounding headache and stumble toward the long grass away from the wall, where there are bundles of trees in the distance. My legs give out before I can get under the shade. My face burns, dirt scratches my face, and I groan as I lie on the ground. I don't even know how to find water or food.

For some reason, I just stay there. I close my eyes while my stomach aches from hunger. I am at my limit. There really is no point in this. I have no idea where I'm going. Isra's won this sick game.

After what felt like seconds, my eyes open to darkness. I shoot up. A howl echoes in the distance, followed by another and my heart pounds against my chest.

"Oh . . . oh shit," I whisper. It isn't the cold or the danger of the demons finding me that makes chills run up my arms. It's the surrounding growls and howling. I can only blame myself for falling asleep, but I can't believe Lucifer would send hellhounds to find me. Or maybe they're just patrolling the area. It doesn't matter. They are here, and they'll rip me to shreds.

I get up, wincing at my aching bones. I narrow my eyes at the wall to see what I am up against. My stomach turns hard. There are black figures of different shapes and sizes strolling among the many torn buildings. I swallow, hair lifting from the nape of my neck. Hellhounds aren't the only things out here. Those are demons.

I turn around. The trees are far, but maybe I can get there fast enough to climb one. And that's if I have enough strength to do so. I'm moving before I can even think of another option, my heart skipping a beat at the sound of another howl. The one time a hellhound had discovered our camp, my dad shot an arrow right between its gleaming eyes, but the damage had still been done. Someone had died.

My legs move faster and faster as I see more and more glowing eyes. There's nobody visible—only two orange dots. Barks start to fill the air, their bodies thundering from behind me. Panic swells inside my chest.

Fumbling up a tree, my heart races, and rapid breaths escape my mouth. I count maybe three pairs of eyes closing in on me. Their barks deafen my ears. Before I know it, the tree shakes. A shriek leaves my mouth as I lose my balance, grasping onto a high enough branch.

The scratches on the tree trunk are obvious. I can only imagine the teeth these orange-eyed creatures rocking the tree back and forth have. The thought makes my heart shrink.

The branch I'm holding onto snaps at another jolt from the tree. The air knocks out of my lungs as I fall to the ground, coughing louder than the growls that surround me.

I think I'm on fire. Despite how weak I am, my arms come out when my eyes meet orange ones. The hellhound tries to nip at me and its jaws snap when it misses. Its paws dig into my shoulders and I feel its hot breath pressing against my skin.

Something drips onto my collarbone, and I scream when it burns. I'm too weak to hold this thing back. Unless, maybe if I think hard enough, I can find that burning power inside me. But I don't get a chance to think. The hellhound snaps its invisible mouth at my neck, and I scream again.

And then I'm pushing nothing.

My chest warms up as another creature rips the hellhound off me, a dark shield protecting him while he pierces a sword into the monster. One by one, the orange eyes begin to disappear, and oxygen fills my lungs once again. Spots fill my vision, but I blink and stare at the sky. I can't fall asleep. Not until I'm far away from here.

"Are you okay?" My head lifts to stare at the other creature. The warmth in my chest is still there, a feeling of safety as I stare at this stranger's hand. I want to move closer and embrace him. I feel some kind of invisible string pulling me toward him. What is this sensation? Does he feel it too? My eyes widen when I finally see what I thought was a shield.

Wings. Black wings.

"What the hell are you doing out here?"

I realize I've shifted closer to him and move backward, still on the ground. He sighs and runs his fingers through his raven hair. He has black horns, but his skin isn't grey. Instead, it's a darker shade of brown than my own.

"You're an angel?" That's the only way he can have wings.

"You're bleeding." Ignoring the question, he comes toward me and kneels. A demon would flash his eyes at me, but he doesn't. He pulls out a rag and dabs at my cheek. I wince and push him away, backing up even more.

"It's all right," I whisper, touching the cut. "I'll deal with it. Thanks for helping but please, leave me alone."

"What?" his voice squeaks higher as if he can't believe what I'm saying. But in this world, no one can be trusted. I don't even know the real reason the demons found out about me back in containment. There was a lot of evidence that I was different when Laurel came out healthy. Maybe the demons had even lied about there being no cameras. But I couldn't rule out that my closest friend might have snitched on me to get something from the demons. It was easy to give in to temptation.

The stranger gets up, his hand coming out once again. "Look, we should really get out of here before more hellhounds come. Thanks to our luck, the demons by the wall weren't alerted. If they were, we would've been screwed. But I don't think luck will be on our side if we stay here any longer."

I take a quick glance at the animal-like demons, sweeping a shaky hand across my forehead to get rid of sweat. I don't want to know what they look like up close.

The stranger's hand is still out when I look back. This time, I stare at it for more than a few seconds. His arm is frozen in place. In two years, no one has helped me unless it was for their own benefit. And despite the warm feeling of safety I feel inside, this odd connection I've never experienced before, I don't know this guy.

But it's either I go wherever with him, or wait here for the demons to find me. In the state I'm in, I'll have no chance.

"Don't tell me I saved you for no reason," he says. A knot ties in my chest.

I ignore his hand and get up. "Let's go."

7

My cheek stings. My eyelids fall every second, and I jolt myself to stay awake. The fire in front of my face calms the recurrent nerves I feel, but a knot remains in my chest.

When there is food in front of me, my eyes widen, and the knot loosens up. I don't look at the stranger as I grab the bowl, muttering a soft thank you. I bring the soup to my mouth. I hesitate for a second, but decide to not make my stomach angrier and drink up without using a spoon. If he wanted to kill me, he never would've saved me in the first place.

It's warm. It's actually warm!

"There's more."

I stop when I hear his voice, my cheeks flushing. I place the bowl on the ground, my paranoia getting the best of me as I look out at the entrance to this cave. The narrow, grey walls make it feel as if I'm cramped inside here. The roof is far too small. And that's coming from *me*.

"You can have more," he says.

It took a while to get into the distant forest since a few more hellhounds attacked, but this stranger knew how to fight. Almost like he'd been doing this his whole life.

When we got to this small cave, it didn't look like he lived here. Although a few of his things had already been inside, like this bowl. And even though I desperately wanted a soft bed to lie on, the stone below me wasn't that bad.

"What do you want from me?" I ask, clearing my scratchy throat and staring at him. He's sitting on the other side of the flames. There has to be a sensible reason why he risked his life to save me.

He swallows excessively. Eyebrows squishing together, he runs his fingers through his dark hair. It takes him a few seconds before he looks away. "Nothing."

"That's a lie." I can't help myself from hissing.

"You're the one who came with me."

I'm beginning to regret that decision. But then again, I would've died if I didn't go with him.

"Everyone wants something. Why'd you help me?"

He gets up, stretching his feathery wings. They are *huge*. He can't even spread them out the entire way. For the first time, I notice the black veins rising from his neck and onto his face. But the fear, the hatred I expect, isn't there. Instead, there's a surreal flutter in my stomach. An invisible magnet pulling me toward him. "Is it because you're an angel with black wings?" I ask. It doesn't feel right to ask the question, since from the time I was born, I'd been told the angels were extinct. And now here one was, standing right in front of me.

He stops stretching and turns, staring at me with a

blank face. My heart sinks. "That's not why. And you're half right."

And now the fear begins to dive in. "Half?"

"You can't sense it?"

I don't say anything. He doesn't need to know anything about me. I just have to figure a way out of here in case things go south.

He walks to my side of the fire and crouches beside me. My heart skips a beat. "I can sense *you*. That's how I knew to come here. It—whatever it is—guided me."

I swallow the lump that's formed in my throat. The words come to me now that he's so up close. "You're half-demon."

His eyes flash black at me. The warmth I feel, the trust, vanishes into thin air. "Looks like I'm not their number one target anymore."

"How can I even believe what you're saying?" I try to hide the disgust I feel. "Demons lie."

"Angels don't."

I'd been told angels were the good guys. But they were all dead, so it didn't matter what anyone said about them. No one would ever know if it's the truth or not.

"Why did you save me?" I ask again.

He sighs. "I don't know about you, but I've felt this weird sensation for two years after I escaped that city. The first time I followed it, I ended up outside a containment center. After that, I decided to focus on survival. But today, this feeling started to become stronger. I usually don't leave my campsite unless I have to, especially this close to the city, but I had to see what this pull was. And when I saw you . . . I had to help you."

A city. That's what's inside the giant wall. "Two

years," I murmur. That can't be a coincidence. Two years ago, I left the hideout that shielded me from demons. He seems sincere, but sometimes demons did. Maybe he saved me for some other reason, like torturing me for entertainment. I rub my face. I wish I didn't assume the worst, but I had to, especially now. That's how you survive.

"Who are you?" I ask, the warm tension arising again. Whatever guided him, didn't guide me. But what he'd described, a pull, was the only thing I could feel right now.

His dark eyes narrow, and he lifts his chin. "I don't know. I'm just a guy trying to survive, but to other people, I'm a monster or a fugitive. The only reason I stay by this damn city is because my father is still in there."

My heart aches from the sudden confession and slows down the longer I stare at the pain on his face. "I'm sorry."

"It is what it is."

I have to change the subject. "What's your name?"

It takes him a few seconds before he answers with a small voice crack. "Kavon."

"I'm—" I pause, my eyebrows furrowing together. My name doesn't exactly mean anything. He won't know who I am. Still, for some reason, my tongue is dry as I think of saying it.

"It feels weird, doesn't it," says Kavon. "I haven't said my name out loud for a long time."

"Yeah." I manage to smile. "I'm Mahi."

"Well, Mahi," he says. "What were you doing out there? Most people know by now not to go out in the open like that. Those that don't . . . they're dead. I rarely see survivors nowadays. Although I doubt most of them would stick near the city."

I avoid his gaze. He saved my life when the hellhounds could've mauled him to death. He'd just given me food, when it looked like he was living on scraps. And why should I ignore this supernatural compulsion to trust him? It had to mean something. Besides, he was an angel. Maybe even the last of his kind.

But instead of answering Kavon's question, I turn to the fire to calm my nerves. "Why are you trusting me?"

I hear Kavon scoff, but it sounds almost like he doesn't believe what I just asked. "Honestly, I have no idea. This sensation is taking over any rational thought I have right now. If only you could know what I'm talking about—"

"I know." I meet his eyes. He looks stunned that I'm finally admitting something. "I do feel it. But it's different from what you described. I only feel it when you are near me."

And although it feels like I can trust Kavon, I can't stop staring at his horns and dark veins. Despite the fire in front of my face, a sudden chill spreads throughout me. The prince could've captured me at containment, but he didn't. He was playing some kind of game. What if Kavon was too? What if he didn't feel anything, and this was one of his demonic powers? My head turns fuzzy, and I try to gulp down my heavy breaths.

"Are you okay?" His hand comes out to touch me, but I push myself back before he can. He doesn't react. "Maybe you should get some sleep."

"No." I shake my head. Not with him here watching me. "I can't."

"I can't either," he says. I stop breathing at his words. "Let me help you."

I meet his brown eyes. I don't even know if they're his. If this is his real body. It has to be. What am I even thinking? He has a father. My heart thumps against my chest, heavy as a rock. I hate the feeling of wanting to be close to him. As if an invisible force is pushing me toward him.

I get up quickly. Kavon twitches as his hand comes out, but he swiftly drops it, and I move toward the exit. "I need to get some air."

"It's not safe to go out at night. You don't even know what's out there."

"I just need to be alone." I raise my voice, mentally hating myself for it. He's been nothing but kind to me. But I need time to comprehend everything that has happened; how close I was to death these last couple of days; what happened with Laurel. A few tears stroll down my cheeks, everything I didn't know I'd been holding in blowing up inside me. The moisture in the air sticks to my skin. "I'm sorry."

Kavon doesn't say anything else. Or if he does, I don't hear it. The wind presses against my face, oxygen struggling to escape my lungs as I leave the cave and run toward the closest tree.

The forest reminds me of home, with nothing but the wilderness around me, long green grass, and enough space to move about. That's all I knew for the first sixteen years of my life. That was all I thought was there, and I never realized how lucky I'd been.

Heavy sobs escape from my mouth, and I'm heaving into my shirt while I fall to the ground, leaning against the tree. I'm far enough so Kavon can't hear me, but close enough that I won't get lost.

My eyes are starting to feel sore. Squeezing them shut, I let out a deep breath. Maybe ending it all wouldn't be such a bad thing. My soul belongs to Lucifer, whether I like it or not. And it's not like I have anywhere to go. I grind my teeth together, heat flushing through my body.

He owns everything. He holds my life in his hands.

I wipe my tears. Sweat forms on my forehead; my breathing is so loud I can hear it in my ears. I press my fingers into the ground, squeezing as hard as I can, accepting that the only way I can escape Lucifer is if he *dies*.

The feeling is gone as soon as it comes. My tense muscles relax, and the weakness I've been feeling engulfs me. Isra was right. I do want to destroy everything for all the things the demons have done to me. And they deserve it, but the humans they've taken don't.

"You're crying."

I hold my breath. I'm not sure if I'm hallucinating but as I look up, the prince of Hell is staring down at me with what seems like kind red eyes. My legs are up before I know it, shaking as I back away.

"H-how?" I can barely speak; my lips numb while he steps toward me.

"I'm not actually here," he says calmly. "I had been waiting for you to think of me so that I could come and speak with you. Right now, all I see is you." He smiles. "That's all I want to see."

"Please leave me alone," I whimper. "I want to be alone. Don't hurt me."

"I let you go." Isra frowns, touching his horns. "Why would I do that—"

"Because it's a game!" I almost scream. "It's a game to all of you! And you've won, okay!"

His face hardens, and he crosses his arms over his black shirt. "Why are you crying?"

I want to laugh at his question. Instead, I scoff. "Why do you think?"

"And what's with the cut?" he asks, pointing at my cheek. "I know you can heal yourself."

I sigh. "And I know you enjoy seeing others in pain."

"Not you." He steps forward, a subtle smile forming on his face. "I want you to have everything."

"Stop," I say. "Please. I'll get on my knees and beg you. Just stop playing with me and take me to Lucifer."

His red eyes darken as soon as I say Lucifer's name. "That's the thing. I don't want to."

"You're a prince, but you still have to obey him."

Isra laughs, shaking his head. "I'm not like other demons, Mahi. I don't have to do anything Lucifer says. I simply *choose* to. Or well, until now."

"The other demons probably told him what you did."

"Oh, they might've if I didn't control the prison. I would've gotten you out sooner if I knew that you were in there."

Control the prison. What does that mean? It's a trick. It has to be. I'm glad I'm not falling for it, although I can't help but be curious and see where it goes. "Why?"

He shrugs. "I'm bored. Lucifer may have gotten us the earth, but he hasn't done much with it. The entire thing is ruined from warfare apart from the few cities he forced demons to remake. He's tried to recreate how the earth was before, but it doesn't work. Besides, if you were a demon, would you really want to spend your time harvesting food and managing human shops so that Lucifer can rule over the 'old' earth. It's pathetic, really."

"I doubt you have to do those things."

"I spend most of my time in Hell these days. Until I was told to go check on a human girl with incredible strength." He starts to subtly bob up and down. "And then to find out she can heal others, I was finally excited."

"Someone new to experiment on." My lips press together firmly.

"You're a weapon," Isra says. His eyes are wild and bright. "To see what else you can do, what else you can become. I can help you overthrow Lucifer."

My heart jumps out of my chest at his words.

"That doesn't make sense." I look away. He could just take on Lucifer himself.

"Maybe," he says, his voice suddenly serious. "Now, tell me where you are. It's not safe outside the walls."

"It's not safe anywhere."

"That's true," Isra agrees, but there is no humor in his words. "But you don't seem to understand. Lucifer doesn't care about what is outside his cities. There are lower-tier demons who feast on humans, and even some who do worse. I can keep you safe."

"I doubt that." I walk toward the cave again, hoping that Isra won't be able to see Kavon.

"Mahi, wait—"

"Goodbye," I say as I enter the cave again.

Kavon notices me quickly, turning around with a confused expression on his face. My tense muscles relax, and relief floods through me. If he heard me yelling, he doesn't say anything.

"Had time to cool off?"

"What?"

"Sorry." He rubs the back of his head. "That came out wrong."

Somehow, I manage to smile. "That's okay."

He opens his mouth as if he's about to say something, then closes it. I gulp and sit against the stone walls, the awkward silence slowly killing me.

After what feels like an eternity, Kavon clears his throat. "Look, I'm sorry if anything I said before offended you," his voice is hoarse. "I didn't mean to."

"You didn't say anything wrong." I shake my head and roll my eyes. "I'm just stupid."

Kavon's eyebrows furrow. "Really? Besides roaming around alone at night, how exactly?"

"Wow, you're really calling me out."

"You don't act like you've been living day to day."

I chew on the inside of my cheek, debating if I should tell him or not. Maybe this is what I need. "I've been through a lot in the last forty-eight hours." I trace my thumb over the number on my wrist. "Even before I was . . . captured. So, I just needed time to think. And then I thought about how the demons should suffer like I did—"

"And they should."

"But that makes me like them." I close my eyes since they begin to feel heavy. "And their vessels don't deserve that."

"Most of their vessels are already *dead*," Kavon says. "And you've been through a lot. Maybe that's why you think it's wrong, but it's not. If one of them were in here, they'd stick your face in the fire, amputate your fingers, leaving you barely alive before taking you away."

A shudder runs through me. "You should get away from me then."

He smiles. "Don't worry. But if you want to leave in the morning, I won't stop you. You should get some rest now."

Leave you barely alive. My heart races, and I flinch when the wind whistles in my ear. He saved my life, and he doesn't deserve to die if the demons find us.

8

I OPEN my eyes to a clear, blue sky. It takes me a second to sit up, raising my hand to shield myself from the sun. Birds are singing, and the sound of water rings in my ears. That's when I jolt and stand up. I'm dreaming. I have to be.

There's a stream not too far from me, connecting to a small waterfall. A few trees surround the area, all kinds of gorgeous looking fruit hanging from them. A breeze, that for some reason, I can't feel, blows against the plants. And is that a—

I squint my eyes. A *lion*, sitting across the stream by a batch of flowers? Its golden eyes stare straight through me. Okay, I *have* to be dreaming. But everything feels so real, as if I'm actually here.

"Mahi."

My lips part and I turn around. Tears form in my eyes. It's been too long since I heard that voice. A grin spreads across my face, and I run forward, engulfing my dad in a huge hug. He squeezes me back, and the warmth that radiates from him is something so familiar but lost to me.

Now I *know* I'm dreaming. The last time I saw my dad, he was heading off to his death.

"I don't want to wake up." I snuggle against his chest. I haven't had a good dream in ages.

Dad pulls away, giving me a small smile. He looks exactly the same from when I last saw him. Except there are bags under his dark eyes, and he seems like he's lost a lot of weight.

"We don't have much time, Beta," he says.

I narrow my eyes. "What? This is a dream, isn't it?" It's *my* dream. For once, I'm actually conscious of it. So why does Dad look like he hasn't slept in a month? That's the last thing I'd want to see.

"Yes—no. Listen." He shakes his head, speaking in Hindi. "The fact that we are in this garden is not a good sign. I'm not even sure if you'll remember this. Do not go to the city, okay. It's dangerous."

He shakes me when I don't answer.

"Do you understand?" He raises his voice and tightens his grip.

"Is this really you?" I whisper, tilting my head. It can't be him. He's as good as dead, but I've never had a dream like this. A dream where I *know* I am dreaming. It feels as though I'm awake.

"Yes." He looks around frantically as shallow breaths leave his mouth. There's a vein sticking out of his neck. "Don't go to the city, Morningstar city, you hear me? Lucifer is there. It's not safe."

I blink. He's okay. But how is he in my dream? And

why does he look scared, as if some monster is about to come and eat us? "Why?"

"Did you not hear me? Lucifer is there—"

The ground cracks before he can say more. I scream, and Dad hugs me again. A hug that is suffocating as the lion's roar deafens my ears.

When I wake up, everything is dark. I gasp, rubbing my arms where my dad last touched me. I feel the warmth fading even though I don't want it to. That dream, it can't be real. No one's ever visited my dreams before.

A huff of a laugh leaves my mouth. I doubt anyone could actually visit someone else's dream. This was just my imagination. It's called a *dream*, after all. Whatever, it was still nice, despite what happened at the end.

For a second, I think I'm still in containment, then reality hits as my eyes adjust, and I glance at the large wings surrounding Kavon on the ground. My fingers twitch to touch them until I realize how weird that is.

My chest tightens as I go through his bag that I hadn't seen earlier, pulling out a small knife. He really trusted me not to kill him. Or he thought I wouldn't be able to do anything, considering he's some badass fighter who's over six feet tall. Whatever, I'm not his problem anymore.

I place his bag back against the cave walls, stealing one last glance at the feathers that surround him before heading out of the cave. A yelp almost leaves my mouth as I slip on the dirt, falling face first into some moss. Sighing, I turn and look at the trees on top of the cave.

That's the direction we came from. Which means the ferals, as Kavon calls them, are there.

I groan, climbing onto the cave with ease. The knife is warm in my sweaty hand, my heart racing as I walk through the trees. I flinch at the sounds of an owl, almost bumping straight into a log. Despite the crunchy noise from leaves being crushed below my feet, it's too quiet. As I carry on, every other sound makes me jump up in fear.

Wiping my clammy hands on my pants, I exhale slowly when I finally see the thinning out of the forest and the long grass field on the other side.

The tree line. At least I won't get lost now.

Taking in the smell of fresh dew, I continue walking through the forest but make sure that I'm close to its edge. Once the sun comes out, I'll leave. But I won't go anywhere close to that wall. Even if Dream Dad was my imagination, I know better than to not listen to his advice.

Maybe I'll magically find my old home. I can already imagine taking a nice, long swim in the southern swamp.

I scoff. *As if.* Once you leave home, you can't get back in. That's what everyone was told, every day. That's why the demons never found us. I never questioned how, and now thinking about it made me squeamish. But it didn't matter if I could get in. It had taken the demons hours by vehicle to drag me and Laurel to containment. I can't imagine how long it'd take to get there by foot.

Shaking my head, I try not to think of anything nostalgic or scary.

Ducks. Just think of ducks. And that one time a duck bit you because you kept touching its beak. And then Laurel and Nate made fun of you—

I groan. I can't stop thinking of home. Eventually, I stop in my tracks, staring blankly at nothing before turning my head toward the forest's edge. The sun is finally starting to rise. I wonder if Kavon is awake. I can't feel the weird connection between us anymore, and I have no idea how far I'm from him now. I shouldn't even be thinking of him anymore. I'll never see him again.

And he'll be safer off for it.

I jump up when figures start to get closer and closer. Those must be ferals. Some of them must come in here during the day. That means it's true, they can't come out in the light, which is why the warden was always inside.

My hands shake, and I fumble with the knife. I back into a tree, glancing at where I came from. It wouldn't be that bad to run back, but then I'd just lead them to the cave—if I managed to get there.

A jolt runs through me when a scream pierces the silence. It's close. Too close. Shallow breaths leave my mouth when I notice movement right at the tree line.

"No!" a woman screams—a gunshot echoes, followed by more. My teeth grit together. Another survivor.

Do nothing.

My legs are wobbly and loose and the knife sticks against my skin.

"Help, plea—"

This was just like when I was being attacked by hellhounds. I would've *died*. My soul would've been on its way to Hell but Kavon saved my life. I squeeze my eyes shut. "Screw it."

Sprinting out of the forest, I meet the glossy eyes of a

middle-aged woman. She freezes for a second, her blue eyes widening at me before a large claw rips her throat out. Blood gushes from her neck before the gun falls to the ground.

Oh man, I didn't think this through. I back up, ignoring the mixture of nausea and fear deep in my stomach as two ferals turn around. One's entire face looks like the creamy skull of a bird, its mouth a pointed beak with razor teeth, and its pale body long and thin. The other one roars at me and it sounds like thunder. Its small horns protrude from its rough, dark blue forehead as the glowing orange eyes sunken into its skull trail me. I step back when its huge rotting external fangs snap at me. Except this one has blood seeping out of its chest.

They look at each other for a second, growling. I take a quick glance behind me. The sky's orange there. The sun is almost up. Maybe I can make a run for it. But the second I look back, the bird lunges at me with a gigantic hand.

I duck, a gasp shooting past my lips. The other one comes at me with its jaw wide open, and I slam my fist straight into its eyes. It takes a few steps back, and I take the chance to jab my knife up from under its jaw. My teeth clench together from the force.

"Shit!" I cry out and jump back, my right arm burns as the bird demon thrashes at me. I fall onto the grass, rolling over to the side just as its beak comes down.

I'm going to die.

As I start to crawl backward, the demon whips at my head, over and over, before freezing and glaring at me with its three glowing eyes. Heavy breaths leave my mouth while I rub the bloody scrape on my right arm.

That's when I notice the growing sunny field. The demon snarls as it backs into the forest, tilting its head to the side in what seems like curiosity when I heal my arm.

Sitting down on the grass, I stare at the woman's corpse. There's a massive bandage on her thin left arm, her light blue t-shirt stained with blood. She's wearing red gloves—I close my eyes.

Did I really think I could save her?

As I rub my forehead, my stomach tingles. It's warm, comforting. It's the same feeling I had when I was around Kavon—

"It takes a very special kind of idiot to pull off what you just did."

I jolt. Kavon stands only a few feet from me and I see the dark blood on his face. "What?" I blink as I get up.

He walks toward me. "Or was it her?" My eyebrows narrow downwards and I follow his pointed hand to the dead demon. "Is that my knife in its jaw?"

"I—yes. Yes, it was me." I close my eyes. If he starts asking more questions, I won't be able to explain how a small girl has the strength of a bear. "How'd you find me? Are you okay?"

"Why'd you leave without telling me?" His voice is tense.

"What?"

"Why'd you attack it?" His nostrils flare. "Do you know how lucky you are that the sun was coming up?"

"Wait." I shake my head in disbelief. "Is this why you called me an idiot?"

"Yeah." He wipes his face for a second before gesturing at himself. "This blood is mine *and* the ferals.

The ones in the woods I had to fight off to get here. You could've died."

"Well, I couldn't just watch *her* die."

"She—are you serious? This is how it is now. You're going to see this everywhere!"

"Can you stop yelling?"

"No!" He gives me a bitter smile. "No, I can't. You don't get it. Do you know how shitty I felt when I woke up and you weren't there? How I felt when I thought you were dead in the forest somewhere?"

I avoid his eyes. "You barely know me."

"That doesn't matter." Kavon walks over to the dead feral. "If you died from this demon, I would've felt responsible. And I'd also feel—" he stops himself. "It doesn't matter."

I wanted to hear what he was going to say. Because even though I don't know him, I'd be torn to pieces if something happened to Kavon. It's this odd connection that keeps fumbling up my emotions but I keep my mouth shut.

Kavon pulls out his knife and walks over to the woman. He then grabs her gun, and storms off closer to the forest.

He crouches down as I follow him. There's a blanket and a dark bag lying on the ground. "Well, on the bright side, we got more supplies."

I frown. "We can't go through her bag."

"Why not?"

"It feels—" He's already rummaging through her things. "Dirty."

Kavon looks over his shoulder, staring at me with confusion. "I'm going to pretend you didn't say that."

I roll my eyes. "I'm serious!"

"Everyone does it," he says. "We can't let it go to waste."

He pulls out some of her stuff, throwing what I assume is useless onto the grass. I bite my lip, looking at her body from the corner of my eye. That could've been me. How would Kavon have reacted? If something happened to him, looking for me, I wouldn't be able to live with myself.

"Self-made bullets," he mutters, examining one in between his fingers. "Nice."

"Look, I'm sorry, Kavon," I mumble as he swings the backpack partially over his shoulder.

"Just please tell me next time." He faces me with a crooked smile. "I'll give you some stuff to help you out. You can even leave now if you want."

"It's okay." I return his grin. After this, I'm not sure there will be a next time. I can't imagine going through this every day on my own. "So, how'd you find me?"

"I already told you. I can sense you."

I press my lips together in a thin line, nodding my head.

"Stay close to me," he says, facing the woods. Then he mutters out. "This is why we stay in the cave."

"Won't they go in there?" I ask.

"Usually, no." He points into the dark trees. "They like staying near the tree line. I guess they can get lost too. Some of them are watching us."

Sure enough, orange eyes are glaring through the foliage. Kavon hands the gun over to me and takes out his sword. The blade retracts from the handle. I'm only stunned for a millisecond when some of the demons growl at him. A few back away when Kavon raises his hand.

The walk back to the cave is a long one. We only encounter three demons, and Kavon kills them quickly but my stomach clenches every second out in the open—especially when I think of that bird demon and its enormous hands.

A bitter taste lingers in my mouth as I think of how we left the woman there. I know we had to because what would we do with a dead body? But that doesn't mean I feel okay about it. There are probably countless other bodies in the field leading up to the city. I feel even more nauseous over the fact that I had no idea this was what Lucifer had done to the world.

I knew about the ferals. And I knew that not all the humans were in containment. They had to bring those new people from somewhere.

Lucifer can't do this. No one deserves to live like this.

But he has, for nineteen years.

9

I'VE TRIED to keep my thoughts off Isra. Whatever powers he has, I don't know of them. Except that he's a prince of Hell, which means he can somehow torment me whenever he wants.

But it's *hard.* He seems to know what I can do—what I am. He might have answers to questions I've had my entire life.

As night approaches and the sun starts to disappear, Kavon hasn't returned from his hunt. We had run out of food, and even though I'd wanted to help, Kavon didn't even acknowledge me before heading out. I had volunteered to help find water, but by the time I reached the exit of the cave, he had disappeared.

With howls in the distance, my stomach begins to feel heavy. I could've helped him out there. I used to hunt animals a lot before containment. That was one of our main sources of food. Maybe now, I can do even more.

My eyes slowly shift down to my hands. They look normal. Human. And yet, I melted those cuffs off. I overpowered someone twice my size. If only I had the shame to ask Isra about it.

"I know what you're thinking."

For a moment, a sudden chill runs through my core. It can't be him. I only thought of him for half a second.

"How are you here?" I get up and turn around.

Isra smiles. He's wearing a casual red shirt and black jeans. He looks like a normal person, besides the glowing red eyes, grey skin, and curving horns. "Nice hoodie."

I ignore his comment on my new clothes. "Tell me how you're here."

He shakes his head and gestures to the walls around us. "Here, where?"

My eyes narrow. "Why can't you leave me alone?"

"You needed me. That's why I'm here."

"No, I didn't." I move closer to the fire, feeling a little safer.

He laughs slightly, shaking his head once more. "Maybe you don't need *me*, but you need me to help you. I felt it. The only way I can be here is if you thought of me."

"I don't understand," I say. "I don't have any bond with you. Nothing at all."

He moves closer. "We do. You just don't know it."

I want to know. I desperately do, but I don't want a demon to give me anything. I just want him to go away. His eyes go lower, and I follow them. My heart stops.

There was a fireball in my hand.

I look back at Isra. He's staring at me with wide, insane eyes, like I'm the most exciting thing on Earth. I gulp, turning away and heading outside. The hellhounds are better than being in a cave with what may or may not be my imagination.

The trees bring me a little more peace, the grass scratching my ankles. I wish I could see the stars.

It's all ruined by Isra.

"Mahi, don't run away from what you are!" Isra's voice echoes from behind me. If what he said is true, then he has no idea where I am. But I can't believe that. He's playing games. They all do.

"What do you want, Isra?" I spin around to face him, rage filling my veins. He's not too far from me. "And I mean actually want. No games. No tricks. Lucifer could have me right now, but he doesn't. Why?"

"I told you," Isra shrugs. "I'm bored. Earth needs a new leader."

"And you want that to be you?"

He shakes his head. "I want it to be *you*. Do you even know why Lucifer created those containment prisons?"

"No one does."

"It's because demons need to be fed or they become feral. They need their dose of pain, anger, hatred, all those emotions humans call negative. And they need a *reason* to do bad things, or it doesn't have the same effect. That's why they had so many rules, so that when you would break one, they would now have a reason to hurt you. The lower-tier demons kill any human they see, leaving none for the higher ones. Lucifer is an idiot. Things worked out better before."

My mouth drops open, and then my jaw clenches. I throw my hands in the air, turning around. "That doesn't make—"

A sharp pain goes through my body as I'm forced

onto the ground by Isra, a branch digging into my stomach. Dirt and leaves entangle in my hair as Isra pushes me closer to him against the grass. A scream forms in my lungs and my body feels like it's on fire. I shake desperately to get away. His hand presses against my mouth. "Shh. They'll hear you."

What in the . . . how is he touching me?

The panic I feel slows down, my ears listening to the multiple growls and snarls that are getting closer. I don't focus on his cold hand against my lips. Or the fact that a demon is holding onto me. But then I think about how Gavril might have had me in this exact position, and suddenly the hellhounds aren't the scariest thing anymore. I begin to squirm, tears starting to pool in my eyes.

Isra shushes me again. "Mahi, calm down."

But I can't.

"I know what you want to do. But if you die, you'll never get the chance to stop Lucifer."

Sweat is forming on my forehead. Isra removes his hand, and I spit out whatever is in my mouth.

He sighs. "Mahi, I'm not here. So I can't help you."

His arms are no longer around me, and as my breathing slows down, I look behind to see nothing but a bush.

He left me. And although I feel relieved, I now have to face a more pressing threat. My fingers wrap around a branch and goosebumps have risen all over my skin. Rapidly looking around, I finally see orange eyes in the distance. Not too close, but close enough to charge at me. I can only imagine the acidic drool dripping down its chin as it growls.

The hellhound stares at me. Our eyes are locked. If it howls, many more will come. Maybe even some ferals. I'll stand no chance.

I take a step forward, my eyes still locked with its own. They are the only things I can see. If I lose them, then I'm lost. This stick will do nothing. All I can do is hope that I can use some type of heat on it like whatever I did to the cuffs.

The hellhound runs forward. My heart leaps, and I jump out of the way, hitting a tree. My breathing is heavy once again. I don't think I can do this.

It snarls at me, and I flinch as it jumps and pins me to the ground. Its paws dig into my shoulders. They rip through my clothes, piercing my flesh.

I'm screaming; my skin burns while tears blind my eyes. I push with all my strength to keep the hellhound's jaw away from me. It only gets closer, but the snapping of its mouth slows as my hands sink into something hot and slimy before it falls limp at my side.

My eyes squeeze shut as its nails leave my shoulders, a whimper escaping my mouth.

I lie there, my body shaking, drenched in sweat. Somehow, I killed it but I couldn't let Kavon know.

I gag as I pull my hand out of the hellhound's body. There is nothing but a visible cavity where my hand melted through. Grabbing a stick, I shove it in the hole and shake my hands to get rid of the dark blood. Kavon isn't stupid, but at least he won't know exactly how I killed this monster.

He's already there when I get back to the cave, cooking something on the fire. Relief floods through my body. When I sit on the ground, he rises quickly. His eyes are wide, and then they fall to my hands. He moves toward me with big steps, then stops and steps away.

"I thought you'd left for good," he says. It feels odd with how much distance there is between us. But a bizarre warmness builds inside me at the fact that he kept away. "Are you okay?"

"Yeah, I'm fine." I cross my arms, wincing at the sharp pain in my shoulders.

"Why the hell were you outside?"

"I was . . . trying to find food." I pull out the excuse quickly, gulping. It feels wrong to lie to him. "I ran into a hellhound."

"Let me clean the blood."

I shake my head. "I'll do it myself. The important thing is that I killed it."

Kavon lets out a frustrated sigh before he grabs onto one of his loose shirts, bundling it into a ball and throwing it over. "How'd you kill it?"

I place the cloth on my wound, sucking in a breath. "I'm not sure. But I ended up stabbing it with a branch."

"A branch?" he repeats.

"Yeah."

His lips press together, and he nods his head. "Must've been awfully strong to do that."

I shrug, my heart racing. "It happened so fast."

"Well, let's see it then." He motions outside. My mouth falls open, and I stand like a rock before turning around.

My senses are heightened as Kavon examines the body. The wind whistles in my ears while looking around to see if any other threat is approaching.

He points at the stick. "You killed it with this?"

"Yeah," I mutter. "Can we cook it?"

"I've never risked it," he says. "And I'm not going to. Are you sure you killed it with a stick?"

I don't say anything. He looks over his shoulder, sighs, and gets up. "They know we're here."

"What? How?"

"Relax," he says. "They don't know who is here. Just people. Hounds only go where there are people."

"So, what are we going to do?" I question.

"We're heading out, first thing in the morning."

10

"We aren't really going in there, are we?"

"Yes, we are."

We'd left the cave about two hours ago, at the crack of dawn, so there'd be enough sunlight to travel. Kavon had realized by now that I had no experience in this world. We'd spotted some demons eating the flesh off a dog, and I'd thrown up at the sight while he snuck by like it was normal. We still didn't have any water, so now my mouth was disgusting. He was also still pissed that I'd almost gotten myself killed when he'd saved me the day prior, which had made for some great awkward silence. But then he'd decided to give me lectures on how to survive. One of them was to never go into darkness.

And now he was telling me to break that very rule.

"A whole lot of ferals could be in there." I gulp, peering once more into the supermarket.

I can't believe there used to be buildings full of food. It was hard to fathom, especially after being raised to hunt and grow crops.

We'd come across three interconnected buildings, pieces of their giant names sitting on the ground along with other trash. Boxes, broken-up cars, and silver carts all litter the pavement. And bodies. Too many bodies. Most had been dead for a long time, except one that was maybe a week old. I avoided looking at it. But even after all that, Kavon kept insisting we go inside.

"Well, we need food, and everything is empty these days," he says, taking out the gun he'd gotten from the woman. "You know how to use this?"

Heat runs across my cheeks. "No."

"We only have four bullets, so you don't have to worry about reloading," Kavon says, shoving something into the gun and cocking it. He hands it over to me. "There's no safety. This is the trigger. Only press it when you have to."

It's heavier than I thought, and my fingers quiver as I grip it. "Hopefully, I won't have to use it."

"Only use it in a worst-case scenario," Kavon whispers, stepping into the store. There's a long row of huge windows at the front, most shattered. At least that'll help with the darkness. "Remember do not—"

"Make a sound," I finish. "I remember."

"One last thing," Kavon says. "No matter what, don't let a feral bite you. They don't just . . . eat you. Some infect you with a virus."

A shiver runs down my spine. "What happens?"

"Infected humans become just like the ferals. They kill anything in sight, and gladly allow other ferals to eat the corpse. The only cure, I assume, is in a demon city. Don't think too much about it. Just stay close," Kavon says, frowning and glancing down at my arm. "You should probably hold onto me."

I'm not sure how I can't overthink now, but I let out a long breath. "Good idea."

Holding onto his right wrist, Kavon and I move silently through the building. We pass a row of odd-looking, cramped desks with screens before entering the larger portion of the building.

There are dozens of shelves. Some toppled over. As we pass through them, my heart thumps against my chest. I can barely see, even with the light coming through the front of the building. Something heaves in the distance. I know we're not alone here. It only makes more sweat drip down my face.

"Find anything like this." Kavon grabs something off one of the fifth shelves we've come across. Almost all the ones we've gone through are wiped clean. I shift uncomfortably, glancing around to see if anything is lurking around. I hate being cramped up between the shelves like this. "Mahi."

"Sorry," I whisper, nodding at the beans in his hand. "Got it."

"This or energy bars, but I doubt you'll find any of those." Kavon straightens his back, and I tense, following his gaze and aiming the gun. "Holy shit."

"What?" Panic swells in my stomach.

"I think I might've found something." Kavon looks back at me with a grin. "Keep looking on these shelves. I'll be right at the end of this aisle. If that's what I think it is, we'll be out of here."

I open my mouth as he walks off, desperately wanting to scream his name. Something is watching me, I can feel it. Or maybe it's just my paranoia. If only I could shrink down smaller than I already am. Letting out a large, shaking breath, I start perusing through the shelves, but there is no point. Everything is gone. I'm not sure how Kavon even found this one. A few non-edible things are lying around. We *are* desperate, though. Maybe this is what it's come to.

My stomach growls like thunder, and I freeze, turning my gaze over to Kavon. I blink a few times to get a better picture of him. He's holding some kind of enormous container. Just as he gets closer, a wave of cool air dances over me from up top. For a split second, the sound of wings flapping crawls into my ears.

Don't do it. I know I'll only regret it. But slowly, I glance up at the ceiling and narrow my eyes. A gasp shoots out of my mouth, and I'm paralyzed for a second. I can barely see it, but it's something of a red man staring down at me with large wing-like arms. That's when I realize that his face is nothing like a man's. He doesn't seem to have eyes. There is nothing but a large mouth with long, baring teeth.

I stumble with my gun as a deathly scream floods the entire building.

"Shit!" Kavon's muffled voice cries out.

The gun falls from my hands, my fingers digging into my ears. The monster's shrieks pierce my brain, and I clutch onto the floor, bawling at the pressure that builds in my head.

I have to shut this thing up!

I look around frantically at the dark floor, my eyes landing on steel. Once I grab the gun, I squeeze my eyes shut at the deafening song. My fingers race to the trigger, and without even looking, I shoot up. The weapon almost flies out of my hand, a flash of light blinding me.

Silence fills the air. I rub my sore ears, heaving as I blink rapidly at Kavon. He takes out his sword and I watch his eight feet wings spreading out, knocking over both shelves before he shoots into the air just as the monster screams again.

This time, it's cut off quickly. I aim at the roof, trying to find any opening where I can shoot the creature, but a growl stops me. I glance toward the front of the store, breathless, as I meet orange eyes.

With the skull of a cat, the huge feral demon stalks toward me, its large paws shaking the ground with each step. At every second, Kavon's grunts and the other monster's screams cut my ear. This time, there was no one to save me. My fingers sweat against the gun.

The cat demon growls right before lunging. I'm not sure if it saw my weapon or not because it bounces from side to side as I waste one bullet. At the last second, it jumps directly in my direction. I shoot the last two bullets, and the demon falls onto me. I shriek while my back lands with a thud on the cold floor. The body is limp, and despite how heavy it weighs against my lungs, I manage to shove it off.

"Kavon!" I scream, my eyes blurring as I get up and desperately look around. I can hear him, and I see two bodies flying above me, but his grunts and the monster's squeals make the tears flow faster down my cheeks. He *can't* die. But all I can do is watch from down here unless I grab something.

It doesn't matter. He crashes into the fallen shelves and is up on his feet before I can even run over to him.

"Let's go!" he yells. I don't wait. I turn and run toward the light.

The blue sky welcomes me, and I clutch onto my chest while I let out huffs of air. Kavon flies out seconds after me, rolling onto the ground. I'm racing over to him before I know it.

"Crap," he murmurs, getting up slowly.

"Are you hurt?" I ask him. Without even thinking, I grab his arms and look for any cuts.

He pulls his arms away. "I'm okay—" A groan leaves his mouth, and he flexes his wings. The right one is bent unnaturally, almost as if it can fold in half. "Never mind. This is what I get for breaking one of the golden rules. The rice is still in there. At least the damn thing's dead."

My fingers twitch with the urge to heal it, but I don't do anything. "Is it broken?"

"Yes, but don't worry about it. Were you bitten?"

"No."

"Are you sure?" His eyes form slits. "You *have* to be sure."

"I'm sure," I reassure him. "What was that? A demon?"

Kavon shakes his head. "It didn't have those soul-sucking orange eyes. This was something different."

"Was it trying to kill us by screaming?" I ask. "That doesn't really make sense."

"I don't know." Kavon rubs his face before his skin pales.

His head whips toward where we just came from, and I follow his gaze. The creature lays inside, just at the edge of where the light meets darkness. It slightly shuffles, before becoming completely still. A chill runs through my body. It looks so *human* but so monstrous at the same time.

Kavon taps my shoulder, and we both turn toward the giant wall in the distance. From here, I can see how wide the city inside actually is. But as I narrow my eyes, I notice a vehicle getting closer and closer.

"It signaled our location," Kavon whispers. He grabs my arm. "Go hide! Now. I'll fight them off."

"What? No! You're injured," I say. "You can't fight them by yourself. Let's hide together."

"Mahi fucking listen to me!" I flinch at his stern voice. "Those are demons. We're out of bullets, and I'm sorry, but you're a liability. Let me handle this."

He shoves me in the direction of a black, broken car. My eyebrows furrow, but I crouch behind it, grabbing a piece of broken glass in case I need it.

Seconds later, a white vehicle pulls up while I peer through my car's broken windows. My eyes widen at the six human possessed demons running out with guns pointed at Kavon. A sour taste forms in my mouth and the back of my throat aches. There's no way he can get out of this. He's outnumbered. But I can't find the nerve to get up.

"If you've heard of me, you know you have no chance," Kavon tells them, his arm coming out. If his wing is killing him, he doesn't show it.

Kavon pulls at the air, and all the demons' guns fly out of their hands. I cover my mouth to make sure I don't make a sound. He just gets cooler and cooler. "I'll give you a chance to retreat."

"That banshee was wired to call for only two people." The demon closest to Kavon grins. Compared to the other demons, he seems older, perhaps middle-aged. "You think we wouldn't come prepared?"

"Well, you don't have your guns anymore." Kavon shrugs. I narrow my eyes, jolting when I see a teenage demon on the side, pulling something from behind him, a flat circle in his hand.

I stand up. "Kavon, watch out!"

The demon throws the item onto the ground and red tubes shoot out. Kavon jumps back just in time, and the tubes wrap around one of the other demons in an instant. It zaps her with some kind of orange electricity, squeezing her together while she falls to her knees. Her yell buzzes out of her mouth. I suck in a quick breath, my entire body trembling when the middle-aged demon meets my eyes.

His eyes flash black as the veins bulge from his forehead. "It's the girl!"

He grabs his radio. "Three-nine-seven is with the Shadow Angel—" Kavon darts in front of him, slicing off the demon's hand before he can say another word.

My head whips to the side. The teenage demon grabs his gun. All the innocence has vanished from his grey face. He aims at my legs. I shriek, backing away as a bullet hits the ground, but the next one drills through my thigh.

I scream, dropping the glass while my eyes water and my hands tremble over the wound. Steam sizzles from the hole in my body. This is some other kind of gun, and I don't hesitate to heal myself. The demon stands before me by the time I'm done, reaching down to grab me. I grip the glass shard and carve it into his throat. I twist. Blood engulfs my hand. My teeth grit together, and I drag the glass down, grunting. He roars and falls against my body before he stares up at the sky and opens his mouth widely.

I gag and let him go. Black smoke escapes from his mouth. My lips try to form words as I watch the darkness invade the air. It's an entity of some kind. The vessel falls to the ground, motionless. My eyes are glued to the smoke, fog, gas, whatever it is, as it seeps into the ground.

It takes me a few seconds before my eyes move over to the vessel. The horns and grey skin are still there, but the bulging veins are colorless. I take his gun, but I am stunned when I look up and see all the demons dead. Kavon is on his knees, panting while he cleans the blood off his sword. His right wing looks empty compared to the left as black feathers litter the ground.

I place the gun down, pursing my lips as I walk up to him. Blood covers his face and clothes, and his eyes go wide when he sees more on my hand. A gasp leaves my mouth when I take in the sight of the blade embedded in his stomach. When he falls, a part of me dies inside.

"I'm sorry," he breathes out. "They . . . they were looking for me."

Every other sound fades as I stare at his eyes. My hands lace over the weapon in his body, and I grimace as I think of Laurel; as I think of the knife that sat in her body. Of what she did to me after she found out.

I pull the blade out before Kavon can say another word. The rest comes with ease. The energy I search for courses through me as I place my hand on his wound. He gasps, and I meet his eyes. They fill with life and with shock. I choke on the pain that fills within me, moving onto his arms and ignoring the itching in my own. Next, I heal his broken wing. I let out a slow breath once I finish, resting on Kavon's warm chest. It's almost peaceful. My cheeks heat up and I move away quickly before fear replaces my embarrassment. I face away from him, uncertain of what he'll say.

"How did you do that?" I hear him ask, his voice laced with . . . excitement? "And your eyes, they look like fire. I've never seen that before."

"I'm not who you think I am," I say. "I'm not human, or maybe I am. I don't know. All I know is since I'm different, the demons are hunting me."

Kavon doesn't say anything. When I turn to face him, he isn't even looking at me. His eyes are glued to the ground while he fumbles with his sword. He bites his lip. I sigh, narrowing my eyes and looking past his shoulder. Two figures sneak out of the store. A man and a woman. Humans. *Survivors.*

Kavon finally looks at me, and seeing my confusion, he spins on his heel. "Stop, that's ours!"

The man holds the big container of rice. The woman and him spare us one glance, blinking at Kavon's black wings before sprinting from the store entrance.

Kavon soars into the sky. I shield my face from the sudden wind that pushes me back, and gasp when Kavon slams on the ground before the humans. He raises his sword, and the man drops the rice while the woman falls in hysterics.

"Stop!" I yell, racing behind the other survivors. Now they are sandwiched between us. "Don't kill them."

"I wasn't going to," Kavon says. He clenches his jaw. "Unless they don't give us the rice."

"You're the Angel of Shadow!" the woman cries. Up close, I see how thin she is. Her skin is rough against her bones, patchy and loose as if it's lost all its elasticity. Her greying brown hair sits in patches on her skull, and she looks back at me with ghostly blue eyes. The man wears a dark grey, scruffy beard and a balding head. He has the same thin frame, and he tremors continuously. Both of their clothes are filthy.

I narrow my eyes at Kavon. Clearly, the demons are after him too for some reason. He glances at me for a second at the mention of his new title before staring at the woman with pure fury. Without hesitation, he brings his sword to her neck. "Are you giving us the rice or not?"

The woman sobs, begging Kavon not to kill her and even though the man is paralyzed, he seems to understand the situation. He finally speaks up. "We . . . have water," he slurs out. "Back at our farm."

Kavon doesn't seem to believe him. "You're from Rivermouth?"

"No." The woman shakes her head violently. "They rejected us."

That only makes Kavon more suspicious. "Why?"

The man turns toward me, raising an eyebrow at my bloody hand. I place my arms behind my back, the hairs on the nape of my neck rising as the man continues to stare. "They said we were too weak," he tells me. "They only accept the strong."

I clear my throat. "You have water?"

He nods his head. "We have a well that collects rainwater on our farm."

I'm used to being deprived of nutrients, but that doesn't mean I don't still feel the pain that comes with it.

I meet Kavon's eyes. "We should go with them. We have to get away from here anyway."

He looks back at the woman, who is still crying. I chew on my lip. I hope he agrees because I know I won't go without him. He's saved my life one too many times to be a stranger anymore.

Kavon lets out a heavy breath, a vein throbbing in his neck. "Fine." It sounds like he's struggling to speak. "But, if you're lying, I won't hesitate to rob all your supplies and leave you for the ferals."

"Oh, thank you!" The woman brings her hands together into a fist, pumping them at Kavon. "Bless you! May God bless you!"

Kavon grunts. "God doesn't exist."

I gulp, walking back to the bodies of the slain demons while Kavon asks the survivors where their campsite was. I take one of the guns, and reluctantly grab a radio from a demon's hand. I'm not sure how to use it, but maybe it'll give me some information. I could always ask—

I stop myself before I can think of *his* name.

"Good idea."

My heart almost jumps out of my chest. I turn to see the man gripping one of the demon's guns.

"Drop it." Kavon is beside him in seconds. His sword is against the man's neck, who struggles to move before finally placing the gun back on the ground. "Take us to your vehicle now."

"We can take this one," I say, pointing at the demon's car.

"I want to see how they got here," Kavon says. "It's better to be sure. And the radio and gun, you should take it," he says then turns his attention back to the man, "But not *you*." He lets him go and the man quickly scurries away toward the store. Kavon nudges his head at me to follow.

"I understand," I tell him before he can say a word. He stares at me in confusion. "That you can't trust easily, but that doesn't mean you should kill them."

"Everyone is a threat." Kavon's sword finally retracts and he sheathes it.

"And me?"

He pauses. "You were—*are*—different."

Heat forms on my face and I try to push it away. It's the way he says it. The way the words roll off his tongue. There's something sweet about it. "About me—"

He shushes me, pointing at the man walking in front of us. "Not now."

I gulp, nodding my head. "What's Rivermouth?"

We turn a corner, now beside the store. "It's a settlement about six hours from here."

"A human one? How is that possible?"

"Yeah. They've somehow managed. You can go there if you want, after this. They don't take in just anyone though."

"Did you try to go there?"

"Yup."

I frown. "Were you rejected?"

He sucks in a breath. "Yes. They thought I'd bring danger, and they were right."

That means I shouldn't go there either, unless I don't tell them anything. It does seem like the perfect place to hide, and it's been so long since I was in a community where humans were the ones in charge. But if the demons showed up there, they'd slaughter everyone. I sigh. I hadn't even seen the place and I was already making up scenarios in my head. I might not even be accepted, like Kavon.

My eyebrows furrow, and I look at the pavement. The demons were after him for some reason. They'd called him the Shadow Angel. And even the survivors called him something similar. Maybe he wasn't as trustworthy as this bond made me feel, even though it made me sick to even think that. Now wasn't the time to ask him any questions.

But I would find out.

11

THE MAN'S name was Luke, and the woman's Natalie. They weren't married or together, as I had assumed. They had met at the peak of the apocalypse and had hidden together. Somehow, they'd avoided the containment prisons, along with some other survivors. Now, they were the only ones left from their group. The farm hadn't been their home for long. About a month, they'd told us.

It turns out they'd ridden bikes to get here but since we needed to get out of here quickly, we placed their bikes inside the demon truck and took off.

Kavon had wanted us to fly behind the vehicle but I begged him to sit inside with me. I wasn't ready to soar through the sky just yet. So here he was, his wings cramped inside the truck. Though his feathers repeatedly hit me in the face, I didn't say anything since I'm the one who'd asked him to be uncomfortable with me.

The radio had said a few words, but Kavon and I

couldn't make it out. Hopefully, it wouldn't be entirely useless.

After an awkward drive, we finally reach the farm. Clear yellow fields paint the ground with long grass and a small red house was positioned to the right of a larger white one. A small broken fence surrounds the land but I know it won't do anything against demons. Behind the house is a far away forest, which means ferals hide inside.

"The well is out in the field," Luke says as we get out of the car.

I stare in awe at the white house right in front of us, despite its worn appearance. Some of the paint has chipped off and one of the wooden steps is broken. Unkempt plants climb the dirty walls, and one of the second-floor windows is broken. I have never been in a real house before, and the expression on my face isn't hiding my excitement.

Natalie gives Kavon and I a nervous smile. "We can cook the rice in the backyard. I'll go start a fire."

"*You* go start the fire." Kavon rips the rice from her hands. "Luke can show us the well first. We did only come here for water."

Natalie nods, gulping and running into her house. Luke gives us both a blank stare but sweat trails down his cheek as he walks in front of us. I'm about to follow when Kavon places a hand in front of my chest to stop me. He waits until Luke is about ten feet away before walking.

"There's something off about these two," he whispers. "It doesn't make sense why Rivermouth would reject them. They clearly have scavenging skills and can source water."

I tighten my grip around the demon gun. "Natalie

just seems scared. She could be faking it though, but Luke doesn't seem right." I glance back at the house, my eyes narrowing at the barn. "There could be more people inside."

Kavon's eyes flash black. "They seem to know about me. Hopefully, they're smart enough not to try anything. Be prepared for anything."

I stop in my tracks. Luke is already waiting for us by the well, but I don't care. "What exactly about you *is* there to know?"

"I've been outside a demon city for two years. I guess word spread about a black-winged angel."

He's hiding something. But I won't interrogate him right now. It's not a good time to make Kavon my enemy. We need to deal with the situation we're currently in.

I sigh. "Let's go see if this well really has water."

I wake up with sweat clinging to my body. My heart is beating wildly and heavy breaths escape my mouth while I run to find my finger scanner.

Then I remember.

I clutch my chest, slumping onto the floor and allow air to flow back into my lungs. My hands move to my hair, as I tug at the strands. I try to think of something else. Anything else. But my heart pounds against my chest, threatening to tear itself out.

As my eyes adjust to the dark, I notice that my bedroom door is wide open. It turns out that Natalie and Luke had been honest with us. They were alone here and they had a lot of water. They'd offered me and Kavon separate rooms upstairs, but I decided to stay with Kavon so that we could take turns keeping watch. I'm not sure what time it is, but I assume it's my turn, yet Kavon is nowhere in sight. I tiptoe away from my bed, leaning against the rusty table beside the empty mattress he's supposed to be on.

Panic rushes inside me, and I race to check my bedside table. When I open the drawer, I turn to stone. Both the radio and demon gun are *gone.*

A lump forms in my throat. I glance at the open door again. He couldn't have called the demons, could he? My mouth suddenly goes dry and I lick my lips instinctively as I walk toward the single window in this room. It's shielded by dusty curtains, and I know I shouldn't open them. If a feral sees me, I'd be putting everyone at risk.

My heart leaps at the sound of footsteps. It sounds like someone is downstairs. Maybe Kavon couldn't sleep? My gut twists with every step I take, but I need to know what's going on.

Luke and Natalie's door is shut, which means they might still be sleeping. I try not to breathe too loud, cringing as the stairs slightly creak under my weight. I've only gone down two stairs when I freeze at the sound of more footsteps. These move quickly. A soft breeze presses against my back, and my breath hitches in my throat when the footsteps come from behind me.

I spin around, throwing my hands out, but nothing is there—except Natalie and Luke's door is open now. My palms sweat, and I frown at the sound of chewing. If they were eating, then they'd hidden food from me and Kavon.

"Mahi."

I jump at the whisper of my name. Without thinking, I turn around and shove the body in front of me. Kavon slams into the wall as bits and pieces of wood fall out of an already broken house.

I clutch my face before racing down the steps and stopping halfway where Kavon sits. "Sorry!"

"Quiet," he says, getting up. He glances at the cracks in the wall, and I look away from his gaze. I'd forgotten all about my sudden strength. "There's something going on here. Luke and Natalie are up to something. The front window is broken."

"Where's the demon gun and radio?" I ask.

He shakes his head. "I don't have it." A vein pulses on the side of his face. "But I'm pretty sure I know who does. Come on, we're leaving."

"No, it's still dark—"

A figure smashes through the roof. Kavon's wings wrap around my body to protect me from the debris. I manage to see what is in here; It's the same monster from the grocery store.

My hands clamp around my ears the second it screams, but it's cut off quickly. Kavon flies toward it, crashing it into the kitchen.

I run my fingers through my hair, practically sprinting to Luke and Natalie's room. I expect to see them secretly eating some snacks, or wide-awake, wondering what the hell is going on, but my heart sinks before palpating madly.

A creature sits on top of Natalie, who's sleeping on a small bed. I can barely see its head, but its orange eyes subtly light up her devoured stomach. It has the abdomen of a spider, and claws for arms that chop

Natalie's body into smaller pieces. The chewing, it sounded so *human* earlier, but now, all I can hear is a monster tearing into human flesh. A hand clamps over my mouth, and I almost scream.

Luke drags me into the bedroom bathroom. Once inside, he hooks his arm around my throat just as the banshee screams again. The creature's cry is short-lived when another crash cuts off its voice.

"Let me go," I whisper. "We have to go! Kavon needs our help." That's when I see it. The radio on the sink countertop. "Why do you have that?"

Luke shushes me. I really shouldn't talk, but more screams go off. This time from outside. Dread sprouts within my gut.

"Why do you have that?" I repeat. A voice comes from the radio and Luke tries to block it, but it's too late. I hear what I needed to.

Thanks for the tip. Hide out until we get there, and we'll fulfill the deal. I know the person is a demon. Luke increases his hold on me, and I gasp for air. I have to get him off me.

A wave of heat overcomes my body, and Luke shrieks as the flesh on his hand starts to burn. Already, some of his skin is like charcoal. I push him onto the floor once his grip loosens.

I grab the radio and smash it against the sink. Luke's whimpers turn into sobs at my sudden strength. "Why?" I ask.

"W-we heard them say they were searching for you," he manages to stammer out. Water seeps from under him. He pissed himself. I almost feel bad, frowning at his tear-stained cheeks. Then he says, "We had to make a deal."

My hands turn to fists, but my mouth drops open when a claw pierces Luke's forehead, cutting through his eyeballs. Half of his face slides off as blood squirts out of the wound. His body goes rigid for a moment and then slumps on the wall behind him. I don't even realize I'm screaming when I glance at the spider creature. It has a human skull with dark hair sitting on top, but its orange eyes glare at me. I try not to move suddenly when a deep roar escapes its black mouth full of monstrous fangs. Its human neck trails down into a spider-like body, and its claws come for me, but I roll onto the floor, pushing it aside. The creature lunges at me again and I escape into the bedroom.

For a split second, I look at Natalie. Except, it isn't Natalie. It's a lump of blood and flesh. The next second I'm racing to the door, but I land face first into the floor when something sticks to my feet.

On my knees, I gasp as I try to desperately tear off some kind of webbing. The monster stands before me, watching as I helplessly rip at its trap, and then its claw comes down, straight for my face but I'm not ready to die.

"No!" I scream, throwing my hands out. Flame erupts from my palms. The creature shrieks monstrously, its shoulder ablaze. I watch as it thrashes around and falls to the floor.

I'm not sure how I did that, but I use the remaining fire in my hand to burn off the webbing. I'm ready to leave when a sharpness digs into my right ankle. My eyes widen at the monster's fangs in my foot. I stomp on its head, squashing it. Gasping for air, I bring a hand to my chest. Once I catch my breath, I heal my ankle.

Only it still stings. Immediately I think of the worst. *Shit. I'm infected.*

Whatever this bite is, I need to focus on finding Kavon and getting out of here. I look back at the door. It's completely quiet. And although it's peaceful, it's also terrifying.

I sprint downstairs, ignoring the pain in my ankle. Kavon's sword sits retracted by the steps. A bad feeling sinks into my chest as I clutch onto it. There's a giant hole where the front door should be, and figures coming toward the house. Escaping from the back, I round the house until I'm hidden on the side, staring at two white trucks and more than a dozen demons. Kavon is on the ground, surrounded by a glowing rope. He doesn't look like he's struggling. I don't even think he's awake. The banshee lies dead, a few feet away from him.

The cool air is perfect tonight, but it doesn't calm my nerves. Two demons grab onto him, taking him to one of the trucks while the other demons get in. My fear keeps me rooted in this spot. It's when they slam their doors and start their engine that the realization finally hits me like a punch in the face.

As the bond that pulls me toward him fades, I squeeze onto his sword and lean against the house. I watch the vehicle head toward the very city Kavon told me to avoid. My ankle burns, begging for attention, but I can't focus. I wait until the other demons are gone before freaking out.

My eyes bulge out of my skull while I stare at the white spot getting smaller and smaller, repeatedly blinking to make sure this is real. I cover my mouth.

"Shit." I shake my head, pacing back and forth. My

legs are weak, and my chest is twisted in a knot as I crouch down. "This can't be happening."

I throw Kavon's sword. The world blurs around me. There's nothing I can do. *Nothing.* He saved my life and now he's as good as dead. And so am I. I can't heal my ankle for some reason. As Kavon told me, I'm infected with some kind of virus, and the only cure is in the demon city.

I rub at my face before getting up. As I walk over to Kavon's sword, I freeze. There *is* someone who can get into the city. Someone who helped me escape containment. I know it's a bad idea, but I'm desperate.

Gulping, I grip Kavon's sword, the name forming on my lips. "Isra."

12

It doesn't take long before he shows up. By the time I'm sprinting along the tree line, back to that forsaken city they took Kavon to, Isra pops up in front of me.

I halt, almost bumping into his chest. My heart leaps from the scare. "Where are you?" he asks.

I take a second to catch my breath, tasting blood in my mouth and pressing my fingers against my stomach cramp. I'd taken the demon car that we'd driven to the farm after figuring out how to use it. But the vehicle had stopped working once I'd reached the supermarket. Maybe it was still functional, but I had no idea how to fix it. Now, I wish I had brought some water with me.

The sun is finally up, and it's so damn hot, but one of the things I like about not being an ordinary human is that I don't get tired as quickly. Anyone else would've been on the ground.

My infected ankle stings at my sudden lack of movement. It hurts more when I'm still. *The infection doesn't matter,* I think once I've regained my composure, hiding Kavon's sword behind my back. My gut screams at me to not let Isra see it.

The prince frowns. He's wearing black cargo pants and a white t-shirt. There is a radio sitting on his shoulder. It's odd seeing him in regular clothes. "Do you know what's going on?"

"I need your help—"

"You don't get to speak until you answer me," Isra interrupts, gesturing at my chest. "You're covered in dry blood. The hellhound, I presume. Or something else?"

My jaw clenches. Why did I even bother thinking he'd help? Time is ticking by. Who knows what they're doing to Kavon right now or how long I have before this infection takes over. Scoffing, I run past the demon, ignoring the flutter in my stomach when I shove his shoulder. "I don't have time for this."

My speed doesn't stop him. He comes up beside me, sprinting with ease. *Is he actually running? But he still can't see where I am?*

"You were with the hybrid," Isra says. I hope I don't give him any reaction, despite my shock. "He's dangerous. There are more risks than I thought about out here. You heard a scream, right?"

It'd be better not to tell him I was there. "I heard something."

"What you heard was one of Lucifer's mutants."

"A mutant?" I give him a quick glance while taking in heavy breaths. Here comes the headache. "Wasn't it a demon?"

"No," he tells me. "This should be a term you're familiar with. That monster was one of his *experiments*."

I stop in my tracks and drop Kavon's sword, heaving

while wiping off the sweat at the back of my neck. "You mean that thing . . . it was human once?"

"Well, some demons were also humans once," Isra says, tilting his head. "But this thing never died. It was *made* into that."

"Why would Lucifer do that?"

"Because it's one of his hobbies."

"How long?"

"He's been making them for around ten years. Hellhounds are another offspring from his experiments, you know. He loves keeping them as pets."

I'm not sure why he's giving me all this information, or if it's even true. "So, in containment, when someone would be taken—"

"They were experimented on," Isra finishes for me. His red eyes narrow, and a frown forms on his face. "Now tell me where you are. Lucifer's growing relentless in finding you."

"Why?" I groan. "Why can't he leave me alone? I don't understand why he's on this manhunt."

"Because of what you are." His lips curl up, and he seems to have gone into some kind of trance. Even though he has no pupils, it seems like he's staring off in the distance and daydreaming. "He's scared of you. I haven't seen him like this in years."

"How many more of these experiments are there?"

"He's dumped a lot of failed ones outside the walls. I'm not sure how many successful ones he's made, just that there *will* be hundreds."

"What's that supposed to mean?" I know what it means. I just don't want it to be true.

"All those inmates in containment centers, he's

turning them into his monsters one by one. All to find you."

The world spins around me. I think about all the elderly I saw. The innocent women and men who just wanted to live a little longer before their souls went down to Hell. Now, they were going to meet a fate worse than death.

Just to find me. All because I healed someone.

"Shit," I whisper, bringing both my hands to my head. "This is crazy."

"Where are you?"

"No." I back away from Isra. I don't know why he's told me all this, except to get me on his side. I still think this is all a game for him. Even if he let me go, it's never good to ask a demon for something, but I have to. "I called you here for a reason. I want you to tell me how to get into Morningstar."

Isra raises an eyebrow. "The city?"

"Yes," I say through my teeth. "I need you to tell me how to get inside, unnoticed."

He glares at me. "And why would I do that?"

"Because if you do," I mutter, letting out a sigh. "It'll show me that I can trust you. Then, I'll start to actually listen to all the crazy shit you have to say."

He studies me, rubbing his chin before a smirk forms on his face. "There are many buildings outside the walls. Wild demons tend to use them to hide from the sun. One of them, the largest house, has an entrance to the sewers right below it. Just be careful."

I'm not sure if I heard him right. "You're actually helping me? Just like that?"

"I'll do anything for you." Isra grins, but there's some humor laced in his voice.

I roll my eyes. "Sure."

His eyes brighten at my words, and then he fades out of existence. A sigh leaves my mouth, my sweaty palm gripping back onto Kavon's sword. I hate holding the thing, fearing that I'll somehow cut one of my hands off by accidentally making the blade come out. As I peer at it, I realize I had never actually taken a good look at it.

The handle is red, and the bottom looks as if it's made of gold. I narrow my eyes to get a better look. The sides of the top part of the grip, just before the actual steel, rise up and there's some kind of symbol on them. It looks like flames.

"That's freaky," I say to myself, opening my palm. If only I knew how I made those flames. I wouldn't be completely useless anymore.

Slouching, I lazily squint at the wall. There's no entrance from what I can see. It must be on one of the other sides.

The numb, tingling feeling in my ankle breaks my curiosity and the sensation slightly rises up to my knee. That can't be good. I need to get inside. These mutants, monsters, whatever they're called, are bound to find me, especially if Lucifer is making an army of them. All those people, transforming into beasts because of me. Shivers crawl up my spine, bile rising up my throat.

I start running again, straight to those sewers Isra told me about.

∾

There is nothing but small, destroyed buildings and a massive wall in the distance once I cross the road. The forest is far behind me now. My body burns up, cramps digging into my stomach. I'm not in the best shape, and all that running sucked my energy dry.

While passing pairs of small buildings, many with shattered glass and huge, gaping holes, I notice the few ferals hiding inside—my stomach backflips. Their orange eyes burn through me as the sounds of inhuman growls quietly come from the shadows. I shift my focus to the ground, taking in the long grass and other plants growing between the cracks of pavement.

How am I going to find the sewers? I run my hands through my hair and grimace while surveying the streets —big mistake.

Bodies. Dozens of them. I even trip over a few. Most of their faces are ripped to shreds and chunks of flesh were torn from their arms and legs. I look away as nausea builds inside me. How many of these people were killed by ferals, trying to seek a safer place? How many were killed by the guards on top of the wall? The more I'm out here, the sicker I see the world is.

I come upon a broken-up road, more grass than cement, if anything. The largest building that I can see is on this street. That's where Isra told me the sewer was. The biggest *house* in this place. Its windows are shattered like everything else on this road. There's a large gaping hole on the right, revealing more debris inside. It's hard to believe people lived in these huge homes compared to the small cabin I lived in before containment.

Still on the street, I walk in front of the house to get a better look. But as I take one more step, my foot goes straight down a hole, and my body follows. I land with a small splash, a whimper leaving my mouth.

I groan at my aching, wet feet. That's going to leave a bruise. I glance back at where I came from, and I see a few leaves and grass slowly falling. It makes sense Isra would hide the entrance. I just wish I had paid more attention.

A disgusting stench fills my nostrils as I get up and I use my hand to cover my mouth. There's nothing but darkness and silence, besides the rippling sound of water echoing close by.

I'm blind down here, and now I don't even have a way out. The hole I fell through is far too high since the natural light barely flows into the darkness. From what I can see, the walls are damp, painted with fungus. It's filthy down here, and the silence only makes it seem like I'm being watched. Isra could've at least warned me about this because, honestly, I'm going to die down here now.

"That's not a pretty face."

I jump up at his voice, a groan escaping my mouth.

"Of course, you'd show up." I spin around to face him. His glowing red eyes light up the environment around us, yet somehow, he doesn't know where I am. Even so, he can touch me and he can affect what's around him. However scary that is, it's also insanely interesting and right now, I need to use him.

"I did what you asked," Isra says, closing the space between us. My eyes trail down to his feet, which walk through the puddles of dirty water as if they weren't even there. "Are you going to tell me where you are now?"

"I said I'd *start* trusting you," I say, the lie easily

rolling off my tongue. "So, for once, you can talk, and I won't try to tune you out."

Turning back around, I slowly walk a few steps, waiting for Isra to come up beside me so he can light up my surroundings. He places a hand on my shoulder, and I shove it off.

"Are you okay?" he asks, frowning.

"Of course," I let out a nervous laugh. "Unlike you, I can't relax. I'm always on the move."

From what I can see, there's a long circular tunnel with shallow water running along it. My shoes are going to be soaked, but I already smell and look like garbage. All that matters is getting into the city quietly.

It takes all my will to keep moving forward. I know I don't want to see what's in this city. I had a freaking nightmare about it, although I can only vaguely remember what happened. My dad was the one telling me about it.

I glance at Isra. "Can people visit other people's dreams?" I ask, cringing as we move along.

"I've never heard of that," says Isra. "Humans are very plain."

"If a human was taken from outside the wall, would the demons bring them inside the city?"

"Sometimes."

My heart skips a beat, a flicker of hope forming inside. I try to push it away, but it doesn't disappear. Maybe, just maybe, my dad is in here. A chill runs through me as I think of what he might be going through. He might be one of the monsters Lucifer has created. He might've been the one in the store, but he also might be alive. There's a chance.

Isra crosses his arms. "Why do you ask?"

"Never mind." I shake my head. "When did Lucifer start doing his experiments for an army?"

"The second he found out we lost you," Isra says. "I'm not his favorite, so granted, I got some heat for it. Nothing I couldn't handle."

Laurel could be one of those things right now. Prickles rise up my neck, my heart sinking at the thought. If she's the reason the demons found out about me, then maybe she got out as a reward. Why else would she turn me over if not for a deal?

"What do they do? Besides screaming," I ask. There are loads more tunnels as I go along. There are so many different paths I can take, but if I get lost, there'll be no way I can get out of here. Straight it is.

"Nothing," Isra sighs. "As of now, they are useless creatures. They're set to scream if they see you but will attack only if provoked. Hellhounds are only useful for killing, and the other abominations he's created aren't conscious enough to take orders."

"That's all you know?"

"You seem shocked."

I can't help the small smile that forms on my face. "I thought you'd be there or something when Lucifer made them—"

A shriek leaves my mouth, and I collide into Isra's body. "Mahi!" he yells.

I breathe heavily, a hand on my chest as I watch a small lizard against one of the walls scurry away from Isra's small light. A grin cracks across my face. "That thing almost gave me a heart attack."

Isra comes up in front of me. "What thing? You made me think you were about to die."

"Maybe I was," I say. "Lizards are one of the creepiest things to exist."

"A lizard?"

"It's funny because I was never scared of the bugs or animals back home." I laugh, walking past him. "Everyone thought I was crazy climbing up trees to look at them."

I gasp when I realize who I'm talking to, what I'd almost done. There was an extremely low chance Isra would find out where I used to live, but it was still possible. He just had to ask the demons who'd picked me up the right questions. Then it'd just be a matter of finding the place. Unless what my dad had told me was true. Once you leave, you can never return.

If Isra's interested, though, he doesn't comment on it. "Where could you be that there's a lizard?"

His tone is hard to detect. He has to know I'm in the sewers after I asked about them. I shrug, narrowing my eyes at the ladder in the close distance. "I don't know."

"You should've tried to burn it."

My cheeks heat up. "I don't know how to do that."

He speaks some more but I ignore it and start running toward the ladder. As my fingers curl around the bars, I suck in some air because of how cold they are. I rush up, turning the circular door at the top and getting out of that disgusting place. The air becomes richer and the stuffiness I'd been feeling fades away.

Clean air. Finally.

The wall is gigantic up close, but I don't spend too much time looking at it. I take in the tall buildings surrounding me. They have at least three floors. I'm trapped between the two of them. For a second, I feel confined in the narrow space, but it goes away quickly. My fingers trail along one of the dark red buildings, its texture alien to my skin. I've only seen tents, wood, and metal-nothing like this. This is so different from out there. In here, life looks survivable.

It's at this moment that I realize I don't know where to go. The morning wind howls in my ear. I shiver, glaring at the clouds while my stomach twists into a knot.

I freeze at the sound of voices in the distance, before I will myself to lean against one of the buildings and peer around the corner. There's a road up ahead, and a group of demons walk by the gap between the buildings. My jaw drops as I notice someone among them. I slap my hand on top of my mouth to silence my sob, my vision blurring.

It's my dad. He's *alive.*

"Make sure to find the weapon." Those are the last words I hear before the conversation fades out, but that voice is unforgettable.

I rub my eyes, my lips forming a smile. This isn't a hallucination. That *is* his deep and intimidating voice. That's the brown skin, dark hair, and pointed nose we share. And for some reason, he's with the demons. They must be forcing him to help. Now my dream makes sense if he really was in it. He's in the city himself, so he knows how unsafe it must be. It doesn't matter. I won't be leaving without him now.

"Amazing hiding spot."

I jump, turning to face Isra. He rests his hands on the

wall, keeping himself at arm's length. His grey skin and red eyes illuminate differently than before. He's physically here. My heart accelerates and I look around for a place to hide, but then I give up. There's no point.

A sigh leaves his mouth. "What are you doing Mahi? You're going to be caught. Monsters aren't just outside the walls."

"How'd you find me?"

He laughs quietly. Controlled. Fake. "You're so cute. I told you where to go, remember? You didn't think I'd let you come here by yourself?"

I glare down at the ground, letting out a slow breath. He'll know where Kavon is. And the cure. The pain in my ankle has gone numb now, but the coldness has climbed up to my knee. If I were a regular human, I suspect I'd be dead by now. Or worse.

I could ask him about my father but he might use that against me. "We have to save Kavon," I finally say.

"Look at that, you know his name. Nothing about him though, I'm sure."

"Please."

Isra narrows his eyes at my frown before glaring at my pleading expression. "You don't have to beg. I'll help you."

"Really?" I question. "What's the catch?"

"The catch is, you shouldn't be here." He grabs me and pulls me toward him just as something invisible snaps from where I was standing. I gasp, but Isra raises his hand. The sound is replaced with whimpers. The hellhound lowers its eyes.

I'm too surprised to pull away from Isra. He's the one who lets me go. I gulp as I stare at his chest. He wasn't cold like I expected. Instead, when I was against him, a comfortable warmth that comes with any hug radiated from his body.

"How did you do that?" I ask, walking away from the demon dog.

"I'm in charge of them," Isra says. "All the animals, actually. Now come on. The hybrid isn't in Hell yet. He's actually pretty close."

He motions for me to follow. I hesitate but swallow any doubts I have. If he's lying, it doesn't matter. I have to trust him.

13

BONES. That's all the feral demon had left to eat, from what I could see. For some reason, I couldn't tear my eyes away from where it sat in the middle of the street. It was similar to the cat one I'd encountered in the grocery store. The human it ate wasn't even a person anymore. The monster had devoured every single cell, and it was now licking the bones clean.

It took Isra shaking me to knock me out of the trance.

"I'm fine," I tell him. "I didn't expect to see ferals here."

He gives me a face that looks like he doesn't believe me. "They make sure humans don't come out until curfew ends."

I nod my head and place my palm against my forehead. We're hiding in what Isra had told me is an alleyway. It's narrow enough that we won't be seen, if we're careful.

"He's in there." Isra points to a row of connected buildings, all different colors. Most, if not all, are three stories high and demons walk along the sidewalk outside.

"I expected a fortress," I say.

Isra glances at me with a smile. "You know what that is?"

I open my mouth but gasp when a sharp pain runs from my ankle to my thigh. I bite my lip to stop myself from making any noise, backing away from Isra.

"Are you okay?" he asks.

"You can order the demons to leave, right?" I blurt out.

"And make it obvious I'm here to save the hybrid?" Isra asks. I'm glad he chooses to ignore what just happened. "If we're lucky, he'll have already escaped. I'll be surprised if he hasn't."

"He didn't look fine enough to escape last I saw him."

The prince shakes his head. "That's not what I meant."

He doesn't provide an explanation and goes back to examining the buildings. I clench my jaw but let out a slow breath. There isn't time. My leg is getting worse and I still have to find my dad.

"What are we going to do then?" I ask.

"Well, I have a mask, but you—" He turns and looks me over with his red eyes. "You're still wearing your containment outfit, so you can't be seen, unless you want to join your friend. However, they aren't expecting anyone to come here. So, there are fewer guards."

"That's a few for you?" I look past his shoulder,

counting at least four but there's probably plenty more inside.

"For me, that's nothing." Isra's wearing a mask when he faces me. It's entirely black, with white eyes and silver swirls printed all over. "Can you burn that car?"

I follow his finger to a grey car not far from us, on our side of the road. Sighing, I stare at my hands. "I don't know how. It just happens."

Isra places a hand on my shoulder. I flinch but don't shove it off. "Do you want to burn the car?"

"What?"

"Answer me."

I frown. "I don't understand."

"If you want to burn it, you can. Repeat that phrase in your head," he tells me. "Once you do that, at least two will come check. That's when we sprint across the street. Stay behind me. We'll have around ten minutes before more demons show up. If you encounter any, use your power or that sword you keep trying to hide."

I open my mouth but close it immediately. There's no time. Instead, I move closer to the sidewalk. Leaning against the building closest to the car, I place the sword on the ground and sigh. My thoughts run wild, but I finally conjure enough self-control to do what Isra told me.

I want to burn it.

Throwing my hands out, fire bursts from my palms and surrounds the car. A boom echoes in my ears and a scream erupts from my throat. Pieces of the car fly in every direction.

Isra grabs my arm and pulls me away from the alley. We crouch behind another car, watching two demons cross the street before sprinting to the connected buildings. Isra only lets go when we're face to face with a horned demon guarding the door. He slams his hand into the demon's chest, pulling out his heart and dropping it on the ground. Black blood covers his hand.

Smoke escapes from the demon's mouth. It's just like the demon from the store.

"Close your mouth and move," Isra whispers, opening the door to a dark green building. My jaw remains dropped and my eyes wide, but I force myself to keep going.

We walk inside a hallway. A few black feathers litter the ground and warmth fills my chest. Kavon's here.

A demon walks into the hallway and appears in front of us, but Isra punches her face in seconds, and she falls to the ground. When she doesn't move, he steps over her body and waits for me to do the same.

"He'll be up these steps," Isra says as we walk up the stairs. "When I open the door, send as much fire as you can into the room. Don't worry about Kavon."

He doesn't wait for me to speak. He opens the first door. In a panic, I try to send bursts of fire, but nothing happens. Luckily, there's no one in the room.

"They would've shot you." Isra shakes his head. "Perhaps I'll go first. You stay in the hall."

I nod my head. My heart races as we stand beside the next door. Isra knocks, snickering when a grunt comes from inside. When the knob turns, he's already through the door. A round of gunshots goes off, but I don't dare look inside.

"Hey!"

My eyes widen. A male demon comes from the stairs.

He aims his gun at me, but lowers it as the realization hits his face. "You're the girl."

He moves toward me but hesitates and bites his lip. I'm guessing he thinks I took down his friends downstairs, but then he sniffs. His mouth forms a grin, and he takes huge footsteps toward me. At least he can't feed on me, but from how anxious I am, he probably smells a feast.

His hand reaches out once he's less than an arm away and then he gasps. His eyes lower to the sword in his chest—Kavon's sword. I grip onto it tightly, focusing on the demon's veins and horns. The human inside was already long gone.

His skin turns freakishly blue as his eyes bulge from their sockets. They almost look like they're going to pop out. I pull out the sword, jumping away as the demon falls to the floor. This time there is no smoke coming out of the vessel's mouth. The swollen veins are no longer black. Instead they are the same color as the demon's skin.

The blade retracts. I take a deep breath before spinning in front of the doorway. Five bodies lie on the wooden floor. Isra stands by Kavon, who sits on a chair surrounded by those glowing tubes I'd seen at the supermarket. He's shirtless, eyes twitching. But the tubes jolt him whenever he opens them. His wings are small, close to his body like they are protecting him. A huge cut runs across his forehead.

"We need to get that off him!" I run to Kavon's side, scowling at Isra, who watches me with crossed arms. Guilt seeps into my stomach. I ignore it and bring Kavon's sword toward the cords. As if it reads my mind, the blade comes out, and I cut the cords easily.

When Kavon falls to the floor, a part of me dies inside.

"What are you going to do now?" Isra asks.

I roll my eyes, pulling Kavon up and placing one of his arms around me and over my shoulder. We need to get out of here. Healing will come later.

"Wow." The prince claps.

I let out a huff of air. "What?"

"I knew you were strong," he says. "Just seeing it in action is different."

"Can we get out of here?"

"Whatever you want, darling." I can hear the smile behind his mask.

Isra leads me and Kavon to the back of the building. We go through some more structures and alleyways. The whole time I keep my eyes on Kavon. My heart beats in my throat at his shut eyes. Finally, Isra takes us to a building full of dusty shelves. A rotten odor invades my nostrils when we enter. Isra covers the windows and doesn't bother turning on the lights.

I slowly place Kavon against the wall. He shuffles slightly, but doesn't wake up. My vision blurs as I stare at the blood gushing from his wound. It's all I can see. A metallic smell fills the room, but there is also a lingering sweetness. I reach out toward his cut, pressing two fingers against it, then bring my hand to my nose. His blood smells amazing.

"Mahi?"

I freeze, realizing my blood-stained fingers are inches from my open mouth. Straightening my back, I wipe Kavon's blood against my clothes and turn to face Isra.

He takes his mask off and tilts his head in my direction with his arms crossed.

"What is this place?" I decide to change the subject.

"It's a bookstore. Not important. Were you going to lick his blood?"

Oh shit. I gulp. "Yeah, uh, it's how I test for poison." Sure, that'll work.

"Really?"

He doesn't believe me but I doubt he's been outside the walls much. He can't know about this virus. I can't ask for his help yet since I'm not sure what he'll do. If he drags me away, I'll never be able to search for my dad.

A sigh leaves my mouth. I rub my arms. "Thank you."

His eyes widen and he takes a step back. "I'm sorry, what?"

"You didn't have to help me," I say. "But you did."

He grins. "As I said before, I'd do anything for you."

My heart races at his words, but I push down any positive feelings that come up. He's a demon—a prince of Hell. I have to remember that. There's an alternative motive to this.

Isra nudges his head. "Come on. You should drink some water."

I follow him past shelves of books. Sitting on a stool, I lean on the table in front of me while Isra pours two glasses of water from a sink. He places the cup on the counter, standing across from me.

"So is the scar a fashion choice?" he asks. My eyebrows raise as my fingers trail over the scar on my face.

"No." My hand falls, and I scowl. "I just forgot about it."

"Relax. I was trying to be funny." He lets out a small laugh but it sounds involuntary. When I look back at him, his eyes have a little less glow. "You're smart not to reveal your power but you might as well heal it now."

"I will," I say. Right now, all I can feel is the numbness in my entire leg.

"Morningstar isn't safe. You should come with me," he says abruptly.

I stare at him in disbelief. "No. Even if you're not taking me to Lucifer, you'll just lock me back inside a cage in containment."

Isra shakes his head before giving me a perfect smile. "Haven't I told you already that I want to work with you? What fun would it be if you were inside a cage."

I press my lips together to stifle a groan. "That is true."

He grins. "I'm curious, do you know about the archangels?"

"Yeah," I say. "Everyone does. Michael, Gabriel, Raphael, and Uriel. But I guess, Lucifer too. Except he's a fallen one."

Isra nods his head. "Interesting. So how do you know him?"

I chug my water down and wipe my mouth. "I was about to die from a pack of hellhounds. He saved my life. And then he saved me from hunger. And also from dying, again," I answer truthfully.

"Did he tell you who he is?"

"No, but I know the demons are after him."

Isra's red eyes gleam directly into mine. There's no

smile on his face. Every inch of mischief is replaced with seriousness. "You have no reason to believe me, but you deserve to know. He was Lucifer's right-hand man. The Shadow Angel. One of the most feared creatures in Hell." Despite the supernatural string of trust I still feel with Kavon, my gut twists at Isra's words. "He loved the power. I could see it in his eyes. And he had it. I'm sure one day the demons would've abandoned Lucifer for him. But two years ago, something happened that made him leave Hell, and made Lucifer desperate to find him. Maybe it has something to do with that sword. Perhaps it's the fact that it can kill demons but I'm not sure."

"He's not with Lucifer now," I say. "He saved me."

"I get it, but even the humans know him as Lucifer's assassin. You shouldn't trust him."

"And I should trust you?"

"That's up to you," he says and glances over my shoulder. "I think he's waking up."

He's right. Kavon shuffles against the wall and groans. He blinks a few times, flinching when he notices me kneeling beside him.

"Mahi?" he croaks out. "What's going on? Where are we?"

"Safe," I tell him. "Let me heal you."

Before he can protest, I place both my hands on his head. One to keep it still, the other to heal his cut. I'm slightly leaning over his legs, our faces inches away. My heartbeat accelerates and I let out a hollow breath. I focus on his wound. Power flows through my veins, radiating on him. He clutches onto my arms, and I wince at the sharp pain on my forehead.

I can feel my cheeks flush when he doesn't remove his hands right away. I don't know why his touch affects me like this, especially after learning what I did from Isra. Maybe due to the bond? But Kavon clearly isn't bad. He saved me, and if he had told me his story, I never would've trusted him. He doesn't even know why the demons are after me.

"Thank you," he finally says, letting my arms go.

I tuck a strand of hair behind my face. "You don't have to thank me."

"Where are we?" he asks.

"Morningstar."

His eyes widen before flashing black. "How did you save me?"

I glance back at Isra. He's not watching us. Instead, he was reading a book behind the counter. "Isra helped me."

Kavon sits up straighter. "What?" he asks through his teeth. "Why would you ask him?"

"I'm sorry for involving him, but he really did help me! He's the reason we're not with Lucifer right now."

"That doesn't matter," Kavon mumbles. He gets up, frowning at me. "He's a prince of Hell."

I rub my strained eyes while Kavon walks up to Isra. I'm not sure what he's going to do or say, but right now, it's more important for us to hide. I follow him to the counter. Isra's back is turned to us as he leans against it. He gives us an unbothered look and continues to read his book.

Before I can react, Kavon grasps onto Isra and snaps his neck. A gasp shoots out of my mouth. My hands clutch my face so tightly it hurts. When Kavon turns, his jaw is clenched, but his features soften when he looks back at me.

"You killed him," I say.

"He's not dead." Kavon shakes his head. He walks behind the counter, taking off Isra's shirt. "We only have a few minutes before he wakes up."

My hands turn to fists. Isra helped us. It doesn't matter if Kavon didn't kill him. He still hurt the prince. I'd always thought all demons were horrid creatures, but Isra wasn't as awful as the rest.

"He helped me. He helped us," I tell Kavon.

"We need to get going." He walks past me, back to where he was lying down before. Grabbing his sword, he heads to the door. "I won't kill him because he helped you rescue me."

I want to yell at him, but I push down the feeling. It doesn't matter. I have to focus. I need to figure out where my dad is. Kavon is right. The longer we're here, the more likely we will be found.

At the sound of Kavon groaning, my eyes trail down to the hundreds of black feathers on the ground. I look back to see a wingless Kavon and discomfort on his face. He bites his lip, trembling while he puts on Isra's shirt.

"They'll disintegrate," Kavon says. "Don't worry."

"Wait, what?" I lower my voice, glancing at the ground and back at his face repeatedly. "I-I don't even—what?"

"I'm half demon. Which means I shouldn't have wings," his voice strains. "My wings can, let's just say, disappear if I really want them to and grow back. It's fucking painful, but it's necessary. If we're caught, though, I won't be able to use my powers."

"Where are we going?"

"Anywhere but here," he says. "You shouldn't have even come to the city in the first place! But you're here now. I know a place. We just need to get a car."

While he stares out of a nearby window, I think about what Isra told me. Maybe he was lying. But why would he? When we're out of here, I'll have to ask Kavon about it. And if it's true, I'm not sure what I'm going to do.

14

"I'm going to need you to trust me."

I look away from the window I'm peering out of and stare at Kavon's stressed face. The bags hiding under his eyes are pronounced, and he looks drained of energy. Even his skin looks paler than usual. I healed him about five minutes ago, so that doesn't make sense unless rushing it somehow messed everything up.

"Are you okay?" I ask.

His eyes close, and his shoulders slump. "My wings aren't out. Another side effect is exhaustion."

My eyebrows furrow. Maybe there's another way to make him feel better. "Do you feed on pain? Like the demons."

He waits a few seconds before answering. "I can when I want to."

"What do you mean?"

"I mean." He sounds angry. "I don't need it like the demons, and it doesn't come naturally. I need to focus on taking in the suffering consciously."

"Oh. Well, you know if you need to feed on my pain —to feel better—"

"Don't think about it."

"—I'm just saying if you need it, you can."

He nods his head at me. "Thanks."

I give him a small smile. "So, what are we going to do?" We're still hidden inside the building Isra brought us to, and the prince of Hell is still knocked out. Kavon's been waiting for the patrols he'd seen outside to leave. "Someone's probably going to find us soon."

He sighs. "Please, Mahi—"

"Okay." I nod before he can finish. He's an expert compared to me. "I . . . I trust you."

Kavon seems surprised by my confession, but after everything that's happened, I really do trust him. My brain nags at me to question his history, which I will, but he's saved my life far too many times. I wonder if he feels the same warmth inside him, the feeling someone gets after knowing a person for a long time. That feeling lingers inside me for him.

He shakes his head. "There's a car right outside. I'm going to get it started. Wait here until I call you."

I take a deep breath, my chest building up with fear once more. He steps outside. I gulp when I see him approach someone. Probably a demon.

I stare at a book to distract myself but my eyes hurt. Only a few seconds later, a blood curdling yell overwhelms my ears. I stand up, stepping away from the wall. I run outside. The fresh air pushes against my face. A body lays at his legs, and a lump forms in my throat.

"Get in the car," Kavon says once I'm in front of him. I'm tempted to look down at the body, sweat forming on my forehead as I open one of the doors. From the corner of my eye, I can see that there are no horns. This person wasn't far gone yet. They still had a chance to be saved.

"Hey!"

I tense up. Kavon places his hand on my shoulder, his grip tightening as someone approaches us.

"What are you doing?" It's a man. I can't see whoever it is, but I know it's a demon. There's too much confidence in his tone.

"Bringing in what Lucifer wants," Kavon says, sounding amused. A gasp leaves my mouth when he turns me around. His nails dig into my skin, and my mind spins as my shoulder slump. I know what he's doing —taking in my pain. That's the only possible reason he'd purposefully hurt me. But I don't know if that'll make him strong enough to get out of this situation. He doesn't have his wings out.

The demon stares at me as the breeze brushes his blond curls toward his face. He also doesn't have any horns or grey skin. Just *very* subtle veins and dark eyes. I glance at Kavon. A smile is plastered on his face as his own soulless eyes stare ahead. Whatever Kavon is trying, it isn't going to work. We need help.

Maybe Isra—

"Why'd you knock out Talos?"

"He was trying to take the credit." Kavon shrugs.

"Well, let me come with."

"Want me to knock you out too?" Kavon chuckles. I close my eyes at the slight distortion in his voice.

The demon scoffs. He narrows his eyes, and when

they widen, I know our cover is blown. "The Shadow Angel!"

I expect him to pull out a knife but instead, the demon bows. Literally bows in front of me and Kavon. My jaw drops.

"I never thought I'd meet you," says the demon. "It is an honor."

"Please, keep this encounter to yourself," Kavon says aggressively before shoving me in the car and slamming the door.

My heart turns rock hard when I hear a thud. A few more minutes pass until Kavon comes and sits in the other seat.

I don't say anything as he starts the car. The air feels cold and I feel the chills spreading throughout my body. My fingers twitch to open the door and run out but that would be crazy. It *is* crazy, yet the shivers in my body refuse to go away.

"I told you," Kavon finally says as he begins to drive. It feels like an eternity as I turn my head and look at him. He smiles at me, not with black, but red blood on his face, not his blood. "You can trust me."

The last time I was in a vehicle like this one was when I was captured two years ago. I shudder at the memory. It's best not to think of that day.

It hasn't been that long in this car, but it feels like it has. In containment, I'd somehow been able to manage all the slow days, but now this single car ride was making me go mad inside. Playing with the window button wasn't enough to distract me, and Kavon said it annoyed him anyway, so I stopped. How comfortable I had felt, began to fade once I sat in this vehicle.

In this world, you don't trust anyone. You couldn't. That was how you survived. Still, no matter how many times I said that about Kavon, this stupid bond between us made me believe him. A bond I couldn't even explain.

"So, what do you think of the city?" Kavon asks me. "Even though we won't be here long."

"It's nice." My voice comes out sounding bored, and I don't even know if the words are true. I've been shaking too much to focus on what's outside.

"Where are we?" I look at Kavon and ask.

His eyes are fixated on the road, and his head slightly twitches. I frown. It must be his wings.

"We're going to my home," Kavon replies. "My dad can hide us for the day."

My eyes widen. "Your home?"

"Where I grew up," he says, glancing at me before looking back at the road. I open my mouth but don't say anything. Kavon sighs.

"I know what you're thinking."

I lick my lips, and I stare at the dry blood on his face. "What?"

"We'll get out of here fine." He grins. I listen to the piercing silence around us, and slowly, his lips curve downwards. I must be frowning. "That wasn't it, was it?"

"Maybe it has something to do with the blood on your face," I murmur.

"The demon isn't dead. I didn't get a chance to kill

it," Kavon says. "I just injured the vessel. It escaped and went back to Hell. I should've taken my angel blade out but didn't get the chance."

Most of the time, demons couldn't die, but *people* could. It wouldn't matter to me if the vessel didn't look human; If the human hadn't still had a *chance* of being saved. That person was dead.

I laugh, but it comes out shaky and forced. "That's not what I was thinking," I say, swallowing my saliva to moisten my throat. Why did I have to bring that up? That had been at the back of my mind until now. Until I saw the blood on his face again. Until he had to mention it.

"Then what?"

"How old are you?" I try to change the subject. Kavon's jaw clenches slightly.

"Twenty-one," he answers in a sharp tone.

"Really? You look a little younger," I say. Kavon's face pinches for an odd second when I say that.

"What about you?"

"I'm eighteen. Are you sure it's safe in your house? It doesn't seem safe anywhere."

"They don't know about it," Kavon answers. His nostrils flare, and he keeps a high chin. "Or well, the demon who possessed my mom doesn't want anyone to know I'm her kid, and in her twisted way, she allows my dad to live away from everything. But he can never leave the city, just like everyone else." He shakes his head. "I don't even know why I say that. Demons are an *it*."

"It's okay." I wish I had kept my mouth shut. It's not okay. "I say she and he too sometimes."

"It's hard not to, when they have those vessels."

I nod my head, looking down at my hands and fumbling with my fingers. Isra's not an it, no matter how badly I want him to be. A groan leaves my mouth. I don't want to think about what has happened so far, but I can't stop. No matter what, the things I don't want to think about resurface in my brain. Even though I was captured two years ago, I'd dealt with that memory for months after. It was finally shoved to the back of my brain.

Now I couldn't help but think about it.

"We're here," Kavon says. He parks on the road, and I look at a small building. There's a little white door behind some grey steps and a larger white door with a red car behind it. The home looks to be only one floor tall, with a few batches of different colored flowers on the grass in front. It doesn't look horrible to me. If I were a human, I'd rather be in the city if everything looked like this.

"I don't get it," I say as I get out. "If the demons leave you alone and don't know about this place, why not just hide here?"

Kavon scratches the back of his head. "Let's get inside."

I frown but follow him up the three steps. My eyes turn to slits as he opens the door with a key he has out of nowhere. A blast of heat surrounds me as soon as I step in, and I welcome the warmth with a huge breath, eyes adjusting only for the light to blind me.

"What are you doing here?" a rough, deep voice asks.

I turn to see an older man. My heart skips a beat but settles when I notice he looks slightly similar to Kavon.

Brown skin, dark brown eyes. He's shorter than Kavon, but still significantly taller than me. He glances my way, wrinkles forming on his forehead.

"Who's this?" he asks. I gulp and look over at Kavon. His eyes are glossy.

"Dad, please—"

"I told you not to come here," Kavon's father raises his voice. "Leave."

"We need a place to settle down for a bit."

"Then go somewhere else." His dad looks at me again, eyes widening. "Wait, this is the girl they're after. Are you turning her in for the reward?"

A release a shaky breath, and I feel as though my heart is going to jump out of my chest. "Reward?" I squeak out.

Kavon sighs. "No, I'm not. And we can't go there. Besides, nothing is going to happen to you. Arrun will never let anyone find out about you—"

"Don't say that name," Kavon's dad says, his voice so low I can barely hear it. "You can stay the night because I'm tired and don't want to argue. But if you know what's good for you, then you'll leave in the morning."

"Come on, Dad—"

"Every time you come back here begging for help, I tell you to stop calling me that," his dad shouts. I flinch. "I am not a part of this."

I shake my head. I can't listen to this anymore. "Can you please stop?"

Kavon's father glares at me. "And I never welcomed you into my house. I can call the demons right now."

He could, but I have a feeling he won't. If he wants

Kavon to leave so badly, he probably doesn't want attention.

"This is your son," I say. "This isn't about me. I'll leave if that's what you want, but Kavon has saved my life one too many times. You shouldn't treat him like this."

Kavon touches my shoulder. "It's not worth it, Mahi. Please, stop," he whispers.

I open my mouth but don't say anything. Kavon sits down on a blue couch. His father shakes his head and walks away into a dark hall.

My chest pains when I see Kavon rubbing his face. I sit down beside him, hoping to offer some comfort.

"I didn't think he'd be up," Kavon whispers. "I thought I'd talk to him in the morning before you woke up."

"Is he always like that?" I ask.

Kavon shakes his head. "No. When I was a kid, he was great. He loved that I looked exactly like my mom. But then my demonic side began to show, black veins, black wings, randomly scaring him with my voice. He began to hate me. Arrun, my demon mother, came by once and scared him too. That's when he found out Arrun had killed my human mom after she gave birth, leaving me with him. And that it was an angel who was my real father. Things got worse when I became —" He brings a hand to his face and sighs. "I haven't seen my dad in months now. I'm just an abomination to him."

"You're not an abomination Kavon." I don't know what comes over me, but I touch his arm. It feels so awkward, but the comforting warmth inside me grows stronger, feeling like a giant bubble of trust and familiarity. Hopefully, Kavon feels it too.

He scoffs. "What angel screws a demon? It doesn't happen."

"We don't know that," I say. "Angels are dead. They have been for a long time. No one can say how they were because humans only found out about them in the war. Just because we are told they were good doesn't mean they were all the time. No one is perfect."

Kavon groans. "It doesn't matter, it's not natural."

"If it's not natural, so what." I shrug. "You clearly turned out better than your father."

"Don't say that Mahi," he whispers.

I chew on the inside of my mouth and move my arm away. All I hear is both of us breathing and my stomach grumbling.

"Kavon, why did the demons capture you?" I ask. "Why do demons and humans call you Shadow Angel?"

His eyes squeeze shut. "My past is why."

Running his fingers through his hair, he sits up straighter. His wings sprout out of his back, ripping his shirt. I gulp down the lump in my throat. His powers will be back now. "I . . . I used to be Lucifer's assassin. I'd hunt down whoever he wanted. If he was busy, I was in charge. That's why I know Prince Isra is trouble."

"Then why are they hunting you now?" I ask.

"Lucifer betrayed me," Kavon breathes out. "He . . . he tricked me. So, I stole his precious fucking sword and escaped the city two years ago."

"A sword that kills demons," I mutter out. It would make sense why Lucifer might be after him. Or maybe Kavon has something else the king of Hell needs. "What did he do to you?" Kavon rubs his eyes. I know I've asked something too personal. "Never mind."

"I understand if you want to leave," he says.

"No, Kavon—" I pause. I don't trust him, but at the same time, I do. It's not just because of this bond that I feel tugging me toward him, making me want to be in his presence. He saved my life. I would've been dead without him; my soul with Lucifer. And Kavon hasn't handed me over to him either when he's had so many chances to do so.

"What about you?" he suddenly asks. "Your power is what Lucifer wants, isn't it? You're different."

I shrug. "That must be why. Even Isra constantly talks about my so-called power. But it's not like I could kill Lucifer or something."

"Have you always been in containment?"

It's not surprising that he'd know that's where I came from. If my clothes weren't a dead giveaway, my lack of knowledge probably was. "It's not something I want to think about." I look down at my hands. "But no. I used to live with my dad before demons took him."

"Live where?"

"I can't say." I really hope he doesn't ask about how my dad was taken. I'll burst into tears if he does. "It was with humans who went into hiding before the war ended. I was an idiot, got myself caught, and ended up in containment around two years ago. They interrogated me to the core, but I didn't say anything."

I remember Laurel telling me that she'd given them false information that they wouldn't be able to follow. If only I'd been smart enough to think of that.

"How'd you manage to live on your own like that?"

"I have no idea."

"Well, you're strong," Kavon says. "Not only because of that, but because most people, even here in Morningstar, eventually break down. You need to be able to handle the world mentally, and you can. If Lucifer catches you, which won't happen under my watch, it'll take something powerful to knock you down. Probably why he's after you."

Kavon places his head down, his fingers running through his hair. I swallow the lump that formed in my throat, feeling a loss for air as I think of something that might make him feel better.

"You know…" I still have a chance to back down—to say nothing. But he looks at me with quivering eyes. "I could be an abomination, too."

He lets out a huff of a laugh. "I doubt that."

I stare down at my hands, letting out a huge breath. Here it goes. "When I was around four years old, I fell and scraped my knee while playing with some kids. I had that privilege, you know, to actually have a childhood. I just remember *wanting* the pain to go away. And so, I touched my knee and healed myself."

"Sounds more like a gift to me," Kavon says.

I sigh. "I don't remember if I kept playing or whatever, but I told my dad later. He told me never to show anyone. Ever. It made me think that it was *wrong*."

"It's anything but wrong."

"I'm just saying that you may think you're an abomination, but you're not."

There's a long pause before he speaks again. "Thanks."

I smile and look up at him, but it vanishes quickly.

Isra stands in the dark hallway, watching us. He's wearing a black shirt now. His red eyes send shivers up my spine as he stares intensely.

"What is it?" Kavon's eyebrows furrow, and he looks behind him, exactly where Isra is. He doesn't seem to see anything.

"I think I'm just tired."

"Right." Kavon gets up. "Let me take you to your room."

A hollow breath leaves my mouth as I follow Kavon, walking past a smirking Isra. He bows, and I narrow my eyes before looking away.

"So, there's some clean clothes." Kavon stands by the door of the room he's taken me to, pointing at the clothes beside me while Isra stands beside him. I sit on a small bed, taking in the white walls with a large mirror in the corner. There's a single brown bookcase, reaching all the way to the ceiling. Some cracks line the edges where an overwhelming number of books sit inside. "You can shower right now if you'd like. I mean, you stink."

"Thanks," I say. No way am I going to shower while Isra is here. "But I'm exhausted. Where are you going to sleep?"

"There's another room at the end of the hallway. Nothing but a mattress."

I frown. "I can sleep in there."

"Trust me, you don't want to. It's creepy as Hell."

I'm not going to lie, I'd prefer an actual bed. "Well, good night."

Kavon smiles. "Goodnight."

He turns the light off and closes the door, leaving me alone with the bright red eyed demon.

"I'm sorry," I say before Isra can speak.

He stares at me, a hand rubbing his chin. "I helped you."

"I didn't know Kavon was going to hurt you!" I try to explain, lowering my voice. "But you are still a prince of Hell."

"He got in your head." Isra closes his eyes. "I should've expected that."

"I can't do what you want me to Isra."

"You don't need him," he speaks slowly. It's chilling, and his eyes shine with excitement. "I'm all you need. We can stop Lucifer together. You won't be running from him anymore. It'll be fun."

"You know nothing about me," I scoff. "You're a demon. A . . . liar."

He flinches, like I just hit a nerve, "I know *you're* not a demon," he says. "Which means you won't have to do Lucifer's bidding. You won't have to do everything he says, against your will like the others."

What am I? I want to scream, but I know better. Isra will never tell me if he actually knows.

I frown. "I can't trust you just yet."

"But you can trust him?" Isra raises his voice, pointing at nothing. "Don't you see I should be the one helping you? I'm the one who set you free in the first place. I can take you to the top where you *belong*."

"This isn't about boredom anymore, is it?" I ask quietly.

He glares at me, and we stare at each other for what feels like hours. "I can support you," he finally responds. "Teach you so many things!"

He keeps rambling on and on, but I've had enough. I close my eyes. "Leave me alone."

His voice fades. I place a hand on my chest. For some reason, I feel guilty about ignoring him. He's a demon. I shouldn't.

But he's also not like any demon I've ever encountered.

15

I DON'T TELL Kavon about my talk with Isra last night. I try my best not to think of it as I take my shower and get a chance to brush my teeth. It's relaxing to freshen up at my own pace, putting on new, comfortable clothes instead of the same thing every day. Even if they are a little too big and there are two holes in the back of the sweater.

Kavon's father stays locked in his room. The one time he comes out, he gives me a fuming glare and tells me to get out of his house. I spend my time on the couch practicing the fire power I have.

But there's one problem, I *can't*.

My flame only comes out during stressful situations, and pretty much whenever I'm about to die. Since there's nothing on the couch trying to kill me, it was a lot harder to do.

"What are you doing?" Kavon approaches me, raising an eyebrow at my hands.

My face flushes and I quickly sit on my palms. "Nothing."

He laughs, sitting down beside me. He turns to face me while his wings stretch behind him. "Okay then. Well, I was thinking we'd get out of here tomorrow morning. They'll be searching all over the city today. But for now, maybe I can show you some fighting tactics."

"Oh." I get up, my stomach swirling with excitement. "Sure!"

"Let's start then." He follows my lead and gets up, nudging his head for us to go in the center of his living room. "Stand straight, but with wide, bent legs," Kavon instructs from behind me.

I do what he says, moving my legs and straightening my back. He comes in front of me and nods his head. "Now show me your fists."

I lift my hands, forming two fists. Kavon's eyes narrow at them, and he raises his hands as if he's going to touch them, but he looks at me first. My heart skips a beat, and I nod before he grabs both my hands and shapes my thumbs. My skin tingles from the contact.

I suppress a smile. Despite his veins and horns, I don't really see anything demonic about him anymore.

"Don't point your thumb at your opponent. Curl it over your knuckles. Now place your dominant foot back," Kavon says.

Ignoring the numbness in my leg, I place my right foot back. My stomach backflips as Kavon places his hands on my hips and angles them. "Keep your fists up to cover your face." He smirks and lifts his hand. "Now, I want you to punch my hand. Quick, move your hip forward while your fist does the same."

A slow breath echoes past my lips, and I yell out as I slam my fist into Kavon's hand with all my strength. In a blur, he falls to the ground, holding his wrist.

"I'm sorry!" I squeak out, clearing my throat and ignoring the exhilaration I feel. "I didn't mean to do that."

"I forgot you weren't human for a second." He coughs, a smile on his face as he gets up. "If *I* were human, I would have a broken hand. Good thing you didn't knock me into anything."

"Kavon——" My body becomes alert when he swings at me. I duck, backing away. "Hey!"

He nods his head. "Good! When it comes to defense, always try to avoid it. My motto is usually evading capture unless necessary. When it comes to offense, I rely on luck and my telekinesis."

His fingers swirl and a group of four spoons float in his palm.

"I'll never get over that," I tell him.

A grin forms on his face. He flicks the spoons to the side and gets in the stance he'd shown me. "Let's keep practicing."

For most of the morning, Kavon keeps me in the motion of defense and attack. Sometimes he does something out of the blue to catch me off guard. I'm pretty sure he lets me hit him a couple of times because he dodges effortlessly. By the time I've gotten decent at dodging, we're both sweating like crazy.

"I'm impressed," Kavon says. "Now, what about your power? What else can you do?"

I chew on the inside of my cheek, a large breath leaving my nose. "I don't know. I think I can make fire, but I've tried to do it when I'm alone and nothing happens."

Kavon shrugs. "Maybe you aren't trying hard enough."

I don't want to show it, but his words sting. "I should get cleaned up."

"Dibs on the shower!" he yells like a little kid, racing to the bathroom door.

"Hey!"

"Maybe you can use the sink," he calls before the door closes.

"I'm not that short!" I shout, groaning in frustration.

My eyes shut as I sit back down on the couch and ignore the urge to try to make a fireball. It'll only make me more upset.

I should plan how I'm going to get my dad out of here and what to do about my leg. I can feel the numbness tingling in my abdomen now and a lingering hunger.

I tense when I hear footsteps. Kavon's dad glances my way and sits a few inches away from me. He leans back, eyes glued to some book. He must've thought I'd gone in the shower and that he'd be here either with his son or alone.

"Hi." I smile. "So, this is what you do in your free time? Read?" *Why am I so awkward!*

"Do you have a problem with it?" he asks without looking up.

"No. I was just wondering."

He doesn't say anything, but his eye twitches.

"What kind of books do you read?"

He slaps his book shut and I flinch. "Go wait for Kavon."

"I am."

"Somewhere else."

I narrow my eyes. "Why do you hate me?"

"I don't hate you," he says. "I pity you. You have no idea who Kavon is."

"Why don't you tell me?"

"He killed his mother."

"You blame him for that?" Bile runs up my throat. "That's hardly his fault. He loves you. He calls you the better man."

"I am. You don't get it . . ." The sound of a heartbeat awakens somewhere, slowly getting louder and louder until I can no longer listen to Kavon's father's nonsense.

My eyes fixate on his chest. Blood flows through his veins. Sweet, savory blood that all comes to his heart only to go out again. My stomach growls. I ate a while ago. I'm not sure why my mouth is suddenly dry.

I realize that I'm moving closer to him. It's only when he gets up, shaking his head, that I snap out of whatever state I'm in. "That's just the least of what he's done. I don't even know why I came out here," his father mumbles.

I lie on the couch as he walks off, staring at the white ceiling. What the hell just happened? The infection is turning me into a bloodthirsty monster. I wonder if I'll turn into the spider creature. It is best not to think of it until I get my dad out of here or die trying. Waving my hand in front of my face, I groan and sit up.

I head into the room I've been sleeping in and shut the door. I notice the closet's open, and Kavon's clothes are on the floor. A smile forms on my face as I examine a photo of a grinning baby Kavon outside, with dirt all over himself. I'd never seen a baby, and I probably never will in person.

I head over to his bed, where he left his angel sword. My eyes land over the flames again. I press my lips together in a thin line. Even the sword is mocking me. I can't deny that it looks cool, though. I wonder if Isra has one or if this is it.

Shit.

"Been a while."

I jump, turning around to see a smug Isra. "You scared me."

"Well, I am naturally terrifying," he says.

I roll my eyes. "Do you like, wait around all day doing nothing until I think of you?"

"Not really. I'm quite busy planning and telling my loyalists about you."

"That I'm eighteen, and you want me to be their leader?"

"No." He grins. "More like how you scream in the faces of strangers."

My mouth falls open. I know he isn't serious, but I shake my head anyway. "I was the calmest person you've probably ever met when I first saw you."

"Yes, but no one will believe you."

I'm not sure what he's trying to achieve right now, so I turn around and study the sword once more, but there's nothing left to look at.

"What are you doing?" Isra comes up beside me.

"Honestly, nothing," I admit.

"Must be boring."

"It is." I pause at the strangeness of our interaction. "Did we just have a normal conversation?"

"Well, I wouldn't quite call it a conversation."

I sigh and sit down on the edge of the bed, blushing when I realize I'm actually comfortable in Isra's presence. "What are you doing here?"

"I came here to see you."

"You want something."

He chuckles. "You already know what I want. I'm not going to get any closer to it by shoving it in your face. Maybe I want to know the kind of person I'll be working with."

I give him a weak grin. "What is there to know?"

"Where were you before containment?"

I frown. "You think I'm stupid, right?"

He tilts his head. "What was your life like?"

I look away. "It was nice. Relaxing. I was going to train to be a nurse. Science has always been cool."

"Oh, it's fascinating the way different organisms work. I can talk all day just about angel anatomy."

"Right." I frown. "You'll probably know more than I ever will."

"I could always teach you," he says.

"I turn to face him, just to see if he's joking. He isn't smiling anymore. He's serious. "Why?"

"Why not?"

We stare at each other. I realize I'm leaning closer to him, but I don't move away. "And what's your life like?"

"Dozing off in my realm in Hell. Organizing Hell's animals. Feeding my pet foxes. I told you—boring." He grins wickedly as his eyes pierce into mine. "Until now."

When I hear the bathroom door open, I jump away

from him. The room's door opens seconds after. My face heats up as if I just got caught doing something wrong. I look beside me to see if Isra is still there, but he's gone. Kavon leans against the door frame, his black wings dripping onto the floor. His dark eyes stare into me, and he looks like some supreme being with his huge muscles and enormous height.

He looks like some kind of savior.

"Why'd you come in here?" Kavon asks. "We should go to the kitchen. I hate how dull this room is."

"You're going to get the floor all wet."

"I don't care."

We have a staring contest for five seconds before I shrug and jump off the bed. But I freeze by the door, narrowing my eyes at another photo on Kavon's bookshelf. I've seen his baby photos, which I made sure to tease him about. Yet somehow, I've never noticed this one. The photo was probably taken only a few years ago. Kavon's in it, rolling his eyes, while a different white-skinned, brunette girl with golden eyes has the sweetest, most genuine smile as she stares at Kavon.

"Kavon." I swallow hard. I don't know why my palms sweat. "Who is this?"

"What is it?" Kavon comes back from the kitchen and a breath catches in his throat when he sees the photo in my hand. A slight gloss forms over his eyes before he shakes his head. "Oh, she's just some girl I was with a few years ago. Forgot I had that photo."

"Oh." My mouth forms a circle, and I place the picture down before the situation can get any more awkward. I've never been in a real relationship. Not that I cared much for it. But after hearing Kavon was

Lucifer's assassin, I didn't expect him to have ever been in one, especially with a human. Clearly, there's still some history there that I don't need to force myself to know.

Kavon gives me a small smile, walking to the kitchen before clearing his throat. Once I'm sitting at the table with him, he sighs. "Here's what's going to happen tomorrow—"

"For you," I cut him off and sit up straighter. "I'm not leaving."

He looks stunned. "You're kidding."

"No, I'm not."

"Are you insane?"

I sigh. "When I came to save you, I . . . well, I saw my dad. This whole time I thought he was dead, but he isn't! And I'm not leaving him in here."

"Mahi, *you'll* die," Kavon says. "You can't help him."

"He's my dad!" I cry out. "I'm going to try. Thank you for all you've done, but I'm staying here. You should get out, and I'll help you in any way I can."

He shuts his eyes and exhales slowly. "I can't stay here. I want to help you, but I can't. Please understand."

"Kavon." I grab his hand, electricity shooting through me. "Stop. It's fine. You don't owe me anything."

"But I don't want you to die. Please, leave with me," he pleads.

Pulling away, I bite my lip before staring deep into his eyes. He doesn't know about the infection. How I'm a lost cause because the cure isn't going to be somewhere accessible. It's going to be somewhere desperate people go, heavily guarded by demons. "I can't do that."

16

I DON'T THINK I'll be able to sleep tonight.

I sit on one of the soft brown couches with a worn-out book in my hands that I pretend to read it for the fiftieth time. My mind is stuck on how I'm never going to get anywhere with my powers; how I'm completely *useless*.

"Mahi, aren't you going to sleep?"

I look up when I hear my name and turn around to see Kavon standing in the kitchen, staring at me with concerned eyes.

I sheepishly grin. "Actually, I was thinking of staying up to read."

I hope that he won't get suspicious. He looks at me warily, frowning. "Are you sure?"

I nod my head a little too eagerly. "Yeah."

He moves toward the bedrooms before facing me again. "And you're okay?"

I avoid his gaze, staring at random pages while my stomach clenches. "Yes. Can you let me read now?"

Kavon mumbles a goodnight, and I glance back to make sure he's gone. The book falls from my hands and onto my lap. Cracking my fingers, I breathe heavily and try to feel the energy inside myself, but my head pounds and I can't focus. I give it a rest, leaning back into the couch.

I look down at my hands. Maybe I could ask Isra for help. It's not like he knows where I am. Maybe it's my turn to use the demon for my own gain.

"You're sitting."

I jolt, my jaw clenching as I look up and glare at Isra's blinding eyes. A maroon hoodie covers his upper body and black joggers are on his legs. He smirks, clearly amused by my small moment of embarrassment.

"Yeah," I say through my teeth. "You didn't have to state the obvious."

He comes closer, taking what feels like a minute to explore the couch before sitting down beside me. He doesn't add any weight to the cushions. I almost question him on how he's doing this. His power is so interesting and confusing. But I stop myself just in time.

Isra sighs. "Why are our encounters always so hostile?"

I give him a fake smile. "Because you almost always show up when I don't want you here." My lips curve downwards. "Except, this time, *I did*. Jeez, sorry. I'm just in a bad mood. You're not even a terrible demon."

"Did I hear you correctly?"

I nod and stare down at my hands. "Look, Isra, I know this is all a game to you, but I feel—I feel so alone right now—" I choke on my words. "You keep talking about my power, and how you want to help me.

And I desperately want to believe that you do, but I *can't*."

"Mahi—"

"But this helps you too!" I blurt out. My cheeks are hot, and I rub at my face. "I—I just *can't* defeat Lucifer because I'm useless. And every second I'm here, there's a chance Lucifer's transforming humans into those monsters!"

"You're not useless."

I look at Isra. His face holds a look of concern; eyebrows drawn together, lips pursed, his body facing me. Whereas I feel as though my cheeks just puffed up like a balloon.

"I've tried so damn hard these past few days." I realize I need to vent. And even though I'm doing it with Isra, it feels *good*. "I tried to make some fire or make my skin hotter than the sun, but I couldn't. And Kavon just kept saying, 'just try a little harder.' I know he's trying to help, but it makes me feel like a failure."

Isra doesn't talk. He's leaning in while giving me a sympathetic smile. "Let me try to help you," he finally speaks, saying each word slowly.

"Why?" I ask

He shrugs. "Just because."

I tilt my head, narrowing my eyes. He's not doing this simply to help me. I already told him that this would be a step closer to defeating Lucifer, which is what he wants. *That's* why he's really helping.

Or is it? I can't forget our conversation in the bedroom earlier today.

"Explain what it's like when you try to use your fascinating power," he says.

"I don't know," I groan. "It's all over the place!"

"What is?"

"This thing," I scratch at my arms. "Inside me! Some kind of energy."

"Mahi."

"What!" I raise my voice, gasping when I remember that two other people are sleeping in this house. "What is it?"

"Take your time," says Isra.

I tuck a stray strand of hair behind my ear and look back down at my hands. "You're right."

"Tell me what you feel."

"I feel this energy coursing in my stomach. I know it's there, and I can direct it to use my powers. But it disappears from my hands as soon as it comes. Unless I'm healing."

"Now, why do you want to, say, make your skin hot?" Did he move closer? I feel as though his breath is against my ear.

"Just, because?" I let out a small laugh when I repeat the same words he said earlier.

"There's your problem." I can hear the grin in his voice. "You need to have *intention*. You can heal because you mean to help the other person. You escaped because your purpose was to get out of there. You created that one fireball in the cave with me because your goal was for me to go away."

I blink repeatedly. "Did you just figure it out?"

"Yeah." He does his attractive smirk. The pit feeling I get in my stomach whenever I'm with him forms. "Now, make your skin as hot as fire because you *want* to burn me. It's as simple as that."

I stare at my hands again, fidgeting with my fingers. A pain forms at the back of my throat as I start to direct the energy toward my hands. I have to show Isra. I need to prove myself.

I notice my veins start to glow orangey and fire-like, similar to a demon's black veins. Sweat runs down the side of my face. The power is awake, spread out. Not directly in my hands, but *there*.

"Is this normal?" I ask Isra.

"Are you normal?" he asks me. I roll my eyes. "Now, let's test if it worked."

"I don't know . . ."

"You are literally glowing." Isra brings out his grey hand, hovering over mine while he waits for me to say something. The back of my mind is saying no, but I need to know if this worked. So, I nod my head.

He places one of his hands over mine. It feels as though hours pass by, but he finally flinches and brings his hand to his chest. There's a slight sizzling noise and smoke coming from it.

"No way!" I jump up, feeling as though my insides are vibrating. "I did it! And I'm still doing it."

"Yeah," Isra says. "I knew you could. You just have to be patient. Soon enough you won't even have to think about it."

He grins, and I smile back. I never noticed that he has dimples. They make him more handsome than he already is.

"Your scar is gone," he points out. "And your number."

I'm about to respond when I freeze at a harsh bang

coming from the front door. I flinch when I hear two more knocks.

Isra gets up, his head shaking. "Mahi, what's wrong?"

I try to form words, but I can't. Kavon is beside me in seconds, barefoot in his sweatpants and a white t-shirt. "You need to hide."

"Tell me what's going on, Mahi!" Isra cries out from behind me.

"Open up, or we'll break the door down." Whoever says those words, their voice is morphed and damn scary. Multiple thoughts keep running through my head.

They've come for me.

They're going to hurt me.

Kill me. And capture Kavon

I want to place the blame on Isra, but he keeps asking me where I am and what's going on. His voice gets fainter and fainter as I think of him less. It wasn't him, so *who?*

"I thought you said demons never come here!" I hiss, pulling the hair on top of my head. "Shit. Shit. Shit. Shit! I'm going to shit my pants!"

"They don't!" Kavon whispers. "But they know we're both in Morningstar. Lucifer must've put a reward big enough out there for Arrun to come here. That's the only person I can think of."

He grabs my arm and pulls me toward the backyard. I look around for Isra, but he's gone. "You go. I'll hold them off."

"No way! Let's just fly out of here!"

"They have feral demons that can fly at night. And they probably also have snipers waiting at every corner,"

Kavon says. "If it comes to it, I can get away on my own!"

He doesn't give me a chance to say anything. He runs to the front door and opens it. I duck behind the kitchen table.

"Sorry," Kavon says as two demons step inside. They're holding guns. I glance at the hallway toward the bedrooms, sighing at Kavon's father cowering. Great, why did he have to come out here?

"We're looking for a girl named Mahi." My heart pounds faster at those words. I glance at the back exit as an unsteady breath runs past my lips. I'm not going to leave. "Also known as Three-nine-seven."

My head spins as I take a quick peek at my wrist. The number is gone, but I can imagine them burning it into my flesh once more.

"Wow, Arrun." Kavon scoffs. "Really going to pretend you don't know your own son? And you brought friends. I'm sure they can't be trusted."

"Shut up." The other demon says, the voice deep and masculine.

"Where is she?" Arrun, I assume, asks, ignoring Kavon. "Is she over . . . here?"

I cover my mouth as she looks around the house. Maybe I can heat my skin up and get the jump on her. But as I try to, the floor doesn't even sizzle.

"She isn't here," Kavon mutters. "You're wasting your time."

"Oh? I think you're lying. Although, I adore seeing you take after me."

I gasp when I hear a thud and multiple protests from Kavon, before a stranger stands in front of my terrible hiding spot. She's grinning at me while her brown eyebrows curve downwards. I take in the image of her horns erupting from her skull and black eyes glaring through me. *This* is Kavon's demonic mother. In the body of an innocent woman.

A scream erupts from my mouth. Arrun grabs my wrist and pulls me up. My skull pounds while I struggle to rip away. I try to focus, but it's easier to make my flesh as hot as fire when I'm not scrambling to get out of someone's grip.

I spin around, kicking Arrun into the kitchen table, but she's too fast. I cry out when she scratches my shoulder with her abnormally long nails. She smirks, about to shoot me when a bowl hits her in the head. And then another one. And then some more. Her gun flies out of her hand, and I look back at Kavon with a smile. But it disappears as fast as it came.

"Kavon, stop!" He follows my eyes to his father. A knife is pressed against his throat by a young man with short black hair and kind blue eyes. The only demonic trait he has are black veins.

"You attack me, and he'll have a nice new red necklace," the demon says. "She comes with us, and we leave you here. We won't feed on his fear, either."

Kavon glances between his father and me, teeth clenched together. His hand turns.

His dad's a piece of shit but I won't live with myself if he dies. "Stop," I say once more. Kavon's eyes meet mine, black as night. His mouth twitches and then he groans. He leans against the front door with quivering arms; his veins pulsing.

I grunt as Arrun brings both my hands behind my back and places handcuffs around them.

I'm forced up, the metal cuffs digging into my wrists. The demon holding Kavon's dad follows us to the front door. Kavon moves aside, his face blank. They allow me to put on my shoes. I gulp when the demon throws Kavon's father deep into the house. As soon as he does, Arrun pushes me outside. There is another demon holding a gun to the door. When he sees us, he walks over to the driver's seat of a black car.

"Please, Arrun," Kavon calls after us.

Arrun ignores her son and brings something to her ear. "The rest of you stay in your positions. If anyone leaves, shoot on sight."

Her hand clutches onto my head and she shoves me inside the car. I sit up quickly before both demons squeeze in next to me.

"So, she *was* here," the driver says.

"Yeah." The male demon beside me grins, a snicker escaping his mouth. "I can't believe Arrun is the one who spawned the Shadow Angel. He was pretty weak in there though."

"That's a shame. Maybe we should capture him too then."

"Shut up," Arrun growls. "You do that and I'll let him kill you." She side-eyes me, and there is a slight quiver in her bottom lip. Slowly, she grabs my shoulder as the two other demons make jokes. She leans in and whispers, "Don't talk," before letting go of me.

She'd be crazy to think I'd say anything about Kavon to anyone. But why does *she* care about anyone hurting him?

Why does she care at all?

As the drive begins, my arms cramp. Silence embodies the car. Not one of the demons says a word, nothing to provoke me or to make me more scared than I already am. The houses start to fade away, replaced by a long empty, wide road. In the distance are glowing, gigantic buildings. I won't deny that they are beautiful.

Eventually, the car stops. The long ride makes the cramps in my arms numb. I'm dragged out of the vehicle, screaming until I'm face to face with one of the buildings I saw on the way here. Raindrops land on my head and my stomach twists as the demons take me inside. Up close, this is the tallest building I've ever seen.

Inside, the floor is white and glossy, with streaks of gold. Crystals hang from the towering ceiling, a fireplace off to the side with rose couches surrounding it. There are a few small plants against the walls and a gleaming brown desk I'm getting closer to. Despite heading to my death, I look around in astonishment. This place is beautiful.

A woman—probably mid-thirties—with pale white skin and a black blouse sits behind the desk. She's shaking, and her blue eyes look like they're about to pop while she glances around frantically. She must be human.

With as much strength as I can conjure, I try to pull away from the demons, but it's three of them. They drag me like a doll.

"We need to see Lucifer," Arrun tells the woman. She nods her head, picking up a phone.

A slow breath comes out of my mouth. It's now or never. I have to melt the cuffs. I *want* to get away. Spreading the power through me as I did earlier, my entire body starts to burn. I resist the urge to scratch my skin, sucking in a breath at the prickling sensation under my flesh. Sweat drenches my hair when we start walking again. I pull at my cuffs. They grow softer and softer. Hopefully the demons will just think I'm sweating excessively from fear.

"What the hell?" one of the demons says. "Her hoodie is drenched."

"Are her veins glow——"

I rip my hands apart as the liquid metal drips onto the ground. I take my chances and kick Arrun's knee, then elbow the other demon's gut. I make a run for the doors once I see an opening. Their screams are horrifying from behind me.

Everything around me is a blur once I push past the doors. The rain is pouring heavily. There are buildings everywhere, and I have no idea where anything is. So, I just pick a direction and move.

I run down the road and turn a corner, my hair soaking wet.

"Please," my voice shakes under my breath. "One hiding spot. Just one."

I'm already heaving when I sprint to the closest car on the side of the road. I attempt to catch my breath as I rest. I've never run like this. For some reason, I can run when I'm dehydrated, but I don't have the lungs to do any kind of exercise right now.

My hands grasp onto the bright red car in front of me. I balance my body against it. A metallic taste forms in my mouth and I feel my shoulder itching as I graze my fingers over it, and I realize it's still bleeding from the cut Arrun gave me earlier.

I don't get to rest for long when something slams onto the car. I'm so unimaginably tired, but I'm wide awake when I hear a deep growl.

I meet the brown eyes of a human, but it has the mouth of an insect. I'm paralyzed. Unable to make a single sound. Two large fangs are in replace of its mouth while its bee-like wings erupt from its back. I can only imagine what the body looks like. Out of nowhere, a web surrounds my left hand.

"No!" I yell, blasting the monster with fire, just as it nicks my right hand with one of its fangs. I suck in a breath, squeezing my fist before melting the webbing off. The car catches on fire from my previous blast and I make a run for it, diving down while the car behind me explodes into pieces. That could've been me right there. I could've been dead at this very moment. And that thing, I don't know what it was going to do. Maybe this time, the demons *are* trying to kill me.

Once I heal the cut from the human spider, I get up and place a hand on my head. More sweat covers my skin, accompanied by rain. Glancing back over my shoulder, I frown. There are no demons. But I can't pay too much attention to that. That monster is still out there. I turn and start running again. Everything is so dark, but from the corner of my eye to the right, I see a light flash for a second, which makes me stop.

I walk back to where the light was and realize that I'm in some kind of neighborhood similar to Kavon's house. Dozens of homes surround me, each connected to the other and bigger than Kavon's. I assume they are full of humans. The light isn't shining from the house anymore, but I don't care. I'm desperate.

I run up the stone steps and slam my hands on the door repeatedly. "Please!" I cry out, hot tears escaping from my eyes. "Please let me in! I'm begging you! Please!"

My left-hand bursts through the door. Not clean through, and I barely feel the pain as I pull it out. Just as I'm about to bang on the door again, it opens.

My forward motion causes me to fall inside. I sit up quickly, backing into a wall as someone slams the door shut.

A little boy stands by the front entrance, a woman who I presume is his mother scolds him in a language I don't know. My jaw drops. He's so young. I've never seen someone so young!

Two more kids, a girl who looks a few years younger than me and a boy around my age are all staring at me with wide eyes. They all have deep, dark skin and short black, curling hair. Except for the younger boy. His hair is shaven. An older man, sharing the same features as his family, limps into my view. He must be the father.

The entire house is pitch black except for a small amount of light coming through the covered windows.

"Thank you," I struggle to say, still catching my breath. "Holy shit—jeez—thank you—"

"You need to leave," the mother says. Her voice holds an unfamiliar accent.

I feel as though someone cut a hole inside my heart. "What? They'll kill me."

"That's why you need to leave," the father says. I get up, my mouth down to the floor as I glare at all of them. The little boy hides behind his mother.

"Mama, Baba, maybe we can take her to them," the older boy says.

"What?" I cry out.

He ignores me, walking over to his mom. "We'll get a reward. And since they want her so badly, she clearly isn't human. So, who cares."

The mother says something in a different language, nodding her head.

Am I hearing them right? They sound like demons, only caring about themselves. "I'll leave if you think it puts you in danger."

"No." The father raises his voice. I gulp, taking a step closer to the family. He doesn't notice and glances at his son. "We can't let her go now. We should take her in."

I have to get out of here. I grab his sister in a quick motion and hook my arm around her neck, as I conjure up a fireball in my right hand. A long, relaxing breath leaves my nose. I take in the power, angry tears strolling down my cheeks.

"Nyah!"

"No, stop!"

"Mama!"

They stare at me in silence after they realize they can do nothing. "Let her go please," the father begs.

I give him a mocking grin. "Really? You weren't going to let me leave. You were going to hand me over to the demons. And now, *I should let her go?*"

I bring my fire closer to the girl's face. Her cries pierce my ears, but I have to do this. Those would've been my cries if I didn't do anything.

"Please," the mother sobs. "We'll let you leave."

I nod my head. "Yes, you will, and she'll be coming

with me. When I finally can't see any glimpse of your house, or you, anymore, I'll let her go."

"No—"

I bring the fire close enough to blind the girl's eyes. She shakes uncontrollably, but I'm strong enough to hold her down. Being this close to her neck, I can smell the sweet metallic scent of her blood. Maybe, when I take her away from here, I'll just nick her finger a bit to see if it tastes as great as it smells. "That's the only way it'll work."

They don't get a chance to say anything. The door slams open. The mother grabs the younger boy, backing away while multiple gasps fill the room, including my own.

"Mahi?" Isra's voice comes out breathy, his red eyes staring at my hand before landing on the innocent girl within my grasp.

"A prince of Hell," the girl screams, shaking madly. I'm frozen. I can barely speak, let alone hold this girl anymore. She breaks out of my arms and runs off but I can't move.

"Isra," I manage to say, my voice croaking out.

He's actually, physically, *here*.

17

"WHAT WAS THAT?" Isra asks me once we're out of the house. My feet sink into a puddle on the street as the rain refuses to slow down. Even when Isra had come inside, his presence overpowering the entire room, those humans still looked at me like *I* was a demon. When he pushed all of them back with the flick of his wrist, they stood there shaking in their skins at a power they'd never understand, yet it wasn't him they tried to hide from.

"I don't know." I refuse to meet his eyes, scratching my hand. An antagonizing pressure eats up at my insides. "Maybe I should go try to stop Lucifer now. Me, an eighteen-year-old, against the most powerful thing anyone has ever seen. That'd be a boring fight. Or, I have a better idea! I'll just turn myself in. Put an end to at least some of the torture he's inflicting on people."

"Look at me," Isra says. I don't. "Mahi."

My eyes widen when he gently grabs my chin, and I look at him. His red eyes gleam, a frown on his face. I pull away. He doesn't seem to care. "At the moment, you're in no condition to do that. The entire city is in lockdown looking for you. Any human is going to be shot on sight, and their soul is going to have a special journey in Hell for disobeying a high order. That's how badly they are hunting you down. We need to get you out of here. Do you trust me?"

My eyes turn to slits. "No."

Isra smirks, chuckles even, but I can see the disappointment on his face. "Smart. But you either come with me, or I leave you with the pack of demons closing in on us. The only reason I found you is because every demon got a message that you were in this zone."

He grabs my right hand and presses hard on where the monster's fangs cut me earlier. I grind my teeth together to hold back my shrieks, trying to tear my hand away. Isra finally lets me go when he pulls out a small bead.

"You had a tracker in you," he says. crushing it between his fingers. "And you weren't exactly subtle when you screamed outside these humans' houses. If I didn't get here, some meager demon would've."

I sigh, the tracker didn't even surprise me. Lucifer has all the resources in the world. When Isra grabs my wrist again, a feral growl leaves my mouth. I gasp, covering my lips with my free hand.

Isra stares at my hand before lifting my sleeve. I follow his gaze, my heart palpating at the black veins all over my arm. "*You're infected*. Why didn't you tell me? It's almost reached your brain."

"Because you would've taken me away!"

He lets go, a slow, aggravated breath escaping his mouth. Despite that, the worried expression on his face doesn't go away. "I can help, Mahi," he tells me. "There isn't time. Are you coming with me?"

I purse my lips together and look over his shoulder. There's a row of vehicles approaching, quickly.

A prince of Hell who *has* helped me, or a hundred other demons who will for sure drag me toward the scariest thing in the world. "How do I know you aren't just going to take me to Lucifer?"

I know he's had multiple opportunities to do so, but to demons, everything is a mind game.

"You don't," Isra says, bringing his hand out. "Clocks ticking. Take my hand."

I bite my lip, glancing behind me before grabbing his hand. My eyes squeeze shut when I feel nothing below my feet. The air is knocked out of my lungs and the cold rain vanishes as warmth takes its place. My legs wobble when they hit something solid.

"Did we just—" I open my eyes and stare at the navy blue walls around us. "What just happened?"

Isra huffs out a laugh. "Teleportation. It's one of the perks of being a prince, although it takes so much energy. We call it phasing."

My stomach feels heavy. It's good I never told him where I was. Despite that, I glance at him with a small smile. "Do you need my consent to do it?"

"Of course."

Quickly, I examine the room for any exits. There's a door at the end of a dark hallway. Just before the hall, there's a large window by a gleaming black table with four small stools. I can't help but stroll over and feel the smooth surface. The building I'd been taken to seemed to have the same material. "What is this?"

"Marble," Isra says from behind me. I can feel his presence, and I'm glad he can't see me because I blush. "Here."

I turn around only to see him holding a needle in his hand. "The cure was with you . . . the whole time."

"It needs to go in your shoulder," he says. "And yes. Maybe if you asked, I could've cured you sooner, but you have this mindset that all demons are cruel, horrible creatures. You're lucky you aren't human. The process was slowed down for you."

The way he speaks makes me shiver. Like he spat out the words because he hated them so much.

I grab the collar of my shirt, lowering it from the left side so that my shoulder is exposed. He places one hand on my back before pressing the needle into my skin. It all happens so quickly, but the second it ends, we share a look. Like both of us just did something extremely intimate. Swiftly, I move away.

The kitchen is behind the marble table, which is decorated in a theme of black and white cupboards. I spin around to face Isra again and notice a small, dark dining table. This one I can tell is made out of wood. It's covered in desserts—my stomach grumbles.

"How is this already set up here?" I ask, walking toward the sweets. Without thinking, I grab a cupcake, then put it back when I remember where I am. On the anniversary of my first year in containment, the demons gave me one. They hadn't fed me in a while, probably to make sure I ate it. It turned out to be poisoned. Of course, I could've healed myself, but I had to get my stomach pumped to let them think it was real.

"Can't a guy have a table full of cakes and pastries in his house?"

I frown. "I don't believe you."

He sighs. "I thought you'd like it if you got to eat some real food—"

"How'd you know I'd come here?" I back away as he comes closer to me, my spine hitting the table. "Were you planning on it?"

Isra rubs his face, shaking his head. "There was an alert sent out, saying that you were here after you exposed yourself. You weren't careful, so I figured the only way you'd be safe was if you came with me. But I wanted you to be able to relax, at least for one night, which is why I set this up, so it'd be ready. Besides, baking is my stress relief."

I try to hide my shock but what he just told me is so *human*. "I can't relax with a prince of Hell around me."

I turn to stone when I see the hurt on his face. "How do I prove to you that I don't want to take you to Lucifer?"

He's helped me in more ways than one. I want to believe him, *but he's a demon*. The thought keeps nagging in my brain. "You want something else."

"Holy—Yes. Yes, I do Mahi, for you to sit on the throne!" Isra raises his voice. His eyes aren't glowing anymore. Instead, they are a deep, blood red. "That's all I've ever wanted for you."

I scoff. "First it was because you were bored. Now it's because you want me to rule. I'm eighteen!"

Isra shrugs. "Well, I mean, the world is still boring, so that never went away. The second thing came later."

"But why?"

"Because you're the most fascinating thing I've ever seen."

I stare at him blankly. I don't know how demons think or feel. I just know that they lie, every chance they get. Yet Isra seems so different. "Then tell me what I am."

He walks over to a different table, decorated with small plants. There are already jugs of water and a few other dishes on it. "Have dinner. *Relax.* And I'll tell you what I think."

My lips press together, but I do as he says, sitting in the chair he stands beside. He smiles, and I can't help but give him a small one back. I have a terrible feeling in my gut, but it also feels slightly like guilt for enjoying this. My shoulder itches and burns, and I suck in a breath when I touch the wound I'd forgotten about.

"Just let me check on the chicken." He walks away. An aggravating sigh leaves my mouth while I heal my shoulder. "You're going to be mind blown. Oh, and I made pasta. I'll heat it up, along with some other food."

"You made all this?" I ask in disbelief, staring at the food he places on the table. I lift the pan from a large bowl, allowing the delicious smell of spicy tomatoes to invade my nostrils.

"That's the pasta," he tells me, running back to bring more food.

Whatever this pasta is, it makes my stomach ache with hunger. I'm already here. If it's poisoned, it's too late. I haven't had a meal like this in my entire life. Grabbing a spoon, I dig in.

After a few minutes of stuffing my face with all kinds

of new tastes, Isra comes back with what I assume is the chicken.

"I'm glad you like it." He laughs.

"I can't believe food like this exists," I cry out. "Maybe I'm overdramatic, but I think I'm going to cry. This beats squirrels and bland bread."

Isra sits next to me. "I'm truly the best chef you'll ever meet."

I don't hesitate to grab a piece of the chicken he brought. "How did you learn to cook?"

He shakes his head and chuckles. "I know you probably picture us demons, especially me, doing sadistic things all day. But that gets boring after a while, and I mostly do these things in my free time. I've had a long time to learn."

I stop eating, my appetite gone. He makes torturing people sound so casual. "But doesn't Lucifer have, I don't know, stuff for you to do?"

Isra shrugs. "There isn't much resistance anymore. And I'm not the first royal he tells anything to. I avoid him, so I don't know a lot."

"What *do* you know?" I ask, taking a sip of water. "About me."

Time to see if he'll actually tell me, and if I should make a run for that window or not.

He lets out a long breath. "Look, I don't know for sure, but I think you are half-angel."

I choke on my water. "What?"

"I think you are half-angel."

My stomach clenches. I think I'm suffocating, or choking. I cough while Isra places a hand on my back. Both relief and sorrow flood my mind. *How?*

"Mahi?"

"But—" I clear my throat and take another sip of water, bringing a hand to my head to relieve the dizziness. "All the angels are dead."

Which means, if this is true, my entire species is gone.

"Well, we missed you. Angel half-breeds shouldn't even exist. They've always, and I mean always, resulted in a stillborn child and the death of the mother. So, angels were forbidden to do it."

I blink at him, swallowing down a lump that's formed in my throat. I'm not sure how he knows that fact, but his words sink in slowly. "You're saying the mother always dies?"

He raises an eyebrow at me. "Yes. Female angels can't have children, so the mother is always the human one."

My vision blurs, a shaky breath passing my lips as I scratch at my forehead. "Is my dad even my real father?"

"I don't know. Most angels had their own bodies and others could go inside human ones. Everything about your birth is unknown."

"My dad told me my mother died from demons. But it was because of *me*?"

I get up and walk away from Isra, pulling at my hair. My stomach feels sick, and my body gets colder by the second. This can't be true. It doesn't make sense. "I don't have wings."

Isra is behind me. "Because you're a half-breed."

"But Kavon has wings," I say, turning to face him. I must look crazy because it startles Isra. His eyebrows shoot up, and his face looks as though he just saw a ghost.

He gives me a comforting smile. "Kavon is something that's not normal in nature," he says, his voice gentle.

"There's never been a demon-angel crossbreed. The number of mutations in his body must be insane."

I groan. "Well, have you seen another half-breed?"

"No," he admits. "You're the first angelic half-breed I've ever seen. And if there ever was another half-breed, there aren't any documents on what they looked like, so what I'm saying might not even be true." He's standing closer to me than I thought. It's the first time I notice our height difference up close. My head barely reaches above his shoulders. "As I said, they're rare."

I rub my eyes. "So, this is only a guess. You don't actually know. I could be a freak of nature."

My heart skips a beat when Isra touches my arms. I should pull away, but my entire body feels awake. "So, what if you are? It's extraordinary."

"Why would I do that—" I choke, the tears rushing out. "Why would I do that to that girl if I was half-angel?"

"Mahi." I meet his desperate eyes, which causes my stomach to flutter. "You're *human* too. And I don't know how much you know about angels, but I was there when you told Kavon that they couldn't have been perfect. And they weren't."

My head is pounding from the amount of pressure building up against my eyes. "Jeez, I shouldn't be crying like an idiot."

Isra gives me a soft smile. "It's not bad to cry. In fact, I think it makes a person stronger."

I break from his grasp and start pacing the room. There's a tightness in my chest. "Why are you so kind to me?"

"What do you mean?"

"You—you're the bad guy!" I stammer out. "You aren't supposed to do this. You aren't supposed to make me feel—" I shut my mouth before I say something I'll regret.

"Do what, Mahi?" Isra asks, his voice rasping. "I know how you make me feel, but you're a closed book."

He's in my space again, but he doesn't touch me. I breathe heavily, staring at him. My eyes roam his face, taking in his lips and his eyes. His smirk grows. "Is there something you want me to do?"

"No," I struggle to find words, looking away. "I don't know."

His fingers delicately grab my chin, and I gasp when he leans in toward me, but he stops halfway. "What do you want?" he breathes out, glancing at my mouth. He smells musky and fresh. It's hypnotizing. His red eyes are the most stunning things I've ever seen.

My mind betrays me. "Kiss me," I whisper hoarsely.

He smiles wickedly before leaning down, and I go on my toes. On instinct, I close my eyes, and his lips press down on mine. It feels as though time slows down, and all the problems in my life have faded away.

His lips are soft. There is a subtle sweetness to them. His hand caresses my jawline before moving onto my cheek. I raise my hands, dragging my fingers against his horns until I start to scratch at his hair. It's still damp from the rain.

My bones are on fire as our mouths move, small gasps escaping past my lips. I shouldn't be doing this, but all I focus on is how addictive his lips feel against mine. Isra smiles into the kiss, and my heart pounds against my chest as he invades all my senses. The harder he kisses me, the more it intoxicates me. We pull apart slightly, staying just close enough that we can breathe in each other's breath. My cheeks fluster. I'm panting while Isra's hot breath soothes my skin.

"That was perfect," he says, joy evident in his voice. I move away from him, and he frowns, scratching the back of his head. "Maybe I shouldn't have actually said that out loud."

"No." I shake my head. "I mean, no, it's fine you said that. What am I saying? I'm sorry."

"Sorry?" He lets out a huff of a laugh. "For what?"

My insides are fluttering and I can feel my heart hammering against my chest. I shouldn't be feeling this way. He's a demon. A demon *prince*. But I can't help but bite down my smile and focus on not jumping up and down.

If only I could tell Laurel. Dating was something we'd always talk about before ending up in containment, even though there weren't many options around. We'd even had our first kiss together, considering everyone else was lame. We tried the dating game for two days but realized we were basically sisters.

Slowly, my lips curve downwards. I couldn't tell Laurel even if she was standing right in front of me. She hates me now.

"Hey." Isra's calming voice awakens me before any more memories can come up. "What's wrong? Did I do something? I apoli—"

"No." I shake my head, moving closer to him. "You did nothing wrong. You saved me from . . . from killing that girl. And you saved me twice from being taken to Lucifer. I was . . . wrong about you."

He grins. "I told you before. We have a bond."

I don't know what he's talking about, because I don't feel anything that could be a *bond*. Nothing like what Kavon and I have, but I do feel myself smiling when I think about the kiss again.

That's when it hits me. I'm here thinking about a kiss while Kavon must think I'm dead. I have to focus on finding my father and escaping the city. Whatever Isra wants, I can't be that. "I need to go," I say, my cheeks heating up as I remember everything that I have to deal with.

"What?" Isra's smile vanishes. "You want to go back out there?"

"I have to find my father." My chest pains as I remember our last encounter. "I saw him when I first entered Morningstar, and I have to help Kavon get out of the city. You should come with me."

"But we have to stop Lucifer," Isra says sternly. "I'll make you into who you're supposed to be." He has that crazy look in his eyes once again. A fanatic shine that makes my stomach churn. Everything I just felt transforms into the need to run away.

"You can." I nod my head, reassuring him so that he doesn't get more upset. "I promise I'll help you after I save my dad, but we need a plan. He can help. And if I speak to Kavon, maybe he can help me understand my angelic side."

I walk toward the door, and Isra shouts from behind me. "Mahi, think about this. You'll get caught if you go now!"

I look back at him. My eyes widen at the terrified expression on his face.

"Y-you can't go now," he whispers, his eyes frantically looking around. "If you go, the demons will be a lost cause."

I pull away from him, and his eyes darken. He has a huge point, and something tugs at me to stay here, but I need to get away from him. My gut is telling me that something is off; that his kindness was really something else this entire time. I turn the knob. The cold breeze welcomes me, calming down only a few of the nerves inside my body.

I'm glad to see that the rain is finally gone. A forest of buildings surrounds me. It makes Isra's place seem irrelevant. Perhaps that's what he wanted.

I only take a few more steps when, with inhuman speed, Isra blocks my way. Gasping, I move away from him. A chain gleams in his hands.

"You can't leave," he growls. His voice is morphed and distorted. He throws his arm out, and I desperately try to control the energy inside me. A spark forms in my hand, but that's all before I'm pushed down by an invisible force. It feels like a knife has sliced into my flesh as sharp pain runs through my back.

I somehow manage to throw a weak fireball at him. "What are you doing?"

I can't see him anymore. I sit up, looking around. My pulse races, and I tense when something cold clamps around my neck. This can't be happening again. "Doing what I have to."

As soon as he places the collar on me, my power fades. I search for it desperately, but it's gone. It's as if I never had it.

I look up at Isra, standing beside me now with

grinding teeth. He's giving me a small pout like I'm a child who just misbehaved. My fists pound against his legs as hard as they can, but nothing seems to work. "I thought you were different!"

I choke as he pulls at the collar around my throat, stroking my hair while he drags me back inside. "I guess we were both wrong."

18

Isra didn't take me down to Hell like I thought he would. I guess he really does want me for himself. Instead, he hauled me into a prison underneath his home.

He gave me food. He even gave me some new clean clothes, but no way, under any circumstance, was I taking *anything* from him. I'd gone weeks without food before. Water, on the other hand . . . whatever happened would happen. It'd only been a day so far.

The cell was a downgrade from containment, but it felt all the same. Grey walls and a cold stone floor that made me think I was sick. I didn't have a bed, but also no scanner. Outside of the cell was a clean, wooden floor and the staircase that brought me down to this nightmare.

I couldn't think of anything I could do to get away. The chains Isra had attached to my arms once we got down here and the collar clamping around my neck somehow blocked my flame.

"There's no point in having a conversation with me," I say for the twentieth time that day, reluctantly turning my head to face him. He's wearing a black collared shirt and what I think are dark jeans while sitting behind the bars that separate us, on the one chair in this dungeon. I'm glad the other cells are empty. The rest of the room is quite spacious, but I can't really see what goes beyond the hallway next to this cell.

"This is for your own good," Isra says for the *fiftieth* time. I'm not sure if he's trying to get me to believe it, or himself.

One of his orange pet foxes sits in his lap, its eyes are closed while Isra scratches its head. If he brought it here to gain some sympathy, it doesn't make me feel anything but disgust.

"I'm flattered," I say just as my stomach growls.

"Eat your food, Mahi," he says. I sigh and go back to looking at the wall, debating if I should bash my skull in it but I'm all talk. There were plenty of times I'd think about ending everything in containment but I'd never go through with it.

My cell door opens suddenly and I back up as far as I can into the wall, watching Isra step inside. "Wha——"

He grabs both my cheeks harshly with his hand, forcing my mouth open as he shoves some of the sandwich he'd given me in my mouth. I shake my head, but he squeezes my cheeks harder. As I start gagging, he lets me go, only to open a water bottle and repeat the whole process.

"Shhto——" I choke. He finally lets me go again, slamming the water back onto the floor. I cough as pieces of the bread shoot from my mouth while Isra leaves the cell.

"Eat," he says. "Or you'll be eating through a feeding tube next time."

"What the hell!" I cry out, rubbing my eyes. I wipe my cheeks, whimpering at the pain. "What is wrong with you?"

Isra sighs, but his lips tug upwards. This is the first time I've continued to speak to him. "I didn't want to do this. Eat, and I won't do it again."

Did I actually start to see Isra as a human? I'm the biggest idiot. "I hate you."

"If you went out there, how would you even find your father? By wandering the streets aimlessly?"

My eyes tense, and I blink at the soreness. I cried my eyes out last night. "It didn't matter." I clear my throat. "I just wanted to get away from you."

He smirks and tilts his head. My blood boils. "Even after our kiss?" he says *exactly* what I knew he would.

My cheeks are hot. I can't believe I forgot in that moment that he's an immortal prince of Hell; that he's done countless harm to so many people and *joked* about it. "I don't know how that happened."

"Oh really?" He leans toward me, resting his head on his hand, a single finger in the middle of his lips. "You don't feel a part of you, I don't know, savors the fact that I, a horrible creature who does cruel, inhuman things, cares for you?"

"I barely know you," I scream so loud my throat hurts. Isra doesn't react. "Chaining someone up doesn't show that you care. Or torturing them! You should've let me leave!"

"And get caught by Lucifer?"

"I'd be in the exact same position I'm in now."

"No, you'd be dead."

I open my mouth but I don't know what to say. He's right. It was stupid of me to leave when the entire city is hunting me down. When, as Kavon said, my face is plastered everywhere.

And even though I wanted to get away from Isra, I could've played along for a little longer. Now I'm back in physical chains. That's worse than containment.

"Do you know what happens when you die?" His words cut through the air. My nostrils flare, and my fingers hook around the bars. I scream, shaking them in an attempt to get out of here. Isra frowns, but he also looks as though he's about to laugh.

"Your soul goes to Hell," I croak out, leaning back and breathing slowly. I need to calm myself down if I want to strategize a way to get out of here. "An eternity of torture awaits you, so I'm told."

Isra's lips curve up. "You don't know that there's something *stronger* than Lucifer? Something you meet before you go to Hell?"

"What?" He has my full attention now.

"You don't know because Lucifer hides it like the coward he is." Isra gets up and leans against the bars. "He doesn't like to meddle with earthly affairs."

"What are you talking about?"

He smirks. "I would tell you and all, but it's not like you're going to help me."

My jaw clenches. "I was going to help you. I just wanted to find my father first!"

"I told you why," whispers Isra. "I can help you sit on

the throne. A demon would never be able to take over Hell. But a half-breed, both human and angel, would."

I pull on the chains. "You don't know that! Do you really think someone like me would want to rule the *entire* earth?"

Isra backs away. "You haven't tasted power. Things could change. And believe it or not, I had to do this for the demons. Every day more become wayward, and Lucifer does nothing."

"It doesn't matter," I mutter out. "I doubt you have a plan, anyway."

"I'll just have to wait for you to come around."

My mind falters at his words. I want to know his ideas and possibly know more about myself. Then again, maybe he doesn't have any plans. Maybe he's just saying whatever he thinks will let me stay. There can't actually be something stronger than Lucifer.

"Why don't you just do it yourself?" I ask. "You could've killed me in seconds. I'm sure you could kill Lucifer."

He pouts at me. "Damn, I'm disappointed. You really don't listen to me."

I give him a smile. If there's a weapon to kill Lucifer, it looks like I'll have to try harder for him to reveal it. "Yeah, I don't."

He smirks at me again, and I hate that he looks so handsome. Pretty things can be so ugly. "He has an influence over me that's difficult to resist. And my followers must obey his commands, no matter what. Not to mention most of the other royals are still loyal to him."

"But some of them aren't?"

"Not enough."

I get up so I can stretch my legs, my heart continuing to race. "And you don't think that'll happen to me?"

He shakes his head. "I'm not telling you anything, Mahi."

I suck in air, closing my eyes for a second to calm myself down. "Well, Lucifer must be a beast if even *you* can't kill him."

"What's that supposed to mean?"

I scoff. "Besides all the basic demonic crap, whenever I thought of you, you came. That's a pretty powerful thing."

"All of the royals can do that. It's quite easy actually—"

"Then whatever you *can* do, I can't imagine what Lucifer can," I clarify.

Isra brings his face closer to the bars. I step back, my legs shaking as I hold in a breath. "Now you know why I need you." He grins. "It'll take a team to stop him. You'll never be able to do it all on your own, no matter how powerful you are. You're so astonishing and yet so idiotic."

I roll my eyes, biting my lip and trying my best to make sure he can't see how afraid I am. "Says the one who seems to know everything about me and won't say a thing. How can I know how powerful I am if you won't tell me anything?"

"I remember the angels." His voice sounds higher, his eyes gleaming while they gaze at me like a laser. "They might be dead now, but they put up a fight. In the end, there were just more of us."

My eyebrows narrow. "You know so much about them. Too bad you aren't an angel." He moves his head away and he *blushes*. It's easy to notice with his black blood. My eyes widen. A smile grows on my face. "You want to be an angel. That's why you're obsessed with my power. That's how you know so much about them."

"Yeah." He blinks, smiling, but it isn't one of his usual ones. This one is weaker, fake even. I don't know if what I'm saying is true or not, but I feel a flutter in my stomach at finally flustering him. "Obviously, it'd be really cool to heal things."

"That's not it." I narrow my eyes at him. "You're ashamed. You want to be an angel, despite everything you have now."

"You act like you know everything." His voice shakes, and he moves back from the bars. "But you know nothing about demons. You probably know nothing about the war. Nothing about Lucifer."

"Then tell me."

He shakes his head. "Forget it." He looks at the clothes he'd given me. "If you're not going to put those clothes on, I'll get you some better ones. Some you can actually fight in."

"Fight who?" I scoff, motioning at him. "You?"

"You're going to be here a long time Mahi," Isra says. "Eventually, you'll find comfort in these talks. Comfort in me. Why waste that time? I'll have to train you if you want to fight Lucifer so that I don't have to worry about you when we face him. Believe me, I won't ever be able to shove a sandwich in your face again when you reach your peak."

I watch as he walks away, leaving me alone in this dungeon. Once I can no longer hear his footsteps, I lie down on the freezing floor and stare at the dark ceiling.

Containment taught me that time moves faster when you sleep. But most of the days, I barely got any sleep at all.

I can't believe I kissed Isra. The memory eats at my insides. He probably had a different goal this entire time. When he helped me understand my powers, it was all because *he* wanted to understand them himself. He might say that he cares about me, but it's probably only my powers he actually cares about.

I close my eyes as my thoughts drift to Kavon. I'd do anything to see him now, especially since I might be half-angel. There might've been other things he hadn't shown me he could do yet. Maybe that was why I felt comfortable around him, because we're both the same. Although, he did say something had pulled him toward me.

I never felt a pull at all.

I don't remember falling asleep, but I can tell that I'm dreaming. My entire body is surrounded by an empty field with a clear blue sky. There's no wind. No heat. Nothing—only the silence that invades my ears.

"Mahi?" I gasp and turn to see Kavon behind me in the distance. His hair is rough, veins pulsing and bags under his eyes.

He runs toward me, stopping about a foot away. I shake my head, my eyes turning fuzzy. I race forward and wrap my arms around his waist. I heave into his shirt, wailing while he places a hand on my back. His wings surround me and all I can feel is his warmth.

"Are you okay?" he asks once we pull apart, rubbing

at his eyebrow while he holds my eyes with a watery gaze. I sniff and scratch my head. A hole forms in my stomach. "How am I doing this? Is this really you?"

Kavon smiles, but it doesn't seem genuine. "Actually, I'm doing it. Dream walking. This is really me."

Makes sense. If I can't use my other powers, how would I expect this to be me? "This is pretty cool."

"Only works if the other person wants to see me," he says. "Where are you? Nothing's been announced, and I felt a pull toward the north. That's not where Lucifer's penthouse is. But last night, the feeling disappeared. And this morning, Lucifer *himself* made a video announcement to everyone in Morningstar. He wants you alive and unhurt."

His voice trails off, like he's unsure if he should continue or not. I don't think I want him to.

I gulp. "Well . . . I escaped your mother, but that didn't stop her and a whole bunch of other demons from chasing me down. A prince of Hell came, and it was either going with him or getting captured. I—jeez, I'm stupid—I went with him, and he placed me in a cell."

He doesn't need to know all the other embarrassing details.

"Did you see anything that might give me an idea of where you are?" Kavon asks, his wings fanning at me. He raises his chin. "Wait, this prince didn't take you to Lucifer?"

I shake my head.

"What's his name?"

I don't know why I tense. "It's Isra."

He runs his fingers through his hair. "Of course, it's him. I should've killed him when I had the chance. Look,

I don't know how much you know about the royals, but he's the demon of passion. He knows what you're feeling and can amplify it. Similar to what I—actually never mind. You have to get away. He can make a small ounce of sadness feel like the end of the world."

It's like Kavon just shot me with the truth. "No way," I whisper, staring off in the distance. That explains why I kissed him. Why I felt safe with him, for a while at least. Which also means a part of me liked him. He just amplified it.

He's so horrible.

"Where are you?" Kavon asks again.

"There are maybe a dozen buildings that look the exact same around me." I pant, placing a hand on my chest. "I'm never going to get out of here! He's put something on me that won't let me use my powers."

Kavon's eyes widen. "I've never heard of that. That's got to be why I can't sense where you are anymore."

"I don't know what to do!" It's getting harder to breathe.

He sighs. "Maybe I can go undercover as a demon. It might help me find out where you are. I won't show my face. Just eavesdrop."

I start to panic when Kavon embraces me in a hug again. "You can't do that," I manage to say through gasps. "You can't risk yourself because I was stupid. Just get out of Morningstar, okay."

It takes him a moment to respond. "I'll visit you every night," he whispers. "We'll figure it out."

I don't tell him in that moment that I might be half-angel because what's the point in making him believe he isn't alone if I'm never going to get out of here?

19

I PULL at the now familiar chains around my wrists. "Since I've been here, for what, forever? What kind of metal is this?"

Isra leans against the wall inside my cage, twirling the chain that connects to the collar on my neck. The first week he'd sit outside and talk to me. Sometimes I'd engage in the conversation. This was only when my anger gave out or I thought I'd get some information out of him.

The second week he started coming inside, feeding me by hand, trying to play games with me like we were friends, and teaching me biology. It was odd how casually I spoke to him now but I had to if I wanted to get some facts.

He pulls on the chain, and I almost fall. He laughs while I try my best to ignore the painful throbbing from my throat. My eyes are glued to the ground because if I look at him, he'll see how much I despise his presence and then he won't tell me anything. Unless he already knows.

"I don't think an angel would do that," I say through my teeth.

"You're cute." Isra scratches my hair. "You think I'm a moron."

"I think you're a lot of things," I say. "Are we going to do this or not?"

Having calmed myself down enough that he won't know what's really going on, I meet his eyes, but there's a scowl on his face. It vanishes quickly, and for the next moment, I suffer as his hands linger over my skin while he takes off the chains.

When he finally removes the collar, I exhale slowly like I'm breathing for the first time and as I close my eyes, I don't care that his thumb grazes over where the metal has dug into my skin. The feeling I get when my powers come back, is like becoming full after not knowing I was starved.

I'd decided a week ago that I'd finally allow Isra to train me. That way, maybe I'd get an opportunity to get out of here. He'd given me so many openings to take the chance, removing my chains and sitting back to watch what I'd do. Every instant, I'd attacked him with a weak fireball. He'd clamp the metal back around my wrists, shaking his head and clicking his tongue while walking away. When I was alone, all I thought about was how I'd locate my dad.

At night I'd escape to Kavon. The first thing he'd ask is if I had any idea where I was. The answer was always no. The collar was only off my neck for an hour at a time, apparently not enough time for Kavon to come find me.

"We're going to try something different today," Isra says, stepping outside of the cage with the collar in his hand. I follow him out even though my arms and legs are stiff.

The cage that's become my recent home is the closest to the stairs out of here. And while my cage looks horrible, the rest of the 'basement,' as Isra calls it, looks quite nice. The beige walls are lined with a few photos of Isra's pet foxes. In some of them, they are even dressed up. Then there's the large blue mat placed by the stairs. There are no windows. I've tried too many times to get out of here. The truth is, the only way I can escape is by getting past Isra and running up those stairs.

I just hate that training so close to his body makes me want to shove a knife up his jaw. I always end up wasting the training session by not using all my effort into learning.

"Like what?" I sigh, keeping my eyes on Isra when he picks up a glowing, white jar. I lean forward to get a better view and my breath hitches at the sight of it.

He smirks. "Do you know what this is?"

"No."

"It's a soul," he tells me, raising it so it's at his eye level, which means at least a foot above me. "I'm basically a criminal like you now for stealing one of these."

My eyes linger over the soul. It's so darn bright, but somehow doesn't blind my eyes. "What are you going to do?" Goosebumps climb up my neck. I rub my arms. It's eerie being around an actual soul, but I can't help but stare at it.

"This is *power*," Isra explains. "That's why demons made deals for them. They're magic. Lucifer used them to build his army, still does. Feral demons come from these."

"Magic," I repeat, shaking my head.

"Is it really that difficult to believe?"

"No. It's just—no," I finish, my face flushing.

"You really think our world is limited to demons and angels?" Isra asks. "You do have the knowledge that your powers are magic, correct?"

I scowl. "It's not like I really had a chance to explore."

"Fair enough." Isra shrugs. "Now, I want you to absorb this soul."

A nervous smile forms on my face as I take a step back. "Uh . . . what? How am I supposed to do that?"

"I wouldn't know." He frowns. "But I have a theory that some kinds of angels can absorb souls."

My back straightens. "What kind?"

He doesn't respond.

I groan. "Okay. But isn't it wrong to use . . . a soul? I mean that's basically a person, isn't it? What happens to it when I'm done?"

"I'll put it back in this jar," Isra says. "Trust me, you won't destroy it."

I chew on the inside of my cheek. If I consume this soul, maybe I can get out of here once and for all. Or I'll fail epically and the relationship I've managed to build with Isra will vanish. *But you have a chance.*

However funny my stomach feels, I don't think Isra's going to take no for an answer.

"Let's do it."

"Good decision." Isra smiles.

"But I have no idea what to do," I say as Isra starts to twist open the lid.

"Just pretend—well technically it—just pretend it's a person and tell it to come to you."

"That totally helps." I roll my eyes, jolting when the soul flies out of the jar and bounces quickly around the room. It collides into one of Isra's photos and the frame falls to the floor.

I place both my hands out and try to stop it. The act itself will not do anything, but it'll help me visualize what I'm doing. "Stop."

The soul freezes above the training mat, almost like it really *is* a physical person. A sigh escapes my mouth at how simple that was. I use the opportunity to grab the glowing orb. As soon as I touch it, it flies into my mouth.

I choke, gagging at the sudden pressure in my throat. It's as if a giant rock just slid into my body, forcing its way into my stomach. My neck feels as though it's being stretched as wide as this room.

"Mahi!"

"I'm—" I cough, holding my hand out to stop Isra from touching me. "I'm, oh my gosh! I'm great."

I tip my head back and gasp as a weightless feeling spreads through my body. My stomach flutters, and everything tingles. "*Wow.*"

"How does it feel?"

"It feeeeels . . ." I smile at Isra, inhaling the sudden

sweet smell in the air. I'm on top of the world. I can do anything. "It feels, really, really great."

"Well, you look captivating. You're glowing more than usual, and your eyes almost look entirely engulfed in fire." Isra stares at me in awe. "Okay, let's master your fire now."

"We alwaaaaaaays do fire," I complain—*which means you know how to defend yourself from it.* "Is that the only offensive I have? I have a literal soul in me. Let's try something new!"

"An angel's primary weapon is an element." Isra's eyes shine. He loves talking about the angels. I try not to throw up. "And I don't know how long you'll be able to contain that soul. We should use it while we can."

"Kavon doesn't have an element." I smile. "Maybe you're not as big of an angel expert as you thought."

Isra returns my grin. "You're forgetting he's half-demon. Since he's the first of his kind, I'm going to have to guess that it conflicts with his angelic side, which is why, according to the documents we have on him, he can do telekinesis. His element must've been air, but since he's a living mutation, he does telekinesis instead. He's also a born fighter. That's one of the reasons he was chosen to be Lucifer's assassin. So, I'm guessing his angelic parent was a Guardian."

My eyebrows curve downwards. I remember how Kavon had slaughtered hellhounds when he first saved me. He made it look easy. "You think I know what that means?"

Isra stretches his arms and yawns. "It means that there were hierarchies in Heaven, just as there are in Hell. Guardians were the warriors, natural fighters in case of a war. And as I told you, the angels *did* put up a good fight."

Wow, he really *does* know a lot about them. "So, what do you think I am?" I lean toward him, trying my best not to shove my fist into his smirk. I wonder if I can break the wall with this soul in me, or if I'll fail and end up in the cell.

He chuckles. "Nice try. But you haven't given me any reason to tell you anything."

I scowl. "Or you just don't know."

He shrugs. "That could be it. Or maybe it isn't. One day you'll find out."

Groaning, I back away from him and get into a stance he'd taught me—legs bent, feet shoulders width apart. I'm not a natural fighter. Against humans, my strength is an asset, but I can barely throw a punch against a demon, so I know I wouldn't be mastering fire today. What I had become good at was making my skin boiling hot to whoever touched me. Whenever I did it now, Isra would bear the pain long enough to lock me back up.

"You look upset." Isra crosses his arms, giving me a frown. My hands turn into fists, but I exhale slowly and tighten my ponytail. I need to keep my cool, but Isra makes it impossible. And my throat is starting to itch as if the soul is trying to climb out.

"Yeah, because I suck at fighting." My words come out stiff and rigid. "And it's because *I'm* terrible, not you."

"Is that a compliment?"

My teeth grit against each other. "Here's an idea. Why don't you talk to Lucifer and tell him what you think could be done better? And then, you can take me to him and gain his favor. Or maybe do that first so he listens to you."

Isra gives me a blank stare, almost like he's sleepy and doesn't hear what I said. It's so quiet that my heavy breathing sounds loud in my ears.

"Let's get to work," Isra says in a flat voice.

My hands clench and unclench as he turns around. I can't control it anymore. Baring my teeth, I use the technique Isra taught me. With my right foot forward and bent, both my palms extend, and a throaty growl comes out of my mouth as a large wave of fire heads in his direction. With the soul, the power comes with ease.

The light consumes me, taking over the room. But as I engulf everything with fire, the swirls in my stomach vanish and I feel something scraping against the inside of my neck. It's not like the huge rock, but something smaller.

That's when the soul flies out of my mouth.

"No!" I cry out.

I'm shaking. My hands fall to my side while I swallow to moisten my dry throat. My stomach cramps, and I want to throw up, but I don't wait a second longer. I race toward the stairs.

Yet before I can make it all the way, an arm hooks around my throat. I choke. Isra presses his other hand on my head. I slap at his arm until he finally lets me go. Coughing, tears stroll down my cheeks. "I'm——" I cough. "I'm-I'm sorry——"

Isra groans, rubbing his face while he turns to get the soul. His shirt is singed and his skin is covered in burns. The soul floats into his outstretched hand before he places it back in the jar. It takes a while for me to notice that the rest of the room is drenched with water. Isra always had buckets full of it in case I lit something on fire.

Maybe I can still make a run for it—

Isra turns and grabs my wrist. His hot breath makes my stomach flip. The dark veins and muscles strain against his skin like the very act is difficult for him as he lifts his other hand.

"Maybe we shouldn't train today," his voice is stern, and I hear the slightest distortion inside it.

"No!" I cry out when I see the collar floating in the air. It clamps around my throat, and just as it does, the glowing veins on my hand fade into nothing. "No, please. I have to train."

He gives me a half-smile. "Maybe you should have thought of that before."

I try to pull away from him as he attaches the chain. Unfazed, he drags me toward the cell before shoving me in. Once I'm in, he tilts his head with a disappointed look on his face.

"One of these days, I'm going to murder you!" I scream.

He doesn't look phased at all. "Well, that's not comforting." He glances down at his chest and sighs. "I really liked this shirt."

I scoff. There's no point in trying to get the collar off now. The deed has been done. "You have a hundred more like it."

"You thought that soul would help you get out of here?" He tsks. "Well, to be honest, if I hadn't moved away in time, I might've been dead."

"I wish you were."

It seems as though his veins just grew from how many are throbbing. "You know what Mahi? Maybe I should just leave you in this cold, dark cell to rot."

"What?" I squeak out.

"Imagine, weeks on weeks." He walks into the cage, forcing me against the wall as I try to get away from him. He pushes me down onto my knees, and I can't help the hot tears that run down my cheek again as I glare at him. "All alone. With no one. Until the day comes that you will *beg* me to say a single word to you."

He strokes my jaw, smirking before his hands move to the collar. He takes the chain off so I can walk freely, and I gaze at the floor as he walks out and locks the door. My eyes squeeze shut, a weep leaving my mouth.

"I'll let you think about it."

I can't help the grin on my face as I listen to Kavon sing, staring at his brown eyes and shaking hands while he slightly sways his body. It doesn't matter to me that he sounds awful, only that he's doing it.

"And that's the song my dad would sing to me to get me to shut up." He breathes out once he's finished, giving me a sheepish grin. "Before I joined . . . Lucifer and he started ignoring me."

"I like it." I clap, nodding my head while I lean against his fake bedroom wall. "Some of my neighbors used to sing. One of them, a younger lady who was the best hunter, had the most insane voice."

This time, we ended up in some kind of house. He

kicks at the red flooring before placing his hands out. "Probably not as good as mine though."

I let out a huff of a laugh, and my grin grows to the point where it hurts. "I remember one time she taught some of us kids how to climb one of the taller trees. She sang to us while we watched the sunset. You would've liked it. It was a gorgeous orange."

"Where did you use to live?" Kavon asks. I realize I've zoned out while staring at his wings.

"It doesn't matter." I look up at the white roof.

"But—"

My eyes shoot open. Staring at the ceiling, I try to ignore the tapping against the bars, but it only gets louder.

Three days of solitary. Now he's back.

"Mahi," Isra taunts. I ignore him, and he continues to say my name over and over again.

After about five minutes, I sit up and smile at him. It's dark, but his eyes are glowing like they usually do. "Please stop talking, I can't hear myself losing the will to live."

He sucks in a breath, but the noise finally stops. He's sitting on the floor.

"That was a pretty impressive blast of fire," he says. "I already had those burns, but it was still extremely strong."

He already has the burns? Is that supposed to make me feel bad for him? I blink, ignoring the tightness in my chest. There's a tiny bit of pity inside me, and my hands make fists. If he's making me feel this way, I might pull all my hair out.

He sighs. "I didn't come here to make you train or anything. I came here to give you company."

"I'm good. Besides, I can't use my powers, and that's the only thing you really care about."

"Is that bugging you?" He frowns, but I know this is humoring him. "Maybe I made it sound like that, but that's not true."

"Sure," I shrug and focus on the wall. "Whatever you say."

"Please don't go back to ignoring me."

Please. I want to laugh, but I don't in case he does something worse to me. "What did I do?" he asks.

"What did you do?" I stare at him in disbelief. "Besides locking me up here, I know you messed with my emotions. You *made* it so I'd kiss you. That's more screwed up than you think."

"I only heightened what was already there."

"That makes it so much better." I press my lips together, my nails digging into my palms. "I hope you know how I'm feeling right now. Not like I have a choice or not. Not like you really care about my personal space."

He groans and rubs his face. "Okay, I *promise* to stop doing anything with your emotions. Does that make it better?"

As if I can trust his promises. I don't respond, biting my lip as I go back to watching the wall.

"Seriously? Is this because you're struggling to learn your powers?"

I shake my head. "You've got to be joking."

"It'd be easier if I was one hundred percent certain on what kind of angel you came from."

"Not like you'd tell me."

I go back to ignoring him. He's never going to see that he's the problem. Or maybe he does and he's just asking these questions to irritate me even more. Yet somehow, he sounds genuine. Just like he did all those other times. It hurts my head.

"Come on Mahi. Ask me anything," he begs.

I narrow my eyes at the wall. He's baiting me in.

"You're stuck here anyway. Why not try to get some benefit out of it?"

I press my lips in a thin line and look at him. His eyes are the only light in here since there are no windows, and I swallow the lump forming in my throat as I ignore his strikingly scary features. Why does he have to be right?

"What was the world like before the war," I whisper. "My dad barely mentioned it. I only learned that there was another world from the other people living with us, but not enough."

Isra touches his horns. "I don't know where to start," he says. "Anything specific?"

"You said things were better before . . . for the demons. How?"

Isra clicks his tongue. "Of course you choose the most boring subject. Humans would make deals and sign contracts with us for favors, like to be more beautiful or have money. In return, the demon who completed the deal got to feed on the human's emotions until they died and their soul would go to Hell instead of Heaven. The demons were given a *reason* to do it. We still do it, but a deal barely goes through now. Humans know too much about us. Their soul goes to Hell no matter what. So they don't care. And back in the day, Lucifer needed souls for his attack on the angels. He'd reward demons who obtained the most but not anymore."

I raise my eyebrows. "And that's all?"

He shakes his head. "We'd also do whatever we want in plain sight. Since humans didn't know about us we'd pretend to be the best friend who'd tempt them to divorce their partner or kill their child. Anything to help strike up a deal."

"So there has to be a mutual agreement. Makes sense." I nod my head. "I had to sign some contract when I got placed in containment. It was either that or they'd kill Laurel."

"Unfortunately, now humans know what we are. Making deals doesn't work, and more souls are turning into demons for no reason. The containment buildings aren't enough to keep demons in check. There are too many demons and not enough humans left to feed on. The angels would kill us, which prevented overpopulation."

I roll my eyes. "I doubt you'd fool humans with your gigantic horns."

"There are things called glamours, Mahi," Isra says. I raise an eyebrow at him and a grin forms on his face. Oh, why does he have those dimples? "So much you don't know. So much I'd tell you if you'd listen."

I try to push my emotions down and clear my throat. "Why even teach me a new word if you're going to keep it to yourself?"

"Because it's fun to watch you squirm."

I'm not going to give him the reaction he craves. "You want things to go back to the way they were before? With angels trying to kill you?"

A grin still rests on his face. *He's totally sensing my emotions.* "Mahi, Hell *does* serve a purpose. Some humans make the same choices as demons, corrupting themselves and ending up in Hell. It's a place for murderers, rapists, all kinds of criminals to be tortured for what they did when they were alive."

"And what happens there?" I sip from one of the three water bottles Isra left in the cell, trying to flush my embarrassment away.

"There are many different things in Hell," Isra says. "It's unimportant."

"Why did Lucifer do this?"

Isra sighs. "He hated angels, considering how they all viewed him like he was a monster. Especially after what they did to him."

"What did they do?"

Silence embodies the entire room as I wait for an answer. I'm not sure how much time has passed. Seconds. Minutes.

Chills climb up my arms. But after what feels like hours, Isra exhales slowly, his face paling. "Nothing," he whispers. I almost don't hear what he says next. "It's not important anymore."

20

"You're getting really good with knives," Isra says while he clamps my restraints back on.

Water drips from my wet hair. Isra had started allowing me to shower and brush my teeth. Well technically, the offer was always there. I'd just finally given in because my hygiene was at an all-time low.

I have to ignore the tug in my stomach whenever I'm in the showers down here, knowing that Isra's waiting for me when I'm done.

"Too bad knives only kill the vessel," I mutter.

"Well, demons in their shadow form can't really do anything," says Isra. "So, it's better than nothing. Feral demon's souls get sent back to Hell though."

"Can Lucifer die from an angel sword?"

"You know about those?" Isra narrows his eyes at me. "And no."

I frown. "I meant——"

He smiles while looking down at my wrist and I can't help but groan.

"He's an archangel." Isra steps outside the cage. "A fallen one. So that's why."

"I never think of him as an angel," I say. "Since he's so horrifying."

"More than you can imagine." Isra sighs.

"So, then what's the plan?" I pull at the chain he has attached to my arm when he shakes his head. "Come on, I've been here for like *two* months. We've been having fun training. With me kicking your ass, even though a majority of the time you're the one who comes out on top."

"I'm sorry, Mahi," he says, closing the cell door.

I sigh. Two months. That's how long I'd managed to keep track of. Although, I could be a few days off. So much time had passed, yet Isra didn't care about Lucifer turning humans into abominations. Why would he? They couldn't track me. Still, that didn't mean they weren't all over the city, and the hope that I'd find my dad was slowly drying out. If only that dream with him hadn't been a one-time thing. It had felt so real, just like the ones Kavon creates.

"Have you even gone to Hell since you captured me?" I ask. "Seen Lucifer?"

He tenses. "No. And Lucifer isn't in Hell, he's here."

"How do you know?"

"I might not have to do his every whim, but he still has—" He twitches. "An influence over me. He's made announcements, promised wishes, and so on, to whoever brings you to him. I'm not going to lie, a part of me wants to hand you over. It's like an innate feeling."

"Well, what's to stop you from giving me up when we find him?"

He gives me a sad smile. "Luckily, I can still make choices. It's more of an urge to please him. I can go against it, even though it might make me want to pull my throat out."

I bite the inside of my cheek. "If he's made promises to get me, what else is going on outside?"

"You don't need to know."

"Isra," I groan. I've been working on gaining his trust, but nothing has done the trick. "You can discuss science with me all night but can't tell me this?" He stares at me blankly, arms crossed. "Okay, I get that you're not going to tell me anything. But maybe, you can tell me a little something about containment?"

His eyes narrow. "What?"

"Laurel," I lower my voice. Do I really desire the truth? My stomach sinks at what Isra might say, but it has to be better than making up an answer in my head. "Is that how you found out about me?"

He gives me an odd look as if he wasn't expecting me to ask, or still worry about that. I guess becoming immortal makes you get over things quickly.

"They were going to take you to be experimented on —which means to Lucifer," he tells me. "But when I visited her since I wanted to see if what the demons had told me was true, she begged me for a deal. And honestly, I was aware that you couldn't sew her stomach back up. That made no sense, but it's not like the idiots would think there might be a half-angel out there—"

"Are you really insulting your followers?"

"She *told* me what you did, and I couldn't let Lucifer get his hands on you," he continues.

"What was her wish?"

"To get out of that prison. In fact, she broke down screaming for me to get her out of there. It wasn't traditional, but a deal is a deal."

I lower my head and grimace. She's out? Does that mean she went back and found our home? That seems impossible. Did she get killed by something instead? I rub the back of my neck, swallowing the lump that formed in my throat.

"Do you know where she is?" My voice barely forms a whisper.

"Yes."

My mouth falls open, and an unknown tension escapes my body. "Can I see her?"

Isra tilts his head and narrows his eyes. "She traded you for a wish, and you still care about her?"

"It doesn't just go away like that," I groan. I wish it could go away because thinking about it makes me want to explode in tears. "I grew up with her. She was the closest thing I had to a sister. And I understand why she gave me in." I swallow excessively. "She probably thought I was a demon. It was her shot to get out of there."

Isra tilts his head, staring at me while his fingers coil around the metal bars. His eyes don't blink for what feels like an entire minute. Finally, he smirks. "I guess there wouldn't be any harm with giving you closure."

"Seriously?"

He shrugs, opening the cage. "You're right. It has been two months. You've made progress."

It's as if I'm dreaming when he steps in. When the shackles drop from my wrists, I'm still not sure if this is a joke or not. Still, he doesn't take the collar off my neck, so I know I won't be able to escape anyway.

Taking your dog out for a walk.

My muscles twitch while I force a smile. Isra cracks a grin. He'd told me about his many pets. He even let me pet his orange fox once.

"Okay, hold my hand." His arm comes out and I stare down at it. He laughs and says, "Don't be so shy, darling."

Darling. It makes me want to burn into a crisp as the word rolls off his tongue. But instead, I look down and grab his hand. If anything, this nickname means he's becoming comfortable with me again.

Isra doesn't even bother to give me a warning. For half a second, I'm floating. A quick breath escapes my lips when we stand on fresh grass and I notice the sun setting as the sky grows dark. A wave of peace runs over me when I inhale the sweet smell that comes after a thunderstorm. Laurel and I would sleep over whenever there was one, thinking up awful pranks. I expect to see the familiar cabins, but we aren't anywhere near our old home.

I'm facing a large fence that squares off the land with towers at the corners. Guards stand on top of them, but they don't seem to be actually keeping watch.

"I thought you were taking me to Laurel," I raise my voice.

Isra closes his eyes, exhaling before giving me a stale smile. "I did," he says. "Squint hard enough and you'll see her."

I narrow my eyes, searching through the fence. Shivers run up my spine at the sight. I can't see her completely, but she stands among many other prisoners in her tan clothes, all alone.

I turn to Isra. "But you said——"

"What I said was true," he cuts me off. "She said, word for word, 'I want to be out of *this* prison.' Truly, if I were a gentleman, I would've let her collect all her emotions and word it better, but I didn't care."

"So, this is another containment center?"

"Yeah," he answers. "Another one under my control."

"You put Laurel here?"

"Yes." He shrugs. "I mean, what did she expect?"

I can barely see her face, but tears pool in my eyes. "Can I talk to her?"

Isra laughs. "Nice joke."

"Please." My hands ball into fists. I don't know how to explain in a way that he'll understand, if he even can. "You haven't been on the other side of things. We adapted to containment because we were there for each other. She has no one here. I just want to ask——" I let out a deep breath. "I want to ask if she regrets it."

He doesn't reply. Instead, he touches the tips of his horns and paces around, but I grab his arm. "Please, Isra."

He frowns. "You'll get hurt, Mahi."

I sigh. "It can't hurt as badly as the first time."

The blue hood covering half my face itches, but I shouldn't complain. It's better than the thin scraps I wore for two years.

The room I'm in is empty. No windows, no furniture.

The longer I stare at the grey walls, the more I think about how much I'm going to piss my pants.

What if she screams when she sees me? Or refuses to talk like she did the last time I healed her? The thoughts spin into a cobweb inside my head.

A breath catches in my throat when the door opens. Isra brings Laurel in, who's looking straight down. Her face is paralyzed with fear, and I can visibly see her swallow excessively.

"You have ten minutes," says Isra, letting both of her arms go. He gives me a quick wink before strolling out of the room. The door clicks, locking us in here.

I glance at Laurel. She's still staring at the yellow carpet. She must think I'm a demon. Her knees shake and she is hugging herself. I realize her hair is in two French braids that have come loose at the ends since she doesn't have any hair ties. Everything else about her looks fine. I press my palm against my chest, rocking back and forth. Relief floods through me. Demons usually don't hurt beautiful people.

My lips form a smile. "Laurel," I say breathlessly. I can't help it. I move a little closer as tears well in my eyes, but I stop abruptly.

Her head shoots up. My grin falls and I go completely still. There's a deep cut at the bottom of her right cheek, trailing down to her jaw. What did she do to earn that?

"Mahi?" she whispers. I can't decipher her emotions. One second, she looks scared. Another second there's something that looks like, regret? Maybe I'm just imagining it. "How are you here? I thought they killed you."

Not even a 'how are you' or an 'I miss you.'

"I got out," I say.

"But how are you here right now?" she asks. Her legs still shake, her eyes bulging while she clutches her neck. "You're a demon, aren't you? You've come to kill me."

I squeeze my eyes shut, shaking my head. "Are you serious Laurel? I grew up with you! I *healed* you. I fucking saved your life! A demon wouldn't ever have been able to do that!"

"Then what are you?" she asks, her voice a hissing whisper.

"I'm—" I pause, letting out a huge breath. Yelling will only make her more afraid, and I shouldn't claim being half-angel just because Isra said it. "I don't know. But I'm not a demon. If I was, I'd look like them. Think about it Laurel. Demons can't heal people."

She hugs herself again. A tear strolls down her cheek and a hiccup leaves her mouth. "You have to understand why I did it," she whispers, avoiding my gaze. "I just wanted to see my mom."

"You're like my sister," my voice quivers. "My best friend, and you gave me up to die."

"I couldn't be experimented on!" she cries out. I flinch and cover my mouth as nausea takes over. "I couldn't be in there any longer!"

"Look where that got you."

"Yeah, I know. They cut my face open like a piece of meat as a welcome message. I never should've tried to get away. No one does." Her eyes trail up my body. "Except you."

If only she knew where I was now.

"Laurel . . ." My throat feels tight. Here it comes. "If you had gotten out, would you feel any regret?"

She twirls her thumbs like she always does when she's in trouble and looks down. "I made myself believe you were a demon because what else is there?"

Classic Laurel, avoiding the question. I clench my jaw. "Are you—" I take a deep breath. "Ignoring isn't going to help—"

"And when I did that," she interrupts. "It was easier to tell them. And sure, I would have regretted it if I got out, but you have to live with your regrets sometimes."

I'd figured out her answer before she'd said it, but that didn't stop time from slowing while I process her words.

She was willing to live with the regret of betraying me. With the guilt. With killing a person. This whole time I've been relieved that she hadn't been experimented on and turned into a painful monster. Then again, I'd almost killed that girl before Isra had found me. I'd done it to save myself.

But I would have never, *never* been able to live with it.

"What's that on your neck?" Laurel asks. I look up, not having realized I'd zoned out.

"Oh, this?" I touch the collar. It stings against my throat, no matter how many times I heal the marks it makes. "It's nothing."

Her lips part before she presses them into a thin line and my eyes go to the deep cut on her face. If only I could heal it. But I can't. Not because of the collar, but because the demons will just do it again before handing her over for experiments.

"When did you find out?" Laurel asks me, breaking the awkward silence. "About what you do."

My eyebrows squeeze together. I want to tell her, and I don't at the same time, but I've been hiding this part of me forever. "A really long time ago. I think when I was four and cut myself." I give in, tugging at my sleeves and letting out a deep, gratifying sigh. "You remember that bird with the sprained wing, by the creak when we were kids?"

She nods her head.

"You ran off to get Kiyo, but when you got back, I said the bird had flown off." I smile as she starts to piece together what had actually happened. "I healed it."

"Wow." She paces around the room. "I'd kill to be that bird now."

My gut twists and I frown. I open and close my mouth, struggling to find words. "Laurel . . ." I blow out my cheeks and rub my forehead. "You don't deserve to be in here."

She stops moving. "What?"

"Even if I can't forgive you." I breathe in deeply. "Even if I'd never think to do the same to you, I understand."

"You do?" A genuine shine spreads across her face when I nod my head. "What are you going to do?"

I don't get a chance to respond. Isra pops in front of me, clicking his tongue. I fall to the floor while Laurel yelps.

"Time to go," he laughs, helping me up.

"No." I glance at Laurel as Isra grips my arm harder. "Isra please, we should let her out of here. She doesn't deserve this."

He glares at me before he shakes his head. "I don't care."

And in a second, we're outside the prison. I look around, trying to spot Laurel, but she isn't with us.

She's in that room. All alone. Never knowing which day would be her last.

I didn't even get to say goodbye.

"No," I whisper, looking at Isra. It's completely dark out now. His eyes are our only light source besides the moon. "No—no. We need to get her out of there. Take me back!"

"Mahi." Isra's lips twist upwards. "I don't care."

"But—" I stammer out, narrowing my eyes at the prison. My eyes blur, my hands turning into fists as I lower my head. "Of course you don't."

I have to be smart about this. Isra let me come here, which means he's warming up to me. Despite how deeply I want to shove my fist in his face, I have to show him that I feel the same way. Feel it in a way that he senses it.

Because despite everything, the smallest part of me wishes we could go back to how things were before he imprisoned me—when I had hoped that a demon could actually be a good person. When I might have actually, eventually, cared about Isra.

"Humans are just shells for demons to fill," Isra tries to explain.

"Is that what I am to you?" Hot tears run down my face. Hopefully, he won't know they're full of venom. "I'm half-human, in case you forgot."

Isra shakes his head. "No. You're more than that."

"I have nothing!" Sobs leave my mouth as the truth

comes out. "And I can't help anyone. How in the world am I supposed to stop Lucifer?"

"Mahi." Isra moves close to me as I let my cries out. Slowly, he wraps an arm around me. I lean into his chest, my throat tight as I struggle to breathe. "It's going to be okay."

"He takes everyone I care about," I say through hiccups. Here it comes. *Remember the old him. Feel it like you mean it.* "What am I going to do if he does that to you?"

Isra goes still.

"How am I going to stop him?"

He sucks in a breath. "You'll do it."

I pull away from him, wiping my face. "You say that all the time."

"Because it's true!" he says. His eyes are still shining. That's a good sign. "Listen, you can put an end to him. There's someone stronger than Lucifer, and he'll help us."

I snort. The tears are gone, but I'm still breathing in quick gasps. It's not like what I said is a complete lie. "As if."

"He's called Death," Isra says. I almost grin. "Whenever someone dies, they go to Death before ending up in Hell. Death can kill *anyone*."

"So, then Death can kill Lucifer," I whisper. *But he hasn't.*

He shakes his head. "Death won't do the deed, but maybe, he can help us."

I narrow my eyes. "So why don't we go find Death now?"

Isra frowns. "It'll take years before your skills are

adequate enough to face Lucifer. When they are, I'll take you to Death. We'll go together."

"Wait." I'm not sure if I heard him right. "*Years*?"

His frown turns into a smirk. "Yes. Years of just you and me."

21

It's hard to ignore the tornado in the pit of my stomach when Isra unlocks my cell, or while I stare at his chest as he goes through the routine of getting my chains off. He's wearing red, his favorite color. While the shirt I have on is blue, which is what he gave me after I told him I loved the color of the sky.

Knowing this information about him makes me want to wake up from this nightmare even more than I already do.

One week has passed since Isra told me about Death. I'd taken the time to make sure he knew how grateful I was. I even made sure that when our skin touched, I didn't swear out loud. I'd already been faking myself around him for so long, but today shivers spread across my arms.

Just go into your happy place.

"Are you okay?" I meet his eyes as the collar finally comes off, and mentally force myself not to push him away or flinch when he runs his fingers along my arms.

I give him what I hope looks like a shy smile and shake my head. "I'm fine. Just been thinking a lot."

"What's on your mind?"

Here it goes. I ignore the sweat under my arms. "The angels."

His eyes gleam at the mention. "What about them?"

"I think they would've liked what you're doing," I lie. "Teaching me about my powers. Choosing to go against Lucifer."

"Oh really." He smirks. "Is that what you think?"

He knows. Did I really think I'd be able to deceive him? That he'd honestly stop using his power on me? A shaky breath comes out of my mouth. Just play it cool. Maybe he won't chain you back up. Maybe he doesn't know anything.

"Let's keep that a secret." I tilt my head, smirking back. He lets out a genuine laugh. His smirk turns into a grin as he steps outside my cage but the second he turns his back to me, I frown.

Think of Dad.

"So, what are we going to be doing today?" I ask, glancing at the knife on the floor on the opposite side of the room.

Isra stretches and moves closer to me. "You want me to demonstrate or explain?"

I give him another smile to hide my hatred. "Show me."

In a swift second, his arm hooks around my neck, and I almost elbow him before calming myself down.

"You need to learn how to get out of here without using your powers."

First, he's obsessed with them, now he doesn't want

me to use them at all? I don't understand, and I'm done with it. The irritation, anger, and hatred I've been holding comes out. It's time to put the plan in motion. Clenching my jaw, I jab my fist into his groin.

"Shit!" His grip loosens and I pull his arm around my neck down and away, heating up my skin at the same time. Isra has a high tolerance for it, but I've learned to do it fast enough so that he won't see it coming.

"Mahi!" He lets go of me, and I move toward the knife as quickly as I can. A snicker leaves my mouth, just so I can make it seem like it was a joke. I don't want him thinking I'm up to something. "What are you doing?"

"Hey, I did what you said. You didn't see that coming though, did you?" I laugh, but my voice shakes. My stomach is doing hundreds of backflips. I grab the knife and turn to face Isra, my smile aching. He stares at me with a blank face.

"Come on. You said I'm getting good with knives," I say. "Why don't we try to have some fun with a sparring match? It'll be a nice warm up."

He sighs but gives me a crooked grin. "Okay. We *were* going to practice with the knife later, but we can do it now if you're really that desperate to be on the ground."

As soon as the words come out of his mouth, I throw the first punch. A weak one that he catches with ease.

"Nice move," he says.

My hand that holds the knife lunges at his shoulder. Isra moves back. I take the moment to pull my other arm away from him, and we go through a swing of motions.

Both our bodies are quick. Isra blocks my every move, and whenever we get to the end of the mat, he spins to keep the fight going. I'm not going to lie, he's going easy on me, but I have gotten quite good at fighting. I'd probably be able to handle a regular demon one-on-one.

Finally, Isra swings at me. I duck, punching his jaw and kicking him in the stomach. I shove him into a wall, right next to the exit out of here. Isra clutches his chest, grunting as he looks at me. Is that a proud smile?

"Maybe I should let you use the knife." I try to laugh, panting heavily while I wipe my sweaty brow.

I take a step closer, and Isra's eyes shine as they look at my arm. I've made my skin warm and my veins are glowing, which means I have his attention.

"Oh, really?"

We're as close as we were when we kissed. He towers over me, peering into my eyes. Isra's right. He doesn't know how I feel, but I know exactly how he does. I wonder if he'll feel the same about angels after this. I place the knife against his neck, glancing at his lips. He breathes into me slowly.

"What can I say?" I shrug, moving my arm down. He keeps his eyes trained on my face while I position the knife by his underarm. This won't kill him. It shouldn't. But if it does . . . It doesn't matter. I *have* to get out of here. "You've been a good teacher."

"You know I could get out of this pretty easily."

"Then why haven't you?"

His hands move and his mouth opens to say something. Before he can, I shove the knife into his right armpit and send a powerful fire blast into his face. This is his real body, and it probably won't kill him, but he can't escape it either. He'll feel this pain.

A breath shoots out of his mouth before a scream fills

the room—black blood spurts on me. The last thing I see is his eyes burning with fury.

As I run toward the stairs, I cry out when an invisible force pulls me back. A roar echoes from behind me.

"You can't go out there, Mahi!" he screams.

I'm going to slip. He's going to put the collar on me, and then I'll never get a chance like this again.

Gusts of fire billow out of my palms, and I aim them backwards. When I feel my legs again, I don't hesitate to race up the stairs. Something shears into my back, but I can't stop. My heart races as I burst outside.

It's dark. Of course it is. I glance around, looking for a hiding spot in the hundreds of buildings. Instead, my eyes land on dozens of transparent screens displaying my photo. It's the picture the demons took of me on my first day in containment. My dark, brown hair is loose and messy, bags under my eyes and my brown skin lighter than it is now. My face looked much fuller then, but if anyone sees me, they'll recognize me right away.

There's nowhere I can hide here. So, my feet are moving before I even know it. I'm turning corners, tripping on sidewalks, but the whole city is like a damn maze. I halt when I shoot out of an alley to see what I assume are two people. They are wearing some kind of red helmet. Every part of their body is covered. Both of them have grey vests that guard their chests and armor lining their arms and legs.

They're armed, but not with human guns. It's some huge, black weapon with something glowing within the barrel. Maybe the same kind of thing they caught Kavon with.

I sprint to the closest building and break its window with my elbow. I can always heal myself later.

Landing with a thud, I slide under the first thing I see. I shake as I bring my legs close to my chest and wrap my arms around my knees. The moonlight shines through the broken window, and minutes pass while I try to keep myself calm with steady breaths. I take the time to heal my elbow, sighing when I touch the handle of a knife in my back. At least I don't feel as much pain as I normally would.

Isra shouldn't be able to follow me. The stab wound was almost lethal. If anything, he's lying in his own blood. At least, that's how a human body would work.

My eyes widen when I hear a small whisper. I turn my head to see three people on a tiny mattress before they quickly crouch underneath what I realize are a dozen tables. My eyes land on a young, maybe around seven-year-old, blond-haired boy. He's trying to hide behind, who I presume is his mother, with what I think is his older sister beside him.

They are all shaking, but not like that family I'd met before. They either don't know who I am, or they haven't seen my face yet.

I flinch when I hear footsteps approaching outside. Quickly, I get up and hide in a closet nearby. Ignoring the multiple poking objects in here, I peek through a hole in the closet door.

"Why's this glass broken?" I look at the window. There's a shadow where the light shines in front of me, I see a glimpse of horns. Demons.

"You want to check it out?" another voice asks.

"There's a bunch of broken-down crap here. This is the shittiest corner of the city."

"We could get a hound—" They fall silent. My heart beats so loud I can hear it in my ears. My skin feels clammy as I cover my face. For a second, I think that Isra might've found me. He's the only one who could make demons quiet down.

"There's three of them in there," a deep, feminine voice says. There's strength and humor to her voice. "Jeez, they're shaking like crazy."

It's too dark for the demons to see the family, but I have a feeling I know who, or what, she is. I've been holding my breath ever since the demons started talking. I need to breathe. I take in a quick, shallow breath and peak through the hole again, but it's too late when I realize my mistake.

"Oh, there's also a fourth, much more powerful than the mortals. Looks like it is a fortunate day," she says.

Before I can anticipate their next move, the front door blows open. Two demons rush in and take the girl and boy hostage, blades ready to slice their throats. I finally see who the voice belongs to.

"I guess I am really lucky," a princess of Hell says, with long black hair, horns and dark grey skin. Her horns curve upwards instead of backward like Isra's, and they're covered in gold jewelry. Her eyes glow bright with a purple hue and glare around the room.

The mother of the girl and boy pleads. "Please don't hurt them, they haven't done anything! Please, hurt me instead but leave my children alone."

The princess grins while the mother begs against her leg, a hand with long, pointed nails touching the tip of the mother's lips. "Come on out, or I'll kill them all," she says, staring directly at the closet. "I already know where you are."

Ignoring my trembling bones, I do as I'm told. "Okay, okay. Please, just le-le-let them go," I say, rasping breaths coming out of my mouth. My legs are weak, and I fumble to keep a good stance.

"Le-le-let them go," she mocks me, tucking a strand of her hair behind her ear. I can't let this family be destroyed because of me.

"Please. Just let them go and I'll go without a fight," I say to the royal.

She gives me a smirk. Then, without even losing our gaze, she slices the head off the mother. The children scream as their mother's lifeless head falls to the ground. "She did say to hurt her instead."

I'm shocked. I've seen so many horrible things, but this was extreme even for me. The next thing I know, anger runs through my veins and my skin starts to glow. I make a fireball in each hand and blast them at the demons, freeing the boy and girl. All three demons stare at me like I'm something they've never seen before. I bet they didn't expect that. The children run behind me.

"Take your brother and go upstairs, now!" I tell the girl. She nods and runs with her younger brother.

"Trying to be a hero? You should know how all their stories end," the princess says.

"I said I would go with you without a fight if you let them go, there was no need for her to die," I yell. I shoot a barrage of fireballs toward her, knocking her back outside and hitting the building ahead. I do the same thing to the other two demons, launching fireballs at them and forcing them to go onto the street.

I run out of the building and shoot two balls of fire at one of the demons. He tries to block it, but it slams him back into the building. I don't know if it is the anger or the pain of what I have done to this family that fuels my strength, but I hope I can maintain it.

The demon stands back up as both he and his partner take small knives out of their vests and throw them at me. I return their gift with my fireballs. I can feel the heat from my blasts. The knives melt before they even reach me.

One of the demons dodges my fireballs and charges at me with a sword. He is fast, but I charge right back at him. He doesn't expect it. I trip him, and he stumbles behind me. To push him further back, I shoot a fireball at him. He takes the full force of the blast and gets launched into a wall.

I focus my view on the next demon, shooting fireballs while advancing on him slowly down the street. All the demon can do is brace for my attack. Once I'm near him, I punch his face and blast him further back. I watch as he hits the street with a thud. He screams as flames take him over. I know I've knocked them out when they both don't get up.

I search for the princess when I hear clapping. She's watching from the entrance of the building we were just in, but she looks different. Her skin is no longer human. She now has red scales covering her entire body. Even from here, I notice her hair has turned white, and her eyes glow a hue of yellow. When I see something moving behind her, I instinctively step back. She has . . . a tail.

"I'm impressed," she says.

"All you had to do was let them go!"

"And all you had to do was surrender."

A breath hitches in my throat when she goes up the wall, scaling it like a lizard. I shoot fireballs at her, missing every shot. She's too fast.

I try to focus and picture my next move. I'm not too sure if this will work, but I have to try. The royal stares at me. "Finally stopping, ready to surrender?"

I put my hands together, forming a big fist. A jet of flame, hotter than I have ever felt, escapes from my palm, continuously going toward the direction of the royal. She moves around and jumps to the street before running toward me.

I continue my rain of fire. *Come on, burn already.* Even Isra would step back from this. Instead, she cuts through it like it's nothing. I don't get a chance to defend myself when she grabs one of my arms and pushes it up. The pressure forces me to lose concentration and I feel the fire disappearing. With her other hand, she grabs my other fist. She grips onto them so hard that I can't focus because of the pain. Before I can retaliate, she hits the back of my neck, turning me around and tying my hands with some type of rope. I feel so dizzy that I can't even resist. All I can do is look at her with her smirk.

She holds me there until a row of cars show up, and more demons pop out in the same fancy gear. Some go to help their friends I took down, while one comes to the princess. "What's going on, Your Royal Highness? We saw fire and smoke from blocks away," the demon says.

"I have the fugitive, she's under my control," she answers.

"Oh, you didn't even use the guns." He sounds surprised.

"I didn't need it. We assumed she was strong because she evaded capture for so long, but she's weaker than you can imagine. Although she did burn my camouflage with her first annoying attack," she says while glaring at me. Her skin goes back to being dark grey; her hair black, her eyes purple, just like before.

"All right, Your Highness. Lucifer's been notified, and we are ready to go," another demon comes up and says. I barely register what he's saying, my eyelids becoming heavier by the second.

"Good. Oh, there are some children in the building. They were harboring this fugitive, so go capture them and place them in containment, but make sure they don't die. We don't have enough vessels as it is."

I know exactly where I am when I wake up.

Lucifer's penthouse.

Almost the entire room is surrounded by windows. The sky has an orange gradient that seeps into the open space.

Strapped to a chair, I pull at my metal restraints and try to burn them off before giving up. They didn't put whatever Isra had to keep my powers in check, but whatever this is, it's still hard to get out of.

That's when I notice the demons standing on both sides of me. They're still in their black suits, except they have their helmets off. I'm not going to turn my head to look. Instead, I examine the beautiful table and dark, wooden floor. There's a blue, furry-looking carpet with four chairs in the same color sitting on top. He's living like this, while others are in a containment center.

"Mahi."

My heart stops. I'm frozen as I tense up, listening to the footsteps echoing from behind me. This has to be a trick. That sounds like his voice. *My dad's voice.*

"How are you?" the voice asks again, in Hindi. With my dad's accent. With his exact voice.

A sob leaves my mouth. "Stop it."

This is a different kind of torture. Can Lucifer imitate voices? Can he get inside my head? He is an angel after all. He took over the entire earth. Who am I kidding? He can probably do hundreds of things.

Someone steps in front of me, but I only see their feet. Slowly, I look up and meet the same brown eyes I have. The same brown skin. The wavy dark brown hair that we share. I'm going to collapse. It feels as though time is slowing down, while my arms pull against my restraints to hug my dad, who stands in front of me.

22

I STARE DOWN at the floor, refusing to meet Lucifer's eyes. My *dad's* eyes.

"You two can leave," he says to the demons. The familiar voice drills a hole into my stomach. *Don't cry.* I take in massively deep breaths, trying to picture this as a nightmare.

Dad is his vessel.

I thought finding him would be a lost cause after being with Isra for so long. It was a lost cause to begin with, expecting him to be alive after two years. Still, I wanted to try, knowing that there was a small chance that I could possibly save him from being experimented on. But instead of an experiment, he was facing something way worse.

My bones rattle underneath my skin when the demons leave the room. Now I'm alone with the one thing that has caused every horrible thing on the earth. My body tenses when he approaches me. Lucifer's presence is hard to ignore, but he just stands there, saying nothing.

"You're finally here." He eventually breathes out as if he's lost all the air in his lungs. "I'm sorry about the restraints. I wasn't sure how you'd react."

A tear rolls down my cheek. A minute passes before his hand grips my jaw, forcing me to look up at his face. After staring at me for what feels like an eternity, he grins like it's his birthday.

He lets go of my jaw, causing a grunt to escape my mouth. "Your father misses you," he says, backing away from me. "That little greeting at the start was him."

"Why—" My voice turns into a sob. "How would you know?" I look away. "How—"

"I'm sorry," he cuts me off. It's not like I could speak anyway. "I just need a second to take it in. I searched Morningstar every second of the day for you, and it's Zyanya, of all people, who finds you?"

"My father," I mutter, ignoring what he just said and meeting his gleeful eyes. "You're using him. This is worse than death."

"It's unfortunate, I know. Your father tried to warn you about me though, didn't he?"

I blink repeatedly. "No. How could he have—" My eyes widen. "The dream was actually real?" I had no idea that humans could visit others' dreams.

"I love it!" Lucifer laughs, clapping his hands together. "Wow, he never told you the truth. This is phenomenal."

"What truth?" I ask through my teeth, heating up my skin. All I have to do is rip through the restraints and sprint to the stairs, wherever those are.

Lucifer raises his eyebrows. "Don't bother trying. That steel is from the hottest depths of Hell."

"What—" I glance at my arm and frown. How could I forget that my veins glow?

Lucifer rubs his chin, the smile refusing to leave his face. "You haven't even reached your full potential."

I grit my teeth together. "Whatever you're going to do, just get on with it." There's no point in prolonging the inevitable.

Lucifer tilts his head to the side, his smile finally disappearing into a grimace. "Do you know why you're here, Mahi?"

I swallow down the lump in my throat, and somehow manage to speak with confidence. "You're going to kill me."

"That is far from the truth," says Lucifer. He sits on his desk and smirks at me. I try to imagine that he's just shapeshifted into my dad. "I don't know why everyone thinks I'm going to kill them."

My jaw clenches. He knows exactly why.

"Have you ever wondered why you're different, Mahi?" he asks, his smirk growing into a smile once again. "Of course you have, but have you ever thought of the possibilities?"

"Yeah."

"I know what you are."

"Nice," I say. I don't need to hear this again. "How about you tell me why you have my dad as your vessel? Did you really go through that much trouble just so you could mess with me? How'd you find him?"

Especially since I thought he was dead. Or well, I

never actually saw him die. We were just separated. I ended up in containment with Laurel, and he . . .

He was taken. And I thought it'd been to his death.

Lucifer laughs. "Now where would be the fun in that?" I frown but give him a blank stare when he mimics it. "It's better if you don't know."

I shake my arms, trying to tear through the restraints. "Why am I here!" I yell, a growl escaping my mouth. My lips slap together, forming a thin line. I've never made that kind of noise before. Not without something powering me, like the soul.

"There it is," Lucifer whispers, nodding his head in what looks like astonishment.

Clearing my throat, I repeat the question." Why am I here?"

His eyes darken. "You're here because you are mine!" It's remarkable how he makes my dad, of all people, sound so monstrous. "Everything on this planet is mine, but it was also once someone else's. You are the *one* thing that is truly mine, something I created myself."

"I'm not yours," I say. He snickers, shaking his head. It only makes my blood boil. "Maybe you think humans are just specks of dust, but without us to use as vessels, you and your demons would be nothing."

Lucifer stares at me, and for a second, I think I've won. But then he laughs, much louder than all the previous ones.

Everything is so funny to him.

"You're not human, Mahi," he says between his laughs. "Of course, perhaps partially. That is probably what makes you weak."

"Please," I whimper out. "Just tell me why I am here! I'm done with the games."

"But it's so much fun making you guess!"

I squeeze my eyes shut, tears building up behind my eyes. I should have listened to Kavon. I never should have come here. I should have taken that dream with my dad seriously.

"Hey, I apologize." Lucifer's voice rings in my ears, the slight humor still there while he places both his hands on my shoulders. "As your actual father, I'll tell you what you want to know."

My eyes open right then and there. Although my vision is blurry from tears, Lucifer's grin is all I can see. Does he mean because he's using my father as his vessel? His smile tells me another story.

"That isn't possible," I say, looking away from his face. Me, Lucifer's daughter? It can't be true. "My dad got away before I was born. He went into hiding! You couldn't have found us. No one ever did!"

"Well, nineteen years ago your father allowed me to possess him freely. He just didn't tell his wife. Oh and technically, you're correct," he says. "This shouldn't be possible. You shouldn't be alive. Nephilim *never* survive anymore. The time when they did, thousands of years ago, they grew to be giant abominations. You're something that shouldn't exist."

"But we got away!"

"Some rare humans—should I call them that?" he questions and then continues. "Some *humans* managed to get away before I installed the wall," says Lucifer as he moves away from me. "I should've been more careful of course, but I couldn't help but feel excited when I found out about your existence. Your dad tried to hide you from me, but well, he's paying the price for that."

"You can't be my father!" I shout. I can't be the daughter of someone who ruined the earth; of someone who caused so much pain.

"Of course, I can," Lucifer says. I look up at him, my nostrils flaring as I listen to his lie. "You seem to know you're half-angel. But you've never wondered why you don't have wings? Why I've been searching for you?"

"This has got to be the dumbest way to mess with someone," I say through my teeth. "If you knew about me, why didn't you stay with my mother as soon as she became pregnant?"

"I didn't abandon you if that's what you're thinking!" he says. "I would never, *never*, do that to my child. The truth is, after I won the war, I wanted to indulge in some human . . . pleasures. I didn't know about you until you were born. By then, all I found was your mother's corpse." He caresses my cheek. "I knew you'd find me eventually. You're my daughter Mahi, and I won't let anyone hurt you. You can live your greatest life now. There's so much I can teach you. You have so much power inside you, which only grows every day. Just come with me to Hell and I'll—"

"Never," I interrupt. "There is no way you want me to live a great life. Just kill me, get on with it. Unless you —" I let out a shaky breath. "Unless you let my dad go."

"I'm afraid I can't do that."

"Why?"

"It's a personal matter," he says. "I'm not the only one who despises your father. He's safer with me. Besides, isn't it nice having both of your dads together?"

When I don't say anything, his lips curve up. "I've heard about your powers. Zyanya was quite surprised. What are they?"

My jaw clenches and I shake my head. "Just kill me."

He stares at me before a sigh escapes from his mouth. He whistles and walks away, grabbing something from his desk.

"It's so sad," Lucifer says, "to see my own child hate me." I suck in a breath when something sharp jabs my thigh. My leg goes numb before I feel the electrifying pain of the knife in my body. "The power you carry," Lucifer continues. "It's just so precious. Looks like we'll have to do this the hard way. I've heard you can heal."

My eyes squeeze shut as I gasp for air. I scream, sobbing while he yanks the knife out and releases my restraints. I don't wait a second and heal myself.

Lucifer nods in approval. "Amazing. Now let's try it again."

He stabs me in the same exact spot, and I screech, hot tears rolling down my cheeks. I gasp for air and try to calm myself down, healing myself when he takes it out again.

My eyes glance at the windows, and for a second, I think of breaking through the glass and falling to the streets to end this misery. I'm actually about to do it when something outside stops me. It looks like a giant bird with black wings. A familiar tug in my abdomen pulls me toward it—a pull of belonging, trust, and familiarity. My eyebrows raise when I realize what, or who, it is.

The glass shatters and a scream bellows from my mouth. A gust of wind knocks Lucifer and me back, and

I land on my side, groaning at the impact. However, as soon as I'm on the floor, I'm back up.

"You okay?" Kavon asks me.

I'm momentarily shocked to see him here since I thought he'd left the city. That had been his main focus, yet he's here with me— saving my life.

His breath against my neck, the warmth radiating from his body. I can't believe it. I engulf him in a hug. "Just go!"

He wraps his arms around me tightly, flying off. I don't even realize what is happening until a line of wind slices at my skin. A monstrous roar then comes from behind us. I don't dare look back. I don't bother to keep my eyes open either. My arms waver, exhausted, but Kavon grips onto me tighter and I realize this isn't a dream. His warmth is real. *He's* real. And finally, for a few seconds, I relax before Kavon lands in an alley, pressing me against the wall and lowering both of us down. "We need to hide out here."

There's that roar again. "What's that noise?" I ask, goosebumps running up my spine.

"Lucifer," Kavon says. "Don't worry. As long as we hide, he won't be able to see us."

"What do you mean?" I ask.

Kavon sucks in a breath. "He can turn into a phoenix. And I know you don't know what that is, but basically, it's a giant firebird. Worse, he has really good eyesight. Similar to an eagle—which is another bird, by the way. He'd spot us in seconds on the road."

I did know what a phoenix was. My dad told me, and now I know why. It shouldn't surprise me that Lucifer can turn into a gigantic bird, but it does. Or maybe I'm still comprehending how he's using my father as his vessel. And that he *is* my father.

That's when it really hits me. I've always wanted to know why I was different. I'm the offspring of the person who destroyed the world; a person who is possessing my dad. How can I save my dad when Lucifer is in his body?

I pace around, suddenly wishing that this was all a dream. "No. This isn't real. This is a lie. It has to be. This *can't* be real."

"Mahi?"

The tears fall uncontrollably, and my head throbs while I cry out in agony. Kavon shushes me, but I can't help it. Snot leaks from my nose, and I rub at my burning face. I thought my dad had died. Why else wouldn't he have ended up in containment? Not knowing was better than this.

"I can't—" I hiccup. "I can't save my dad."

"It's okay. Some things are too hard."

"It's not that." I shuffle closer to Kavon. "Lucifer—" I break down into sobs again. "My dad. Lucifer's vessel is my dad!"

For a second, he doesn't react, but then Kavon wraps his arms around me, and I lean into his chest, wiping my soaking eyes. The mysterious bond between us swirls in my stomach, making the pain subside a little. But not enough.

"It's all my fault," I whisper.

"Don't say that."

"But it's true." I pull away from him, rubbing my face. "Never leave the forest. Once you leave, you can never return. I was always told that. Everyone was told that! But this one time, this one stupid time, I just wanted to see what was past the border. So, I went with my friend Laurel. And, of course, we got lost. A hellhound found us. We couldn't find the camp. After what felt like hours of running, we both ran onto an empty road."

"Keep going," Kavon says when I stop.

I let out a slow breath. "My dad caught up to us since we'd been lost for so long. If it hadn't been for him, my friend and I would've been dead. He killed the hellhound, but it didn't matter. It had already alerted demons. They were waiting for us on the road."

Kavon purses his lips and nods his head. "That's how you ended up in containment."

"They didn't take my dad with me and Laurel," I say. "I thought they killed him. But now, Lucifer's *using* him as his vessel." I close my eyes. "It was easier to accept that I'd die trying to save my dad. But now, I have no idea how I'll do that."

"Then don't."

"What?"

Kavon sighs and runs his fingers through his hair before they linger on his horns. "Your dad was one of Lucifer's number one targets before I'd even joined him. It'll be impossible to rescue him."

"But you were helping me—"

"I just wanted to get you away from Isra," Kavon corrects. "Look at what the demons are wearing. They're patrolling the city carrying around guns and your face is all over the place. The humans are doomed anyway."

My eyebrows furrow. I wipe away my tears. "You don't care?"

He looks away. "As hard as it is to believe, they aren't much better than the demons."

I take in what he says. And, of course, my mind shifts to that family I'd met before Isra had taken me. They were going to hand me in to die. And Laurel, she knew me better than anyone, and she gave me up to save herself. She probably didn't even think twice.

It was selfish.

Maybe humans were cursed. I mean, nineteen years under Lucifer's rule, and no one has done anything?

I hadn't seen Lucifer's firebird. But if I couldn't even fight a royal from Hell, what could I do to the king of Hell himself? At least, right now.

It's hopeless.

"We can just run off," Kavon says. "There are other cities, other places we can go and hide. And I'll keep training you. Maybe someday, you'll reach your peak. But not here."

A frown forms on my face. "But all those people he's turning into monsters . . . Your dad."

Kavon shrugs. "I stayed here for him, but he doesn't give a shit about me anyway. You saw that."

I don't say anything. I'm not sure what I can say.

"I know you feel this pull," he says. "I felt like I could trust you the second I met you, which is why I'm here. I'm not ready to give that up."

"You really mean that?" I ask, giving him a crooked grin. "I mean, he's your dad."

"He isn't," Kavon says, walking off and motioning me to follow. "I'm just the monster who killed the love of his life."

23

It's late at night when I walk into my cabin. The light turns on the second I step in, and there sits Dad on the floor, a scowl on his aging face.

I halt, closing the door slowly behind me. I've seen that face one too many times. This isn't good news. Hopefully, Laurel didn't get caught by her mom. She only stayed out late because of me.

"Where were you?" he asks in Hindi, his voice a small whisper. He wants to yell. I know he does, but I'm lucky he doesn't want to wake anyone else up.

There's no point in lying. I lean against the door and debate if I should walk over to the fireplace for some comfort. Because of Dad's glare, I decide against it. I don't want to risk walking past him.

"I was by the southern lake." I sigh, the Hindi feeling foreign to my tongue for some reason. It shouldn't. I speak it all the time.

"All alone?"

"Yeah."

Dad stares at me, and for some reason, I know what's coming. He's going to scold me, and then I'm going to have to help all day tomorrow on the eastern advancements. I was already going to stop by since I could easily lift things, but now it wouldn't be a choice.

Instead, he smiles. "Okay, as long as you're safe."

"What?" I narrow my eyes at him and rub my arms. "Aren't you supposed to be—I don't know—angry? You *hate* lying."

"Actually." He gets up and walks over to me. I tense up. Is that . . . fire in his eyes? "Lying is a specialty of mine."

He grabs my arm and places something in my hand —a small box.

"What's this?" I ask, ignoring the shivers running down my spine.

"Well, the day this happened, it was your birthday."

"Was?"

"Just open it." He nods his head, a huge grin on his face.

This isn't like Dad. And for some reason, it doesn't feel like I'm actually here. It's as if I'm inside someone else's body, but my fingers fumble with the box anyway. A small pair of white wings sit inside.

"You like it?" he asks quietly.

"Where did you—oops!" The wings fall onto the wooden floor. I bend down to grab them but freeze as Dad hovers above me. This isn't how this happened. I don't get gifts. I never have. Dad was supposed to yell at me. That's how this already happened.

I look up slowly to see Dad still smiling, but his skin turns red, eyes sunken in, and bright orange flames are coming from them. His flesh peels off, teeth rotting. A scream runs past my throat.

That's when I wake up.

Sweat drenches my body. My hand rests on my chest while I breathe uncontrollably. I lean back, groaning when my head collides with stone stairs.

Blinking, I start to relax when I see Kavon coming up to me.

"Bad dream?" he asks.

My heart slows down as I rub the back of my head. "How long was I sleeping?"

"Almost two hours."

We hadn't left Morningstar, waiting an entire day since we'd be spotted in seconds. We hadn't gone back to Kavon's Dad's place either. Instead, we sat in an empty building made of grey stone. The walls are covered in what Kavon told me is called graffiti, all kinds of different sayings and shapes of different colors crowding each other, and glass littered the ground. Before sleeping, I'd shown him my powers and he'd watched with astonishment.

Pressing my lips together, I place a hand on my head and let out a groan. "Jeez, I don't think I'll be sleeping again for a while."

"You want to talk about it?"

I shake my head. "No, it's okay."

Kavon gives me a half smile, his wings retracting while dark feathers fall to the ground. A grunt leaves his mouth. "Well, it's calmed down a little. I'm heading out to get food. You stay here."

I'm already on my feet. "No way."

Kavon shakes his head as he puts on a green jacket.

"Did you forget that you're the most wanted person right now?"

"So are you."

Kavon grabs my arm as I take a step ahead of him. "Mahi, it isn't curfew yet. This isn't something you should see."

I tilt my head, narrowing my eyes. "There's something you aren't telling me."

His blush and shallow breath give him away. "It's nothing."

"No." I cross my arms. "What is it?"

His tendons stick out of his skin, and his face grows noticeably pale. "Besides the demons walking around with guns, Lucifer releases different monsters in the city at dusk. And—" He stops and rubs his face.

"And what?"

He looks away. "When you weren't with me, Lucifer made an example of two random humans."

My heart leaps out of my chest. "How?"

"He wanted to show everyone what would happen to them if they helped you."

"But no one helped me!"

"I know. He never said they did. He just showed what would happen *if* they did." Kavon closes his eyes. "It was on live television. He tore the head off one of them, and the other one he injected with some substance." He lets out a groan. "The way her bones twisted and her face mutated, I don't even wish that on any human. She's probably roaming the city, hunting for you."

I suck in a breath. It doesn't sound like there is a way back from that. If Lucifer had chosen to experiment on my father, there wouldn't be any way to save him. But being used as a vessel is a different kind of torture.

"I thought he told everyone to bring me in alive," I say.

"Maybe the monsters won't kill you," says Kavon.

A shudder runs through me as I think of the humanoid spider. I don't know if it was going to kill me, but it did place a tracking device in my body.

Kavon sighs. "I still haven't figured out why he wants you alive."

I gulp. I don't even know why. Maybe it's because I'm his daughter, but honestly, that can't be it. There was a desperate look in his eye when he asked me to go to Hell with him. And would he really be searching so frantically just for me to be with him? It doesn't seem right.

"I didn't tell you this." I'm not sure if I should continue. What if Kavon looks at me differently? But I've already said it, and he deserves to know that he isn't alone. "I'm half-angel, Kavon."

His lip's part, and he touches the base of his neck. For a few seconds, he doesn't say anything. My heart accelerates until I can hear it beating in my ears. His eyes dart all over the room, eventually meeting mine. "This isn't a trick, is it?"

"Why would I do that?" I shift on my feet. "It's the truth."

"But you don't have wings."

Neither does Lucifer. In his . . . in his vessel, at least. If he really is my father, it makes sense why I don't have any. After all, he is a fallen angel. Whenever someone would mention him, they'd never describe his wings. Why would his offspring have wings if he doesn't?

"Lucifer told me——" I close my eyes. Here it comes. "That I'm his daughter. That's why. He could be lying, but it makes sense."

Kavon doesn't say anything. All I hear is him exhale slowly and the shuffle of his feet. He probably doesn't know what to say. How would anyone? He probably wants to kill me.

"Shit," he silently curses. "This changes everything."

I chew on the inside of my cheek as I watch Kavon pace, his hands in fists. I don't know what's going on in his mind right now, but if he decides to throw me against a wall, I don't know if I'll be able to fight him. "What are you talking about?"

"Nothing." He faces me, running his fingers through his hair. "Nothing changes. It doesn't matter if you're his daughter. We're still getting out of here."

My shoulders slump. Relief floods through me. "Then let's go."

"You're not coming with me."

I race to stop him from leaving, ignoring the glass crunching underneath my feet. "Why is it okay for you to go out there and risk your life, but I can't?"

His face twists up in a way that looks annoyed. "Because you're forgetting the obvious. Your face is *everywhere*. I know you haven't gotten the time to see what I mean, but I'm serious."

Grabbing my hood, I shove it over my face and place my hair inside. "Well, now no one can see my face."

"And what if a demon stops us?"

"Then we get away," I say. "You haven't seen me for more than two months. I've shown you what I can do. I can fight."

"No. I'm not losing you again."

My stomach flutters, and the sudden urge to be closer to him takes over, but I ignore it. "You can't stop me."

"*No.*"

"Either I go with you, or neither of us do."

He glares at me with black eyes. Hard. I think back to when the demons would flash their eyes at me in containment, but this is Kavon and his demonic side no longer makes my bones shake. My mouth forms an innocent smile. I almost give up, but luckily, he does so before me.

Kavon groans. "How can you not see that it'd be better if you didn't go."

I'm not going to admit to him that I know it'd be better if I didn't. But it's going to be my last night in the city. I may be selfish, but I want to see everything, and I'm not letting Kavon risk himself while I stay safely away.

So, I cross my arms and grin. "You were going to teach me how to sneak around. Think of this as the final lesson."

"We didn't even start the first one."

My face is, in fact, everywhere.

Hands in my pockets, hood covering my face, I try my best not to stop in my tracks and look around at the posters. There are also giant TV screens and signs with my picture on them.

The same picture I'd seen when I'd escaped Isra.

As I follow Kavon, there are demons around every

corner. Some are in the special gear I'd seen last night. Others are in regular clothing, walking among the hordes of humans who bump into me to get home before the curfew. Besides the evident fear on every human's face, it seems like there really is civilization here. There are dozens of shops and vehicles, just like how I was told the world was like before the war. But the demons look angry, and some even seem bored. From a demon's perspective, it's dumb of Lucifer to make demons recreate the old world after destroying it. I cringe at the fact that I'm agreeing with what Isra's told me.

Shivers crawl up my spine as the sun sets. It doesn't help that small strands of hair keep popping out of my hood. Kavon told me we'd be going to the heart of the city. I never expected it to be this crowded, and I never expected to see this many people.

I gasp as another body collides into mine. I mutter a quick apology and keep moving. There are too many people, and I don't have time to tell which ones are actually human. If I look up, I'm dead.

I sigh with relief when Kavon turns into a building. There are a few people already inside when I push myself in. I follow Kavon past a line of people and we step into one of the multiple sections. There are stacks of food on what seem to be shelves. Just like that trashed-up, empty store we'd gone to outside the wall. Except this time, instead of ferals, we have to worry about humans and demons.

"Grab what you can," Kavon whispers. "Don't worry about paying. They'll let me take anything since I'm a demon."

Nodding, my hands grab onto large bags of food. As

I grab more and more, I realize it'd be better to plant seeds. Just as I'm about to ask Kavon, the music playing in the store gets extremely loud. I drop whatever is in my hands and I cover my ears until it's finally silent.

"Citizens of Morningstar," I know that voice. A small gasp leaves my mouth while Kavon places an arm on my shoulder. I fight the urge to look at him. "Most of you should've stopped what you're doing by now. And if not, well I'm sure the dead ones among you provide enough persuasion."

Lucifer makes my dad's voice sound so light and friendly, but with a lingering sense of disgust. "As you know, the criminal who goes by the name Mahi Sharma —" He even knows my last name. "—is wanted for a very high-profile award. Turn her over, and you gain a single wish of *anything* you want as long as it does not harm me. No games. No twists. A simple deal. I give you my word, which from an angel, means everything. I know Mahi is listening to this. She claims to care for you humans but because she fails to come within anyone's grasp, I've decided to test her loyalty to you all. This city will be destroyed in five days. There will be no evacuation. It'll be burnt to ashes. Unless, she turns herself in."

Meeting Kavon's eyes, he shakes his head.

"I'd advise you, Mahi, if you truly care about the lives of these people, to bring yourself forward. They won't hesitate to bring you in themselves."

The quick-paced music of a random female singer starts playing again. All I can think about are the hundreds of threats around me. Every person, every human on the street outside, this entire city, is a bounty hunter now. They capture me, they get a wish. They don't, this city burns to the ground. Countless children, people who may not want anything to do with this, will die.

Unless I turn myself in.

"Don't even think about it," Kavon says as if he read my mind, voice low. "We have enough food. Let's get out of here."

I'm about to protest when Kavon walks past me. Suppressing my groan, I follow behind him. I'm not sure if I'm ready to see the countless corpses I know are outside.

The air is cooler, and I keep my head low to hide my face while I follow Kavon. He grabs my hand when I trip over a body, but I ignore the sinking feeling in my stomach and the heat in my cheeks. Kavon turns into an alley and his pace quickens. I struggle to keep up with his long legs. Along the way, rotting garbage keeps invading my nostrils.

"Why aren't we going the way we came?" I ask, my free hand sliding down my thighs. I flinch when I spot a rat. "Can you slow down?"

Kavon grunts. "No. After that announcement, I think it'd be better if—"

An ear-piercing scream deafens both of our ears. This time I don't cover mine, but Kavon does, letting go of my hand and yelling out. I sweep a shaky hand across my forehead. My heart pounds in my ears.

The sound is very human.

I push past Kavon, who barely touches my shoulders to stop me and turn a corner.

There's a girl with long black hair and dark skin. She

looks like she's in her late teens. She's trying to climb up the fence behind her while some creature walks toward her on four legs. Two arms sprout from its grey back, and it tenses before turning to face me with what is simply a giant, red, glowing circle for a mouth. I finally realize the girl; *she looks like me.*

As the creature stands up, a sour taste forms in my mouth. It looks like it was once human. And however much I want to deny it, I can't. This *must* be one of the other experiments. One of the things I'd feared I'd end up as when I was in containment.

The creature raises its head, pausing as though it's thinking of something. It doesn't make a sound when it takes a step toward me.

Its long, claw-like nails get closer and closer, and I take a deep breath before I root myself to the ground. The fireball appears in my hand, and I wait as it slowly lurks closer. The girl is almost up that fence. If I just keep this thing occupied—

"Are you crazy?" Kavon comes up behind me, pulling my shoulder. My eyes widen when the monster stops moving.

No.

I don't care if this thing was human once. It isn't now. I run forward just as it turns its head. Blasting its legs with fire, it screeches and gets on four legs again, running toward the girl.

"No!" I scream.

"Shut up!" Kavon slams his hand on my mouth. I scrape at his hand. He struggles, but in the end, he is strong enough to ignore my attempts.

All I can do is watch the girl barely make a sound

before one of the creature's back arms claws into her throat.

My eyes almost pop out of my skull, but all I can do is watch while Kavon restrains me. The monster jumps over the fence, its hand still digging into the girl's throat. Her crimson blood drips onto the ground in little droplets from the wound.

Kavon finally lets me go and touches my shoulder, but I brush it off. "We have to go."

I'm not sure if I feel anything but the emptiness inside. "I could've stopped that."

Kavon glances back at the street. I follow his gaze. There's a line of four people with their hands behind their heads and knees on the ground. Others try to run away, but demons shove them into the concrete. A demon in one of the special uniforms holds a gun against someone's head, and when he's about to look over at us, Kavon shoves me into the wall.

"We need to go back," he whispers, staring down into my eyes. "It's past curfew. They are rounding everyone up."

"That girl—"

"I don't care about that girl. I care about *you*."

I tense, my breath catching in my throat. I can tell by his discomfort that he didn't expect to say that. The bond between us, the invisible line that's tying us together, the one I'd become immune to, intensifies. It's the sound of gunshots that makes us both flinch.

Kavon pulls back, avoiding my eyes. "We have to go."

My face is burning, and I probably look like a tomato, but I need to think of what's important right now. This is going to keep happening. Even if I do run away, what will happen when Kavon and I encounter another banshee? What's to stop Lucifer from turning humans into those monsters? How is this even living?

"No." I shake my head.

"What?"

"I need to figure out how to kill Lucifer in these five days," I say. "Or I'm going to give myself up. It's the only way."

"Mahi, think about that—"

"Isra has a plan on how to kill him," I say. "And if we leave, how am I ever going to find him again? I came here to find my dad. I came here to save him. If I leave, he'll be stuck as a slave forever."

Kavon clenches his jaw. "This isn't the place to talk about this."

I give him a weak smile. "There's nothing to talk about. I'm going to go find Isra and get his help. I'll help take these supplies back to where we were hiding out, but after that, I'm not asking you to come with me."

He opens his mouth but nothing comes out. I brush past him, and he scoffs. "So you're just going to go back to the monster who imprisoned you? Do you even know where he is?"

"There's no choice," I say.

"Yes, there is. We can leave through the tunnels like we planned."

"It's my life for all these people." I throw my hands in the air. "Out there is nothing. Isra's the only one who actually has a plan. Unless . . . you know about Death?"

Kavon gives me a pinched expression. His jaw clenches. "So, you're going to leave me alone again?"

His words sting, and I don't know what to say. Except

that he thinks I'll die. Maybe I will, but that doesn't matter. Isra has a plan, and I at least need to find out what it is, if he's still alive. "I'm sorry, Kavon."

He frowns and shakes his head. After a minute of silence, I hear him whisper, "I'm coming with you."

24

"Are you sure this is the place?" Kavon whispers.

We're hiding inside an abandoned building across from Isra's. Now that I get a good look at it, Isra's place is small, with dirty yellow brick walls. It's invisible next to the other buildings. I wouldn't look twice if I didn't know what it was. There are many small windows I hadn't noticed before, but the entire building looks off. The streets are empty and the whistling wind makes my stomach jolt at any sound. My fingernails dig into my hands as I try to repel the memories that swim up. I don't want to go in there, but I have to.

"I'm pretty sure. But the more you question me, the more I doubt myself."

Kavon sighs. He's more annoyed with me than usual. But on the way here, I constantly reminded him that following me was *his* choice. This 'suicide mission,' as Kavon called it, was mine alone. He didn't have to come.

"Hopefully, I won't have to use this sword." He holds the one he stole from Lucifer; the one that kills demons.

"Isra's actually pretty clever for hiding in this plain place."

My eyes linger on the handle's design before I say, "We don't want to kill him."

I bring both my hands up. My eyes flick back and forth between them. There are small cuts on my left palm from my nails, and I dig in a little more before healing myself, but the pain doesn't do anything. The tightness in my chest is still there, no matter what I do. I look at the house again, knowing that Isra might already be dead. Our one shot against Lucifer, gone.

"Use something else," I say.

Groaning, Kavon takes out a small blade and shoves it up his sleeve. "If we get caught, things will get ugly."

"If anyone is going to get us caught, it's you, being a giant and all."

"Congratulations! For once, being the size of a mouse isn't horrible."

"The only reason I'm short is because you're the one who's like six-foot-five. Is your brain damaged that badly from all those times you didn't duck through doorways?"

He smirks. "Yeah, yeah. Let's see you put those ninja skills to use."

I actually know what he's talking about. Some of the other kids used to talk about ninjas and assassins all the time. "Let's go."

After making sure there aren't any demons or monsters around, I jump out of a window close to me. Kavon follows from beside me. I don't know why he denies it. If anyone sees us, it'll be because of his gigantic height.

Or maybe it'll be me, from fainting in the middle of

the empty street. Well, technically, it isn't empty. There are a few cars along the road, but that's it. There's not a single light, not even a streetlight, to show if anyone is around. And that's one of the things making me lose my balance. The closer I get to the building, the more my mind spins. I think about the countless nights I spent in that basement. The relationship Isra and I grew. We know each other's hobbies, embarrassing stories, and dislikes. I wish I could wipe it all from existence.

Once we reach the steps, I turn around and grab Kavon's arm. He pulls back for a millisecond at the sudden touch before relaxing. "What if he's not even in there?"

What if he's dead? Could a royal demon even die from blood loss?

"Then we'll leave."

I swallow excessively, letting him go and walking up the steps. I should be more like him. Indifferent. Worse case, we'll have to escape the city. But at least we'll both be alive, for a while. Lucifer has probably planted dozens more of those banshees all around. I never want to see one of those again. They're the whole reason I had to call Isra for help and come into Morningstar.

Just as I reach the door, my eyes turn big, and I gasp. I spin around. "Isra knows we're here!"

Kavon's face goes pale, his body tensing. "How?"

I see him. In the distance, standing in the darkness with his eyes gleaming as bright as the sun. Isra's power gets more and more annoying. I wonder how long he's been there. Since I first thought of his name? He knows we're here, but he isn't *doing* anything. The bottom half of his face is covered in shadows, and I can't see his arm.

I'm not sure if he's happy I'm back or waiting to kill me. Probably both.

"I don't know what to do," I say, glancing back at the door. "He knows we're about to walk in. Why hasn't he done anything?"

"Well, we can't stay out here," Kavon hisses. "Anyone can spot us."

"Anyone can spot you," I correct before taking a deep breath and placing my hand on the knob. We need him. It's the only way to find Death.

I'm surprised the door is unlocked. I step in quickly with a ball of fire in my hand just in case. The rooms around me are dark, but I continue to the light in the distance that leads to the kitchen. Kavon's footsteps are loud behind me, and I prepare myself for a fight as I turn into the room.

But he's not there. My stomach backflips and I ignore my racing heartbeat. It won't be hard to find him, but what if I was just imagining what I just saw?

We dig through the entire building. His bedroom, the bathroom, until nothing but the basement remains.

"I can go down alone if you want," Kavon says while we both stare at the door. I face his worried eyes. For once since we got here, he actually looks like he *cares*. "I assume . . . Down there is where . . . Yeah."

I take a step toward the door but back up as memories flash through my mind. More importantly, the memory of stabbing Isra. I can picture him still down there, lying in a pool of black blood. I don't want to see another dead body. "I can't."

"It's okay." Kavon half-smiles. "I'll go alone."

I shake my head. "No. I thought he was in here, but

—" That's when the realization hits me. "Unless he was outsi—"

"Welcome back."

Kavon spins around, and I make a fire whip. Isra tilts his head at us from within his kitchen, a large bandage around his arm.

"We need to talk," I say.

"I don't remember teaching you that." Isra grins, and I groan. "I'm not surprised you figured it out on your own."

He moves toward us. Not in an unfriendly way. In fact, his bandaged arm sags, and I think that maybe we won't have to fight him. Maybe he'll cooperate. But before I can stop him, Kavon pushes the prince back without touching him. As Isra lands with a thud against his drawers, I grab Kavon's arm. "Don't!"

But he pushes me out of the way, dodging the pair of knives that come hurtling toward him. They dig into the wall behind him, and before I can react, he is thrown into the ceiling. He falls face-first into the wall. I blast balls of fire at Isra, but he knows exactly what to do to avoid them. His wooden cabinets catch on fire, but I don't care. I'm not sure what we can do against a demon thousands of years old. I don't think I can use his emotions against him this time.

I glance at Kavon, and he smirks at me before his eight-feet wings sprout from his back, sending the kitchen table into the wall. Creating another fireball, I split it into what looks like a plate and send four of them to Isra. He manages to avoid them, but not the heavy gust that comes after Kavon flaps his wings.

The wind extinguishes every flame. It's enough to

knock me off my feet and send Isra into his fridge. A screech of pain comes out of his mouth, and his jaw clenches when he slowly gets up.

I muster another ball of fire while random objects float beside me. I assume it's Kavon getting ready to attack again, but Isra just stands with his arms limp, glaring with tight eyes.

"So hostile every single time." He sighs. "Let's cut to the chase. You need my help."

"You're really still alive," I whisper, narrowing my eyes in astonishment.

Isra tilts his head. "Don't sound so happy Mahi, I might think you like me."

"You'd be delusional to think that," Kavon cuts in, gritting his teeth against each other. I've never seen him this angry before.

Isra shrugs. "Honestly. I'm a prince of Hell. I kept Mahi in a cage. I've done countless other things that you'll view as horrible. There's nothing I can say. I don't know how you managed to convince her you're a saint, Kavon."

"Because I didn't torture her. And you're right, there is nothing you can say." Kavon steps beside me while the knife floats back into his hand. "Tell us how to get to Death."

"Or maybe, I can just take you both to Lucifer."

"Please," I whisper. I don't want to beg, but that might be the only way to get Isra to listen. And if the past tells me anything, emotions always get the best of him.

Isra glances at me, eyes darkening. "I told you I wanted to do this together."

"We still can."

Isra laughs and shakes his head. "Mahi, I suggest you leave before I can't control myself any longer. The Shadow Angel though, killing him will get Lucifer to listen to me for five minutes."

"You won't do that." I *know* he won't. He had his chance when Kavon was captured but he didn't. I let my fire go when he clenches his jaw. "I don't like it either, but we need your help. And you need ours if you want things to change. Lucifer's going to destroy this entire city, an entire city full of humans. *Vessels.* Do you really want that?" I motion at his arm. "Besides, I'm sure you could use a healing session."

Isra's lips curve upwards. "*Or,* I'll turn you in. Tear your arms off as a souvenir."

"You wouldn't."

"Someone sounds so confident."

"You want to be an angel." He tenses as the words come out of my mouth. "Which means there's some kind of humanity in you. Maybe all these years of causing suffering changed you, or maybe Lucifer messed up when he created you. But there's something there."

He doesn't speak. Instead, he fidgets with his horns. Seconds feel like hours. A small fireball forms in my palm once again. I don't want to do this, but with Kavon inching closer to Isra, I have a feeling things might go south.

"I'm not sure if those are the words you wanted to hear." I break the silence. "But I meant them."

He swallows excessively. Sweat trails down the side of my face, and I glance at Kavon. His eyes are locked on

Isra. He isn't planning on giving the prince a chance to surprise us.

"You'll never trust me," Isra says quietly.

"That's true." I nod my head. "But you can't trust us either. Tell us Death's location and take us there, and you won't lose all these vessels."

His next word comes out soft, but I hear it clearly. "Okay."

Certain of our temporary alliance, I blow out my flame, ignoring Kavon's protests. I stroll over to Isra, my veins glowing as I press my hand on his right arm.

"This is going to hurt you," he says with a rasp.

"It's okay." A thousand needles prick at my body once the healing begins, and with every breath, more pain overwhelms me. A searing pressure digs under my right arm, followed by a piercing silence that invades my ears. As I finish healing him, my legs give out, and I fall to the floor.

I would've been so much angrier if I was him.

"You probably wish you'd never done that to me now," Isra says as my hearing comes back to me.

Kavon helps me up. "I'm okay," I tell him, rubbing my head. "I never asked for your opinion, Isra."

"Where's Death?" Kavon gets straight to the point again.

Isra leans against the wall and gives us an annoying smirk. "I don't exactly know where he is—"

"Isra, I swear if you play more games—"

"—but I know someone who can help us," he finishes.

"Who?"

"If you let me talk, I'd tell you. I'll have to go alone,

of course." He sighs, grabbing a black coat off the hook. I glance at Kavon and nod.

Before Isra can get another word out, he's against the wall. Kavon holds a knife against his throat. "A little too forward, aren't you?" Isra teases. "I know you have a thing for royal princes but come on. You don't want to break Ozanith's heart. Although, it is frozen—"

"Shut up," Kavon says through his clenched teeth. "Ozanith meant nothing."

Isra smirks. "Are you blushing? Now that is utterly disgusting—" He doesn't get to finish. Kavon digs the knife into his neck.

A thing for princes?. Everyone knew who prince Ozanith was. He's the one demons would tell stories about to make sure you didn't fall asleep. My initial disappointment fades after hearing Isra's words. If Kavon really was with Ozanith, it's none of my business. I try to keep my confusion off my face, but clearly, I can't. Isra catches my look and grins.

"You didn't—" he chokes. "Mahi, you didn't know? I thought he told you everything. I guess he didn't tell you he used to fuck prince Ozanith."

I know he is doing this to be spiteful, and yet a small part of me misses what I used to think he was, even though I remember that he is the one that locked me up.

Kavon is already moving to kill Isra when I place a hand on his shoulder. "You're not going anywhere," I tell Isra. "Who is it?"

"I have to be the one to go," Isra says, grinding his teeth and struggling against the blade. "You won't get in without me."

"*Who is it?*"

"One of my followers," he says. "Someone who wants Lucifer gone as much as you and I. Someone who —" he grunts as Kavon presses the knife against his throat. "Someone who wants to meet you."

"Where?" Kavon asks. "No more vague answers."

Isra meets his eyes. "Club Enigma."

25

KAVON'S ARM is warm around my back, and his hand squeezes my shoulder. The gesture is a nice comfort against the cold night air, although it doesn't stop me from jumping up when I spot another circle-faced monster in the shadows. Something that used to be human. It's hunting for prey.

And Lucifer's only going to make more.

"You're going to attract attention like that," Kavon whispers in my ear, sending goosebumps all over my skin. "Relax."

"Can't we go any faster?" I ask Isra. We'd teleported to some popular demon area of the city but still had to walk on the actual streets. It was drastically nicer than what I'd seen before; beautiful tall buildings, clean roads, sidewalks, and gorgeous plants lining the middle of the street.

Isra and Kavon stand next to me while I try to keep the blonde wig I have on secure under my hoodie. Kavon is wearing sunglasses and a hat. His mask covers half of his mouth, though I'm not sure if that's enough to disguise ourselves. The fact that it's dark helps. It is a big risk to be out here, but we couldn't let Isra go off on his own.

"It's a three-minute walk."

Another group of demons on patrol passes us. I glare at the ground. This area of the city was alive. Demons are chattering among the streets, cars are rolling by, and it seemed as if there wasn't a world full of man-eating demons outside the city walls. But that didn't stop my face from being plastered on every screen. I don't know how many heart attacks I have left in me. "It's been like ten minutes."

"You didn't have to come." Isra sighs.

"We don't trust you," I say at the same time Kavon says, "we're not dumbasses."

"I never said you were. But you both coming is very unwise."

"We'd be stupid if we let you go alone," I say.

Loud music creeps into my ears as we get closer and closer to a glowing building. The one demon we needed to talk to happened to be in some party place. Kavon had been reluctant but, in the end, wouldn't let me go alone.

Isra brings us to a halt, pulling us against the side of the building next to the club. I shove his arm off the second I can. "Stay by me so if things go south, we can zap out of there."

Ahead, there is a long line of demons outside the brightly lit building. Glowing blue letters shine the word, *Enigma*. And as we walk back onto the sidewalk, demons start to peer over and whisper about us. I forgot that Isra is royalty to them.

"Aren't all demons supposed to be looking for me?" I ask. "Isn't everything supposed to be closed?"

"Lucifer's too busy to punish people for keeping clubs open. And those aren't all demons," Isra says.

It takes me a second to understand. "Those are *humans?*" I don't bother to hide the disgust in my voice.

"Yes," Isra says. "The wealthy ones. The ones who a demon may have a relationship with. The ones that helped extinguish the rebel forces. They are in other cities too."

I scoff. Kavon rubs my shoulder. "I told you they weren't so great." He sighs.

"I know people can be cruel." A chill runs up my spine. "But this—I can't believe it."

"Yeah, it's awful," Isra says in a monotone voice. "And since the city might get blown to pieces, some demons are also trying to have fun before relocating. I assume some of these humans are attempting to hitch a ride. The ones trying to get past the wall are probably in a bloodbath right now."

Kavon's grip tightens around me. "I can't believe we're standing outside of a club," he murmurs in my ear. If he's trying to change the subject, it's working.

"Took the words right out of my mouth," I say, even though I didn't know what a club was until now.

"How do you know your guy is even in there?" Kavon asks Isra.

"He's the bartender."

"A demon, a *bartender?*"

"He likes making drinks." Isra shrugs, a small smile forming on his face. "He's really going to miss this place."

I don't bother asking what a bartender is. Isra doesn't say anything as he passes the guard. The humans are fawning over him like he's the greatest thing they've ever seen. I make sure not to look around too long.

"I feel so stupid," Kavon says, keeping his head low as we follow Isra. Kavon keeps his arm around me, but it doesn't stop me from bumping shoulders with anyone. We've barely come inside, and already sweat sticks to my skin. My legs wobble when I spot some chairs, desperately wishing I could have a seat to rest for a few seconds.

"You are!" I yell. This high-energy music isn't so bad, but it's too loud. "You're wearing sunglasses at night."

Kavon pushes his glasses up his nose. Finally, I step into a giant room. It's packed in here. I think I might go blind from the thousands of neon lights flashing every half second. Two grey-skinned demons with bulging veins grind against each other and most humans are paired up with horned creatures. Around every corner, demons are dancing. Some sit by the tables set to the side, and some have their bodies pressed against humans. Luckily, I don't see any ferals like the warden. We pass two sets of stairs, one heading down and the other up. A gasp shoots out of my mouth when someone grabs my arm, pulling me over to the side.

"Don't touch me!" I pull my arm away from Isra.

The color drains from his face, before he looks up at Kavon. "The bars in the center," he shouts. Besides a few side tables with people serving drinks, it must be the huge table in the middle of the room. "That's where my contact is. Let me go alone."

"No way," Kavon responds, flinching for a second.

The longer he's without his wings, the more pain he'll feel. We need to hurry.

"You're a big guy," Isra says. "And I don't mean that in a bad way. But you're going to draw attention to us."

"Yeah, right. We're almost the same height."

I glance into the room once more. The path to the bar has too many demons. There's too much risk of getting caught. Already, from the corner of my eye, I can see people looking over at Kavon in admiration. He's more handsome than he realizes.

"I'll go with him," I tell Kavon. "It's too crowded for all of us."

"Are you crazy?" He snarls at Isra. "Are you using that emotion power on her?"

"No." I touch Kavon's shoulder. He looks back at me. "He isn't."

Not like I'd actually know if he was.

"I'm not," Isra confirms. "If I was, I'd only be manipulating what's already there."

Kavon's chest heaves. I sigh and glare at Isra. "Can you shut up?" I turn back to Kavon. "I don't trust him to go alone. Just stand here and watch us. I'm sure that a giant like you can see the bar from here."

"What if I go?"

"No," I say. "I'm going."

"She's right." Isra smirks as I shoot him a dagger. "She's the last person who should be left alone."

I watch Kavon's face, desperately wishing I could see his eyes and lips. Finally, he groans. "He doesn't have any of that metal, does he?"

"No," Isra says, rolling his eyes which are dimmer than usual.

"I'll be okay," I reassure Kavon. He unwraps his arm. Taking a deep breath, I grab Isra's sleeve. He swallows hard as he watches me refuse his hand before moving through the crowd.

I resist the urge to look back at Kavon. Guilt seeps in me, but by how many people bump into me, our cover might've been blown if all three of us walked through here.

Once we finally make it to the bar, I rest against the table. A tan demon with a long dark beard and full set of hair comes toward us, nodding his head to Isra and side-eyeing me.

"We need privacy," he tells the demon, who nudges his head to follow him.

We walk over to the back of the room, where the demon holds a door open for us. As soon as we're inside, I tug my hand away from Isra's arm, discreetly rubbing it against my shirt.

We're in a small room, but there are hundreds of weird items sitting on shelves. Jars full of powders and strange liquids. Weapons behind a glass cupboard. I stray away from Isra, walking over to a box of different kinds of blades. One of the swords looks a lot like Kavon's.

"That's a fake," the demon says.

Great. It could've been useful.

I turn to face him, leaning on the glass counter like Isra. "What is this place?" I whisper to him.

"You're free to talk in here, Mahi."

My eyes widen at the mention of my name, but the demon doesn't move. Instead, he watches both of us from behind the counter. "What are these things?" I repeat

"Magical items," the demon answers, his brown eyes digging into me. I look away since I don't particularly enjoy being stared at like an animal.

"Magic?" I repeat. "Like, powered from a soul?"

"No," says Isra. "Far from that."

I frown. "Then what's all this?"

"Ingredients," says the demon. "Tools, enchanted weapons. All kinds of things that anyone can use."

"Why is it hidden?"

Isra sighs. "Because even though we're going to use it, most, if not all, comes from mages. Rare humans who used magic. And Lucifer killed most of them off since they helped the angels and humans in the war. Another amazing mistake of his. Luckily, Tannik here is casually dating one of them. Must be fun. I heard they're crazy."

"Too crazy," Tannik mutters.

I chew on the inside of my cheek. *Rare humans.* That's what Lucifer had called the humans, like my dad, who'd gotten away. And my dad had visited me in my dream somehow. Just like Kavon.

I laugh at the idea. I know my dad. He snorts when he laughs, he loves scary stories, he never ties the laces on his shoes. He was an engineer before the world went to shit! And secrets were something he despised. Magic was something he would've told me about.

Although, for years, the demons never found us. And all that we'd built, it couldn't be made from a couple of tools and some hands. Dad had avoided my questions on materials all the time. But magic, magic would've made all the houses. Magic would've made the barrier that protected the hideout.

It shouldn't be hard to believe that humans could use

magic in a world like this, but a tiny sliver of doubt remains in the back of my mind. My dad would've told me. If not, someone else would've.

"So, what do you need, Your Highness?" Tannik cuts through my thoughts. He's still staring at me like he can't believe I'm standing here.

"I need to find Death again." I tense as Isra exposes our plan. "I should've kept that mirror."

Tannik smirks. "Luckily, I still have it."

He turns around and starts going through the shelf behind him. It's odd seeing a demon act so normal. The only demon that I'd ever had a normal conversation with was Gavril. Thinking of him opens up a floodgate of bad memories. I think of all those times he was nice to me, and all the times he wasn't.

"Here it is." Tannik holds out a small, rough mirror. It's shaped like a diamond, with silver edges and some non-English words written at the bottom. "Haven't packed it away yet."

"Why not?"

"It's difficult, Your Highness. It's not like I want to relocate."

"I don't think anyone does——"

"We should hurry," I interrupt Isra. He can chat with his friend when there isn't a timer in the back of my mind. "Kavon is going to start worrying."

Isra lets out an aggravated sigh and grabs the mirror. "I just think of who I want to find, correct?"

Tannik nods his head. "That's what the inscription says."

Isra presses his lips together firmly. For a second, a glimmer of fear crosses his face before he grips the mirror with two hands. Bringing it to eye level, his eyes narrow.

I glance at Tannik. For once, he isn't glaring at me, but he meets my eyes and smiles. He—his vessel looks friendly. I wonder if the human has any kids.

"Of course!" A groan comes out of Isra's mouth. He places the mirror on the glass counter and I catch a glimpse of what looks like destroyed buildings.

"Thanks for the help." Isra's frown turns into a grin as he hands back the mirror. "Same spot as last time. I'll come back for the mirror some other day."

They start talking about something else I don't have the energy to pay attention to. Instead, I drift toward a steel bracelet behind the glass counter. There's nothing around it, like it's the last of its kind.

"What is this?" I interrupt whatever conversation they are having.

Tannik glances at Isra before giving me a fake smile. "An astral bracelet. Worth a fortune. You can only get these bad boys from Heaven. Or, you can find them on some dead angels in the rare case Lucifer hasn't destroyed them."

"Why would he destroy them?" I ask. "What does it do?"

"It takes away your powers, Mahi," says Isra. "It's what I used on you when I—in our time together. It's also used on angelic fugitives."

"What would an angel do that would make them a fugitive?"

He sighs. "There are hundreds of things. Murder. Theft. Any crime a human can commit."

"And then what?" I press on. "What happens if they

are guilty?"

"Well . . ." He stares at me for a second too long. "I wouldn't know, would I?"

My lips tug upwards before I look at Tannik. "I'd like to get this."

Tannik's eyes shift between Isra and me, his face paling. "Uhh . . ."

"You can't even touch it without losing your powers," Isra says, giving me a grimace.

I cock my head. "Well maybe this is something we can put on you know who."

"He's an archangel."

"And I'm *half* archangel," I say. "It worked on me."

Isra shakes his head. "Tannik, it's fine. We can just use the ones I already have."

"No Tannik," I say. "I think it's better carrying around a small bracelet than a giant collar."

Tannik looks between us with frantic eyes. "What do you want me to do, Prince Isra?"

Isra ignores him and continues staring at me. I know we should get going, but I'm rooted to the spot.

Finally, Isra chuckles, his dimples popping out. "Okay, you have a point. We'll take the bracelet."

Tannik pulls the metal out from under the glass counter, places it in a brown paper bag, and hands it to me. I turn toward Isra and nudge my head. "You can carry it."

"Who else would?"

Isra gives Tannik a nod and I follow him out the door, scowling as the loud music deafens my ears once again.

"You really trusted him?" I yell over the music,

gripping onto Isra's sleeve.

"He's one of my followers," says Isra. "For a long time now. I actually met him when I was investigating him for Lucifer."

"Really—" A large girl bumps into me, ripping me away from Isra. I shriek as I fall to the floor and my hood flies off.

Panic takes over. I desperately shove my hood back on over the blonde wig. I try to get up while thousands of feet stumble around me. The fear of being trampled takes over until I feel Isra's hands helping me up. He faces the girl, hand in the air.

I'm not sure if she even saw me and yet I freaked out. How will I react when I see Lucifer? He's countless years old. He knows there's nothing I can do. Doubt seeps into my chest but I shake it off.

"Stop." I place my hands on his chest before he can do something to the girl. "It'll blow our cover."

Worse, I don't want Kavon to come over here.

Isra meets my eyes and his face softens before he lowers his arm. "Are you sure you want to do this?"

"Do what?"

"The plan," he says. "You're not ready. Be smart about this."

"I have to," I say. "Or the city—"

"It's just one city."

"And what about the humans being turned into monsters?" I frown. "What about all those vessels you want? We're doing it my way."

"Yes, I want vessels. But I also have to be smart. Your way will get you killed."

I scoff. "Can we talk about this later?"

As we push through the crowd, I manage to spot Kavon, who has a girl tracing a hand against his arm. She flips her long dark hair, fluttering her big eyes. She's beautiful. But she's also a spectator to everything bad around her.

Kavon stands up straighter, alert, when he sees us approaching. The girl glances at us, or well, Isra. Her eyes bulge from her skull.

"Let's go," Isra says to Kavon.

"Holy shit." The girl covers her mouth with her hands. "You're . . . You're—"

"I know," Isra sighs. "But we need to get going, love." He smirks at the girl before all of us head out. Kavon wraps his arm around me again once we're out of the crowd.

"What did you guys do?" he asks me as we walk away from the club.

"I'll fill you in when we're out of here," I whisper, clearing my voice and staring at Isra." So, once we form the plan, are we going to find, you know who, now?"

"Nope."

My blood turns cold.

"I told you he wouldn't help us," Kavon tenses. I almost think he's going to sprout his wings and fly us out of here, but Isra speaks before that can happen.

"You're so vexing," Isra says. "We're heading out in the morning. Get some rest, take a shower Kav—you demon." He clears his throat, looking around us. "And then we can go."

"Do you really have to be an asshole?" I ask him as Kavon sucks in a breath.

"I mean, I don't have to like him, do I?"

26

A BONE CRUNCHES under my foot.

My eyes squeeze shut, and I let out a shallow breath. I wasn't prepared to see where we'd find Death. I thought maybe it'd be a place with a few bodies or some dark forest. Not the place where Lucifer had marched out with his army of demons and slaughtered millions. An old human city, destroyed beyond repair. Almost everything was either rubble or overtaken by nature.

We're in a place of history right now. One that had never gotten the chance to be written down, but everyone would always know.

"You okay?" Kavon asks from beside me, stretching his closed mouth as he tries to hide a yawn. Both of us only got a half night's sleep, taking turns to keep watch in case Isra tried anything. Probably wasn't the smartest thing to do but we had to deal with it now. Kavon tried to persuade me into backing out of everything every time we'd switch turns, and despite his disapproval, he didn't bother leaving. Just like he'd been doing from the day he'd met me.

"It's hard to see," I say.

"Yeah."

I glance at his face. He doesn't seem bothered, but he has a shaking hand around his sword. I'd told him to put it away, but he insisted on holding it the entire time. I didn't blame him. Sure, we're walking during the day, but storm clouds are gathering. It's going to rain soon. Who knows what feral demons are lurking in the shadows, waiting to come out early and find their next meal?

We're not currently in a city, but a neighborhood. Tilted houses and crushed cars circle around us, with tall grass growing between the many cracks in the road. The countless bones covering the ground are hard to ignore. I trip over cracked pavement every five minutes.

And then there's Isra. He's walking a few feet in front of us, taking in the view. I don't know why I expect it to bug him, even just a little. And I don't know why it bothered me that it didn't. He's been here already. He's one of the things that caused all this destruction.

"What did I do?" he asks once I leave Kavon and catch up to him. "I can't even walk alone without being harassed."

"Shut up." The words flow out before I can stop myself. "Tell me the truth. Lucifer told me he's my father? Did you know?"

He stops walking and faces me, but he doesn't speak. Of course, he doesn't. What he does do is *stare*, tilting his head with those red eyes of his. And then I blush, like an idiot, and shame creeps up on me.

He scratches the back of his head, fumbling with his satchel full of weapons. "I had a feeling," he admits.

"Is it true?"

"Yes. Angels, pure ones, can't lie."

That's something new. Which means Lucifer really will destroy Morningstar. I didn't have any doubts, but now it's confirmed.

"Why didn't you tell me?" I ask, kicking a rock as we start walking again. "Is it because you didn't trust me? Because what would I have done with that information?"

"I didn't want you to feel bad on a hunch," he says. "Since he's the reason all the angels are dead. I'm not heartless."

I ignore the sting in my chest and roll my eyes. "I don't believe you. When did you decide to become a good person?"

"I also enjoyed the leverage."

"There he is." I sigh. "It would've helped with training."

He shrugs. "It doesn't matter. I wasn't sure. The soul was a risk, though. Technically, anyone can use a soul. But if their body can't bear it, well, they'd be heading to Hell. Archangels though, they could do it."

My eyes form slits. "So, I might have died."

"Maybe. But I highly believed you were his daughter. And I'm usually right."

"What gave it away?"

"He can do *so* many things. Among them, manipulate fire and make his skin boiling hot, two things that you do very well." He gives me a sad smile. "There's probably so much more you can do. So many things we could have discovered."

I frown. He didn't list the most important power of all. "Can Lucifer heal others?"

Isra's face turns blank, jaw clenched. A vein bulges in his neck before he relaxes. "I don't know. He's never done it. All I know is that he can heal himself and his vessel."

His vessel.

The cold wind cuts through my face as I trip. I place my hands on my thighs, letting out slow breaths. It takes everything in me to bite back my anger as Isra keeps going. It gives Kavon time to catch up to where I am.

"What happened to your feet? You need these wings more than I do."

"Yes," I say. "That would be amazing."

I think he notices something is wrong because he frowns. "Did that asshole say something?"

"Jeez." I close my eyes and stand upright, rubbing my temples. "No, he didn't."

Kavon says something but I don't pay attention to it. What I'm thinking right now is entirely selfish, but I have to ask Isra. If there's any chance of us succeeding, I have to take it.

Slipping on dust, ash, and bone as I skid downwards, I grab Isra's arm. He jolts and looks at me with wide eyes, and I'm a little surprised too. I never thought I'd touch him again after I healed him.

"Can we force him to change vessels?" I ask breathlessly.

Isra's lips part, confusion spreading across his face. "Sure." Hope floods my stomach. "If you damage his current vessel enough. He'd actually be weaker without one."

Just like that, it's gone. It finally sinks in that my dad is going to have to die. Isra steps away just as Kavon comes between us.

"What did you say to her?" Kavon says through his teeth. "Do you really have to make everything shittier than it already is?"

"I didn't say anything to offend her," says Isra, placing his hands in the air. "You should know better than anyone that I can't feed on her emotions unless we have an agreement. Besides, I'm sure she'd shove a ball of fire in my face if I pissed her off."

There's amusement laced in his voice. Kavon gives him a smile before shoving his chest. "Well, you've pissed me off." He lifts his hand, and Isra skids back without Kavon laying a hand on him.

"Stop." I move so I'm in between them. "Are you kids?"

"I wasn't doing anything." Isra shrugs.

Kavon's nostrils flare. "Does Death even exist? Or are you trying to buy time, so we don't kill you?"

Isra tilts his head, his lips curving into a bitter smile. He walks past both of us, strolling down the hill of bones we'd been standing on. He turns to us, stopping in the center of it all. Everything around him is pure destruction—piles of sand and gravel, pieces of houses and stone resting on the ground. Kavon and I share a look before following him. The clouds above close in on us as the shadows grow larger beneath our feet. I look up and a raindrop lands on my cheek.

"Stand in a circle," Isra tells us. "Death's in his dimension. We have to summon him here."

"How?" I ask as I step up beside him. It's probably

going to be something horrifying, like cutting off a limb or bringing some kind of gruesome offering.

"By each one of us telling our deepest secret."

Kavon lets out a huff of a laugh. "You're kidding, right? How is that going to summon him?"

"It makes you vulnerable." Isra stretches his arms backwards. "Have you ever heard the phrase 'bare one's soul?' Telling a secret is giving away your innermost self. In the place where Death, the very entity that collects souls, collected millions of them, it should summon him here."

I purse my lips and nod. I don't really have that many secrets. Both of them know my life story. "So, who goes first?"

"You're actually doing this?" Kavon scoffs, staring at me with wide eyes. "We're outside the wall, Mahi. We should just get as far from here as possible while we still can."

"You're free to leave." Isra gestures toward the distance. "It won't work if all of us aren't willing. But you'll be locked out."

Kavon glances between both of us several times, his mouth wide open. He struggles to form words. His eyes slowly turn glossy while black blood runs to his cheeks. "I'm not sure—"

"I'm a prince of Hell," Isra cuts in. "Surely mine is worse than yours."

Kavon rubs his forehead, fear evident on his face. His secret can't be that bad. But he's starting to breathe quicker and quicker. A few more raindrops land on my face, and I jump as the sky thunders.

"I'll tell mine first," I say, my sweating hands forming

fists. "Might as well get it over with." Kavon's shoulders relax. Both of them lean toward me, intrigued.

Healing has been my secret my entire life, but they both know about it. And they know about my dad and that I've been in containment. And the hideout? I can't tell them that. I can't tell anyone that.

I glance at Isra, looking away when he gives me a lopsided grin. I tense. No. That can't be it. But what else do I have? I sigh, wishing I couldn't talk. But I *have* to. I meet Isra's eyes.

"I wish that Isra was a good person," I say. His face softens. I watch his grin fade away. "So that the feelings I have for him, buried deep inside, the feelings that I loathe myself for, would be okay to have. But they aren't. Because he's a horrible person." I look away as soon as I finish, a heaviness filling the air for a full minute.

"Ouch." Kavon finally breaks the silence with a grin on his face. Well, at least I made him feel better.

"Well." Isra clears his throat. "I wish I was an angel. Now it's the hybrid's turn."

Kavon's eyebrows narrow downwards as his black veins bulge. His fists are so tight they turn pale. "Screw it. Aida—" his voice breaks. He takes a deep breath and closes his eyes before speaking again. "She was my first partner. The perfect girlfriend, actually. Knew everything about me and didn't tell a soul." Another shaky breath comes from his mouth. "And I'd been doing things that disappointed her. So, I stopped for her because I wanted her to be happy. But then one day . . . It'd been one week since I'd seen Aida. When we met at our usual place, that's when I found out a demon possessed her."

My heart breaks when he opens his eyes. They are

heavy with tears. Kavon clears his throat. "Aida barely had horns yet. She wasn't far gone. So while the demon was trying to murder me, I was trying to hurt the love of my life to the point where this disease would leave her body, but nothing worked. Eventually, it was either me or . . ."

"You have to say it," Isra says.

A lump forms in my throat as Kavon mutters the words. "I killed Aida."

Silence fills the air. Kavon doesn't look up at us, and I have no idea what to say. All I think about is how he froze when I asked about the photo. This is why he's so hopeless sometimes. And here I am, drowning in the thought of killing my dad, when Kavon's been holding this in the whole time.

Minutes pass, my eyes lingering on Isra, who stares intensely at the center of the circle, but nothing happens.

"We bared our souls. What could we have done wrong?" I ask. I glance at Kavon, whose eyes are red and puffy, but at least the crying is gone.

"Someone's secret didn't work," says Isra, side-eyeing Kavon. "The hybrid's maybe?"

"No," I say before Kavon can speak. "That was a secret. But Isra, yours wasn't. I already know you want to be an angel."

"Kavon didn't."

"Actually I did," Kavon says quietly, running his hand through damp hair. "I found out when we were at your house."

Isra sighs, letting out a huge breath. "Why do I even care? The truth is, I . . . I *was* an angel."

I don't get a chance to say anything. A chilling wind

presses against my face. Black fog seeps out of the ground and surrounds us, and I instinctively conjure up a ball of fire in my hand. The rain sizzles when it meets my flame. Thunder roars from the sky, and the second I blink, something stands in our circle from a puff of smoke.

The ends of its gigantic black robe have a faint smoke trail, like a fire had been snuffed out; the hood it wears makes it seem like it has no face. When I look at Death, there's just never-ending darkness. In his hand, there is a long weapon of some sort, with a hooked end. The fire vanishes from my hand, and my legs can't help but shake. Of all the things I've seen, ferals, demons, and so much torture, this sends shivers up my spine like never before.

Instantly, I start to look around for a way out of here. Thick grey fog surrounds us, and I have a feeling that it's more like a wall than anything else. A metallic smell fills the air, but I can't quite place what it is.

"Did you bring us here to die?" Kavon snarls at Isra.

"Obviously," he replies.

The back of my throat pains. "I can't tell if you're joking."

It doesn't matter. Death is close enough that one swing of his weapon could kill us all. He floats before us, at least seven feet tall, his hand stretching out to me. I don't move a single muscle as his black, claw-like finger grazes against my cheek. I try to focus on something else, my mind landing on the racing heartbeat paining my chest.

"At last," Death speaks with what sounds like one thousand voices, each echoing after the other. Child, woman, man. "I was awaiting your arrival."

I glance at Isra from the corner of my eye. He isn't saying anything, and I'm too scared to try to look around Death to get a good look at Kavon. "You know me?" I manage to croak out. I mentally punch myself. What a stupid thing to ask.

Death tilts his head. "Of course. Your very existence is by my doing."

"I—um. I-I don't—"

"Speak freely," Death tells me.

I desperately want to move my head away from his ancient finger. But instead, my question comes out in quivers. "How am I alive?"

"Because I made it so."

"But why?" I ask. "What makes me so special?"

Lightning flashes, a heavy sheet of rain pouring onto our faces. While all of us are getting drenched, the rain runs through Death like he's not even there. "You should not waste time. I have other needs to attend to. Why have you come here?" asks Death, moving his finger from my face.

"You can answer her question," Kavon says, his voice shaking like mine. "It'll take only a minute."

"You should silence yourself, Kavon. Unless you wish to lose your tongue."

Kavon doesn't say anything else. I'm not sure why Isra chooses to speak after that, but he says, "You know why we're here." He narrows his eyes at the ancient being, not a smidge of fear in his voice. My shoulders relax. If Isra isn't afraid, maybe I don't have to be. But it'll take a while for my clammy hands to go away.

"There's a reason I didn't answer your questions when we first met, Israkiel. Mahi alone shall speak."

Isra's face pales, and he meets my eyes, nudging his head for me to talk.

I press down the urge to ask my question again. Now my lips don't even want to move. I shiver from the cold, but also from staring at the darkness that is Death's face. He doesn't rush me, and eventually, I say, "We need your help in killing Lucifer. Is it true that you can kill him?"

"I can kill anyone."

"But you won't help us," Kavon speaks up. He's braver than I could ever be to talk after that threat. Death's shadowy head snaps toward him, a hiss coming out of his mouth. Even though there's no face to look at, I can sense the hostility. "Why would you help us kill the one thing that brings you countless souls."

"You should think before you speak," Death's voice thunders. "Reflect on what he's done to life. Perhaps, in the short term, he brings countless souls. But once he terminates all human life, there will be no more left to take. No more wars or murders. And the animals will be the next to go extinct. Their population has increased in these nineteen years with no hunters, but it won't be long before Lucifer unleashes his anger on them. Feral demons are already dwindling their numbers. He does not care for the natural order of things. And without natural order, this world will destroy itself. I'll be too powerless to save it."

"Sounds like humans are a problem on their own," Kavon mutters quietly.

"So, you gain power from both the living and dead. But—" A breath catches in my throat when Death turns toward me. "Why not kill him yourself?"

Isra sucks in a breath. He has history here; history he should've told me and Kavon.

"I would have done so the second he slaughtered all the angels, but I could not. I was foolish and made a deal with Lucifer in the past," Death says. "A deal to obtain something he stole in the first place, for his immunity against me."

I wipe off the rain that clouds my eyes. "Then how will you help us?"

He floats toward the ground, slamming his weapon into the many bones we stand on. "This scythe can turn into any weapon to kill any being."

I stare at it with wide eyes. A weapon that can kill anything. That's too much power. I shake my head. "And you'll just give it to us?"

"Yes."

"How do you know we'll give it back?" Isra asks, raising one eyebrow.

"It's simple." I can hear the grin behind the shadow. "We make a deal."

"What kind of deal?" I ask.

He stares directly at me. "I give you my weapon, and you must give it back once your goal is accomplished. If you don't meet your end of the bargain, I take your life. Your soul will give me more power. Perhaps enough for me to stall the demise of this world."

"But what if someone steals it?" Kavon asks.

"It will be useless since I did not give it to them," says Death. "A recent advancement."

"And what if we take off with the weapon?" Isra says.

"I won't. But how will you know it isn't lost somewhere?"

"You think I wouldn't be able to track my most

important possession?" Death asks Isra. Although, it doesn't sound like a question. I frown, jumping up when Death lowers himself to be face to face with me. "It's the only way. You asked me what made you so special—why I used a great amount of my magic to let you live. It is because Lucifer's weakness is his family. You are the only one who can return Earth to how it used to be. Now, do we have a deal?"

I glance at Isra, squeezing my fists repeatedly. "I don't know . . . what if we fail?"

"We'll just have to bring the weapon back," Isra reassures me.

And why would any of us, except Isra, who I'm sure doesn't want to die, need to keep the most dangerous weapon in the world? "Okay." Sighing, I nod my head. "We'll make the deal."

Death leans toward my ear. "I should tell you, if you use this weapon, you will lose part of your soul," he whispers.

I glance at Isra and Kavon and both give me confused looks. Gulping, I nod. "I understand."

Death backs up toward the center of the circle. His hand extends, and I grasp onto my throat. Something small comes out of my chest. I watch as a glowing orb floats from me, into Death's palm. "Part of your soul stays with me, so if I must, I may exterminate you at any time."

Lowering toward me, Death's scythe molds into a small knife. He divides half of the orb into two and places one on the knife. The weapon absorbs it. His black claw emerges from his sleeve, and I grab the weapon with a trembling hand.

"This will make it easier to carry," says Death. "It can mold into any weapon. A gun, sword, even a pencil, if the situation requires it."

I stare at the knife. It looks like any other thing, but if I narrow my eyes and really examine it, there's some kind of glow to it.

I'm knocked out of my thoughts when Isra opens his mouth. "One more thing. You need to open—"

Death's laugh sounds like a thousand cries. "Who knew a prince of Hell could be so predictable. I won't be opening the gate to Hell."

Isra's eyes flash. "But you told me if I brought Lucifer's heir—"

"That I'd show it to you." I chew on the inside of my cheek as Death motions us to follow. Isra teleported us here. He can't do the same to Hell? "Mahi will be the one opening it."

"What?" I let out a nervous laugh as we walk back up the hill of destruction, slipping on wet rocks and bones. "I don't know how to do that. Why on Earth would I know how?"

"You have Lucifer's essence inside you. You can."

I'm not sure what that means, but seeing how Isra looks annoyed and uncomfortable, I'll ask him later.

"I'm sorry, I can't do this," Kavon says from behind me. "I've been hiding from him for two years. Some vague plan is not going to defeat him. We'll all be killed."

I turn, frowning at the sorrowful look on his face. The connection between us is all I focus on—the tingling in my stomach; the invisible string screaming at me to move closer, to beg him not to leave because we need him.

"Go," I say. "Get your dad out of the city in case—just get him out."

He stares into my eyes, his face holding a pained expression that is full of regret, before he shakes his head and spreads his wings.

"Take this." He shoves his sword against my chest. I don't have time to protest. He backs away and shoots into the sky.

And just like that, he's gone.

My chest aches. For some reason, I don't want to do this anymore. I clear my throat and face Death. "So, once I learn how to open it, we can enter whenever we wish?"

"Once it's open, you must go in," Death says. "This door hasn't been opened in nineteen years. Hell is another dimension, which is why even demons can only get there by using it. This is the only one Lucifer does not guard or own. But he will know that it has been opened."

I frown at Isra. "Do you know where it will open?"

Isra shakes his head. "No idea. Hell's been transformed since Lucifer got the earth. There are different levels and some lower-tier demons that are stuck down there. We'll be lucky if we end up on my level. Although, I doubt he'd be generous enough to give mine a secret gate."

My stomach is heavy. It's only now hitting me that everything is happening so quickly. Isra's plan to train me over a few years is starting to sound better by the second, but this has to happen now. If we don't open this gate, the city will be destroyed. Countless people will die. And even if Lucifer wasn't going to do that, I can't hide forever. He'll keep sending his experiments after me. My life won't even be *lived*. Anyone I encounter will be in danger just by interacting with me.

We turn a corner, passing a grey brick wall with a giant gaping hole, with what seems like a garden of weeds inside. "You should be able to see the door," Death says.

I squint my eyes and I notice there is a single black door in the distance, with nothing attached to it. Surrounding it are masses of destruction from what must've been more buildings, stone, mud and gravel.

"I just have to open it?" I ask, tilting my head as if that'll give me a better look at the door. Now that we're closer, nothing has changed. It looks like an average door. One that anyone could open and stumble into.

"Yes," Death answers. That seems too easy. But maybe it is. Maybe not everything will be so hard. Or maybe that's too hard to believe.

I meet Isra's eyes. "But the plan."

"The plan is the same," he says. "We get in Hell, I'll phase us over to my realm. My followers will attack Lucifer's realm, which will allow us to sneak into his room and wait. Unless you want to leave like the hybrid just did, which I am still voting for."

I don't bother looking at Isra. My shaking hand moves toward the silver knob. I clench my teeth when I feel some kind of force between my palm and the door pushing against each other. Death doesn't say anything, so I carry on.

I gasp once I clutch the knob. It feels as though my hand is glued to it. And the energy I feel inside makes it seem like I could take on anything that comes in my path.

"Why is she shaking?" I hear Isra ask. I don't know what Death says as I open the door.

A sucking air takes hold of me, and I scream. I'm engulfed in a black void. Someone grabs my arm, but they follow me in and let go.

Landing with a thud, I groan when sand scrapes at my face. My eyes are squeezed shut, a blasting warmth taking over my body in seconds. Someone grabs my ankle this time. Their fingers are like grains, with a hint of softness. Light blinds my eyes, and I sit up quickly. Someone is still holding my ankle. If it's Isra, I swear he's going to—

"Help me."

I glance at my foot, gasping when I see a hand of ash hooked around my foot and a person forming from the ground.

27

THE MOUTH IS the most terrifying thing about this ash person. It screams when I kick its hand off, all of its particles cluttering back into the orange sand.

I stand up, but my eyelids can barely stay open. Hot, humid air pushes against my face. After seeing the orange sky above me, there are sudden booms of explosions in the distance with shadows of people roaming about. Cries of agony surround me, sweat sticking to my skin and ash floating through the air. Gritty hands stick out from the ground, some vanishing and others forming bodies before breaking apart and starting all over again.

And then there are the dark figures walking around, kicking down those struggling to reanimate themselves.

"Follow me." I jolt when someone touches my arm, grabbing their hand and twisting it behind their back. It's Isra. His hair clutches to his face as though he just had a shower. "Glad to know the training paid off. Now grab my wrist."

"Where are we?" I yell as I follow him, using my free hand to shield my head. My eyes roam the land, stepping over forming bodies and trying to find any trace of black wings. There are hills in the distance, embers sitting on the ground. I choke back a scream as an ashy face almost touches my leg.

"We're in Hell!" Isra yells back. "Land of The Forgotten! This is where Lucifer dumps anyone he wants to punish. We're going to have to cross it! Phasing only works in that shed."

I don't take the time to look where he's pointing. "These are all souls?" I question, but he doesn't respond. If they are, I can't imagine being in this wasteland And this is just one level of Hell, from what Isra has told me.

Isra faces me, his nose shining and sweat dripping from his chin. The heat is affecting him way more than it is affecting me. "Mahi, you need to focus. You see those shadowy things? The ones walking around?"

I nod my head.

"They've lost their humanity. And they won't hesitate to grab you and turn you to ashes."

"What are they?"

"Lower-level demons."

I bite my lip. "How do you kill them?"

"You can't here," Isra says. "This is their territory."

"Can't you order them to stop?"

He scoffs, shaking his head. "There's a reason they aren't on the earth. They're like animals. They don't listen to anyone. Let's go now! These demons are closing in around us."

Sure enough, the roaming shadows are looking at us, getting closer and closer while pushing the struggling ones on the ground. Soon, I'll be able to see what their hollow faces look like up close.

I take Isra's hand. He guides me through the land, pushing rocks and other things away with his telekinesis. It feels as though we're just walking deeper and deeper into this place. Laurel's mom told me what the desert looked like since she had lived there. This is exactly what I imagined, except ten thousand times worse.

"Isra—" I gasp. One of the ash people grabs my leg, their fingers hardening and their skin scratching my flesh.

I fall. Small rocks scrape at my face. The gravel, sand, ash, whatever is on the ground, warms my flesh. "Those things look like they are closer than before."

I hear no response from Isra. Irritation floods inside me. We may not be on each other's good side anymore, but he can still—

Something grabs my foot again. But this time, it's like hot steel. And it *burns*. I tear my ankle away and get up, blinking away tears. Something else grabs my shoulder and the same jolt of pain vibrates within me. I jerk and spin away. Hollow, orange eyes surround me, black bodies that look like strings of dark wood and vines put together. Each one has a dark, hollow smile that's covered in the black strings. One of them touches me again, its palm glowing orange underneath all the dark wood while I scramble away.

They are all around me. I have a pretty good idea that blasting them with fire won't do anything and Isra is nowhere to be seen. Did he leave me here to die? He couldn't have. Not while I have Death's scythe.

That's it! Digging through my pockets, I take out the

dagger. In a blur, it turns into a lightweight gun. I pull the trigger just as one of those things lunges at me.

Its entire body freezes and starts to melt immediately. As I continue shooting at the countless others pouncing on me, there seems to be more and more showing up. They scrape at my clothes and scratch at my face. I wince at their burning touch. This weapon isn't going to be enough. I'm going to be overwhelmed.

The closest demons to me suddenly fly in the opposite direction. Relief floods my stomach. I turn and almost collide with Isra. He grabs both my arms.

"I'm disappointed," he says. "I thought I trained you better than this."

"Let me go." He complies, and I shoot a demon behind him a few times after missing twice. "Thank goodness it's you."

He raises an eyebrow, a smile playing on his face. "Never thought I'd hear that. Now let's go."

I take his hand again, and we sprint for what feels like forever. After creating some distance, we burst into an empty, one-room cabin. I pull my arm from Isra's and start healing myself.

"We need to leave, Mahi," Isra says.

"Then let's go," I say. "Oh wait, yes, I give you permission."

I take Isra's hand. And just like that, the hot air is replaced with cool freshness. Dark brown takes the intense orange's place. Rows of shelves filled with all kinds of books surround us, and bright chandeliers hang above. The shelves go all the way up to the roof, where there is a second floor with even more.

"Where are we?" I ask, resting against one of the bookcases.

"My realm," says Isra. "But as a precaution, I didn't phase us to the throne room. Time works differently in Hell. Lucifer *may* already know what's going on."

I pull out a book from the shelf behind me. *"The Ultimate Animal; The Fox."* I can't help but laugh. "Don't tell me all your books are about foxes. Man, you really have an obsession."

"You're in the animal section," Isra mutters, walking toward a large door with beautiful silver engravings. "Now come on. I instructed my second, Vadreel, to summon everyone in the throne room. There will be demonic animals, so please ignore them."

"I'll try my best." I roll my eyes. "Hopefully I don't bump into a hellhound."

"They are actually not invisible here."

Leaving the room, we walk along a wide hall with a bright red carpet. Purple walls surround us with yellow, red, and pink roses hugging them. I'm surprised they look fresh and alive.

"I didn't choose how this looks, if that's what you're thinking," Isra says.

"I wasn't thinking that," I lie.

"I can sense your embarrassment without even using my power."

I scowl and, for some reason, mutter an apology. "Sorry."

"Everything here is to remind me of what I can never be," says Isra. His voice lowers at the end of the sentence.

I freeze at the familiar pull in my stomach. A warmth

that makes me safe. It makes me feel like I belong. It's a feeling I only got when I was close to Kavon, but he isn't in Hell, which means Isra has been stashing away an angel for nineteen years. I'm not sure if that's good or bad, but I'm eager to meet someone from my species.

He stops in front of two huge doors. Golden statues of what I think are hellhounds sit on both sides. They actually look kind of cute until you notice their furious eyes and sharp teeth.

"It's too quiet," says Isra. "There should be guards stationed here, but it feels like the entire castle is empty."

For a slim second, a breeze presses against the back of my neck, but I don't react. I wish I did because quickly after, Isra and I are both pushed forward and we slam into the doors that open up. My palms ache from the impact.

"Nice to see you again." My eyes widen at Zyanya's voice. She walks in front of us, taking a fist full of my hair and forcing me up. I screech.

"That's enough!" Lucifer's voice echoes from further in the room. My eyes blur from painful tears, and I can barely see anything, but I can still comprehend who stands beside him. My heart stills and my lungs ache for air, yet I can't breathe.

Kavon stands beside my father, with no shackles or chains. He wears a metallic black suit with a tint of blue and a circle in the center of his chest. A special suit that isn't of human technology or resources. He isn't a prisoner. Which means, he turned us in.

28

IsRA and I stand in front of Lucifer. The room is eerily quiet. All I do is stare at the red carpet. There's no point in examining the room for escape routes. I'm going to die now, and my father will be forced to watch as Lucifer does it.

A knot forms in my throat. I thought I'd be ready when I saw him again, but as I stare at our shared brown skin and dark brunette hair, pointed nose, and big eyes, I have to fight the urge to cry. He's trapped in there, and I have no idea how to get him out.

All this time, thinking he was dead without really knowing. If only I could talk to *him* one more time. Instead, he'll be watching himself kill me.

"I'll be honest." The king of Hell breaks the silence. He sits on Isra's throne, which I didn't get a very good look at since I didn't want to accidentally meet Kavon's eyes. "I didn't expect you to try to kill me, Mahi."

"You—" I clear my throat, ignoring the urge to cough from how scratchy it is. "I had no choice."

"There's always a choice." I hear him get up. "Like Kavon. I knew he'd come back to me eventually."

I finally force myself to look up. My watering eyes lock onto Kavon's. His jaw is clenched as Lucifer pats him on the back. He stands next to another prince of Hell, who I assume must be Ozanith.

He's so beautiful, but chills spread across my arms at how horrifying he looks at the same time. Long white hair cascades past his shoulders, glowing white pupils piercing at me with a bored expression, and black veins coming from his eyes and spreading to the rest of his face. He has darker grey skin compared to the other royals. His matching grey horns tower high before curving backwards. Isra looks like an elite demon, but Ozanith is something else entirely. He looks like he truly is a *prince*.

Besides him, Zyanya is the only other royal in the room. Twelve other demons, if they even are, stand around the room. They have black masks covering their faces with lines of gold forming swirling designs, and their fully black eyes glare straight ahead. It's similar to the mask Isra wore when we rescued Kavon, but not exactly.

I hope Kavon is smelling my negative emotions right now because all I can do is shake from the anger and betrayal.

"Why?" I ask. My voice comes out in a frail whisper. "I don't understand. I saw you minutes ago."

"Time is slower in Hell," Lucifer says. He frowns, his left eyebrow twitching just like my father's would when he was disappointed in me. "Everyone always wants something, Mahi. Kavon is no different. He came and told me your plan in exchange for his freedom. It's too bad he lost something I needed."

The sword. That's why he gave it to me. The second Kavon left, he probably went straight to Lucifer. But he still gave me his weapon. A weapon Lucifer wants desperately. *But why?*

A vein pops in Kavon's forehead. He didn't truly get his freedom. He's stuck with Lucifer.

"Zyanya, take Israkiel to the dungeons under my castle," Lucifer says. "I need to check on Earth quickly. Ozanith, you know what we need to do."

I'd almost forgotten about Isra. I turn my head to see him staring straight at me. His red eyes are glossy, but no tears cover his cheeks. His eyebrows point downwards, and I realize that he won't be able to save the demons now because he'll be dead.

Zyanya comes up behind him. She doesn't look so malicious this time. With a frown, she places cuffs on Isra and takes him outside.

When I turn my head back, I meet Ozanith's chilling eyes. He stands right in front of me, an exhausted smile plastered on his face. "I have the honor of escorting you. Allow me to phase."

"No." I hate that it feels as if I'm in containment, shaking as I wait for some kind of punishment.

Ozanith's silver eyebrows narrow downwards, and an annoyed sigh comes from him before he grabs my arm. Instantly, it's as if my flesh is ice. I try to hold it out, but can't.

I scream. "Okay!"

The ice instantly shatters. I wish I could reach into my pocket and kill Ozanith with Death's scythe, but I can't. Even if Kavon doesn't attack me, the twelve other demons here will. I'll never get to use it on Lucifer.

"Where are you taking me?" I ask.

Ozanith says nothing. Instead, he grips my arms tightly. I take one last second to glance at Kavon, whose eyes remain glued to the ground.

The jump causes me to lose my balance, but we aren't anywhere I thought we'd be. A bright blue sky surrounds me. I gasp when I look down at the puff of cloud I stand on, my head spinning. How in the world am I *floating*?

It doesn't matter. Looking up, I meet golden eyes.

I spin around as I search for Ozanith. Or anyone at all, but there's no one here. No one but the fallen archangel.

"Don't be alarmed," Lucifer says. Hearing him use my father's voice should sound reassuring, but it only makes my bones rattle.

He closes the small distance between us so that he's only a foot away. He trails a hot finger against my face as he circles around me. I flinch when he tucks a strand of hair behind my ear.

"Where are we?" I ask, trying to make my voice confident, but my words come out cracked and quiet. No matter what, I can't bring myself to stand strong. Instead, I'm Three-nine-seven, the number back in containment who would act like she wasn't weak. Yet deep down, a tornado of fear lingered every second of the day.

He stops behind me. I tense when he places a hand on my shoulder. "Where you've always wanted to be."

My fingers twitch, but I hold myself back. I'm not sure if the weapon can transform into what can easily kill Lucifer, but he'll grab my wrist as soon as I move it to my pocket.

So instead, I try to buy time. "Where did Ozanith go?"

"I wanted to give you something nice for all the birthdays I missed," he says. I lick my lips, although my tongue feels dry as I try to avoid thinking about that dream. He couldn't know about it. It was just a nightmare. But as if he reads my mind, he walks up to me and says, "That memory in your dream was taken from me. I never got a chance."

"As if you care." I back up, putting space between us.

He frowns. "You don't like it?"

My heart pounces as the clouds turn into concrete. Laughter surrounds me, and there are more children than I've ever seen running around. There are different kinds of large structures everywhere and small booths with people serving food. While I'm stunned looking at all the happy folk around me, I don't notice Lucifer behind me until he pats my back.

"This is a carnival," he says. "I can take you to one if you'd like. That over there is a rollercoaster. I think you'd enjoy it."

I say nothing as we walk over to one of the booths. A middle-aged man hands what looks like a blue cloud on a stick to a young girl. I watch her run off, trying to examine the happiness on her face. "This isn't real."

"I got you this."

My heart skips a beat, and I turn around to see

Kavon holding a drink out to me. There's a small smile on his face, and he's wearing entirely different clothes.

"K-Kavon?" I don't know how to react when he wraps an arm around me and kisses my cheek. A blush forms on my face, and a fuzzy feeling warms in my chest. "But you were just—I don't understand."

"This could be real. You just have to give me a chance," Lucifer says. Kavon backs away from us, only for Lucifer to grab my hand. I let out a relaxing breath. "My greatest creation," he mutters.

I glare up at the sky, staring into the bright sun that's blocked by clouds, and I realize that I can't feel anything. Not the heat, wind on my skin, or Kavon and I's bond. Nothing at all. All these happy people around me, it's not real. It'll never be real.

I pull away. "This is a lie. You're a disease. A monster. The one thing on this planet that every single creature despises. Even your own demons! The only thing you care about is making others suffer."

He gives me an annoyed stare. So do the other fake people around us. "I tried to find you. I honestly did! But your human father was a step ahead of me. I didn't know when I used him as a flesh bag that I'd conceive you. I just wanted to let off some steam. He used his magic to hide you."

Even though I'd been waiting for it, the reveal stabs at my heart. "So, he really was a mage."

"He was one of the strongest. Probably the only thing he was good at. He got past the wall with it," Lucifer continues. "And when he got to wherever your hideout is, he placed a magical barrier. I underestimated him."

"Why didn't he tell me?" I ask, looking away. What

reason could he have had? Dad told me everything. He could've taught so many of us how to use magic so we could fight back. I wouldn't be here right now if he did. Instead, he told me to hide my healing powers. I could've spent years developing my skills.

Lucifer smiles, like he's proud of me. "Because he's the one who is the true monster."

I scowl, raising my hand before I can stop myself. I send a ribbon of fire his way, which he evades easily by turning to the side. I notice that wild look in his eyes when he faces me again. It's crazier than the one I'd seen in Isra.

"Yes!" A gigantic grin spreads across his face. "That was amazing."

The carnival disappears, and once again, we're floating in the sky. I form tight fists and send more columns of flame, but they do nothing. Lucifer either avoids the fire or fades it away with his arms. The more I do it, the more prickles form along my body, like small needles slowly digging into my skin.

He sends a wave of fire my way, catching me off guard, and I lose my balance. My heart almost leaps out of my chest when I face down. Seeing the endless sky causes my head to pound. I close my eyes as the pressure builds behind my skull.

My lungs, throat, mouth, everything burns with pain. "I can't do this anymore," I whisper to myself, bending down to one knee. I send another blast of fire, but it's so weak that it doesn't even reach him. I can't fight. All my energy is going to waste. "Please," I beg, wiping my glossy eyes. "I'm here. Just let my dad go."

Lucifer lets out a small laugh. "It's actually quite

funny. I feel him in the back of my mind, itching for a way out."

"I get it," the words start to vomit out of my mouth. "You don't know what it's like to love someone. I'll do anything, just please, let him go."

"You're special, Mahi." I force myself to look up, expecting to see a smirk on his face. Instead, he's frowning. "I know you don't believe it, but I do love you. I'd never abandon you, unlike what happened to me. And I truly wish your uncle, Michael, could see you. I know he'll thank you someday for your sacrifice."

"Uncle?" the words feel empty in my mouth. "Please—"

As a last resort, I form a fire sword while he forces me up, but he waves his hand and it dissipates. I try reaching into my pocket, but he grabs my arm.

"Come on Mahi." He shakes his head. "You really think I wouldn't know it's with you?"

A sharp pain resides in my wrist before it goes limp. He does the same to my other one, and a searing pain in my neck takes over. The world spins, spots painting my vision.

This is it. He's going to kill me in the most painful way possible.

Burning coughs come out of my mouth when Lucifer releases his hold, tears coming out of my eyes. But after only a few seconds, every part of me is scorching and freezing at once. I can no longer move or talk. It's as if my skin is being ripped from my body, and I can't move. All I can see is my dad—Lucifer's—intense glare as he holds both his hands out to kill me.

"Goddammit, I'm sorry," Lucifer says. His eyes are watering, a single tear strolling down his cheek.

I try to speak. But instead, I inhale deeply to replenish the fading life inside me. Lucifer opens his mouth again, just as a knife cuts through his shoulder.

29

ALL THE ENERGY I'd lost is sucked back into my body. One second, I'm in the clouds with limp legs and drowsy eyes. Next, I'm on my knees, looking down at a red carpet and breathing like I had just been born. I try to take in as much air as I can, heaving into the floor. When I look up, I meet red eyes.

Isra is speaking to me, but his face is a blur. Sharp, hot pain stings in both my swelling wrists. Liquid fire flows inside my skin, burning until there is a slight numbness in my hands. It could've been worse. Instead of breaking them, he could've cut them off.

"Shit—" I close my eyes, tears flowing down my cheeks as I lower my face onto my hands and heal them as soon as I meet my flesh. As the bones crack and twist back into place, I remember what's really going on.

"Dad!" I get up quickly and reach out toward the body on the floor, but Isra grabs my hands, wrapping an arm around my chest.

"That is not your dad," he whispers in my ear, backing us away.

Dark walls hung with paintings of flowers surround us. One painting of a single black rose covered in thorns, is noticeably larger than the rest. Huge windows reveal a red sky. The ceiling is higher than what a normal room would have, and as I follow the crimson carpet, I notice the white bed. Beside it, Ozanith lies on the floor with his neck in an unnatural position.

"I never should've sent Zyanya alone. You're an idiot." Dad—Lucifer heals his shoulder, getting up slowly and leaning against a large desk. The knife had gone through his body. "You always have been. You've signed your death sentence, Israkiel."

"Then I'm not alone." He takes Death's weapon from my pocket, which forms into a small blade, and places it against my neck. An unsteady breath leaves my mouth. One cut and I'm dead.

I struggle against Isra's hold. "Trust me," he whispers.

Trusting him in the past has never done much, and I don't know what's going on, but I find myself nodding my head, leaning back against Isra's chest.

Lucifer flinches before his nostrils flare and he snarls. "Release her. Let my daughter go now."

Isra is rigid. With Lucifer's influence, this is hard for him, yet no one moves. Lucifer clenches his jaw, taking a step toward us and bringing his arm out. The blade twists in Isra's hand. I whimper as Isra presses the blade harder against my flesh which makes Lucifer stop in his tracks. Even if he has telekinesis like Isra, he won't get the knife without cutting my skin.

"Why?" Isra asks through his teeth. "You were tearing her soul out. What's so different if I kill her like this?"

"Give her to me," Lucifer says quietly, flames engulfing his eyes. "That's an order."

My chest hurts from my racing heartbeat. I don't know how Isra doesn't sink into the floor from fear. "No." He exhales. "I'm going to walk out of here with her. Where's the portal? In your throne room?"

"Portal—" I accidentally lean into the blade. I've never feared more for my life than in this moment.

Lucifer glares at him before his face softens. He takes a step toward us again and smiles when Isra doesn't do anything this time. If he did, I'd be dead. "You're bluffing."

"You need her alive," says Isra, tightening his grip around my chest. "It wasn't only her soul you were taking, was it? And why would you need something other than her soul? Where's the portal? We're leaving."

"And how are you going to do that?" Lucifer's lips curve up. He's enjoying this because he knows he's going to win. There's no way they'll tell us how to leave. There's no way we're getting out of here. My palms turn to fists, and I start scanning the room for some kind of advantage for the fight that's bound to happen. "I presume you killed—or knocked out—the knights like Ozanith here, but every portal out of Hell is guarded. And the hellhounds won't listen to you either anymore."

"You think I'm brainless," Isra says. "And maybe I am, for following you all those millennia ago. But that's why I didn't know what you're up to, right? And that's how I didn't know you're trying to resurrect Michael."

Lucifer's face falters for a second.

Archangel Michael?

He turns to one of the windows just as the sound of a large explosion goes off. He presses his lips together while his head subtly bobs up and down. "What did you do?"

"The demons are growing restless," Isra says. "And I'd tell you, but your ears were always absent. What do you think they'd do if they found out you've been lying to them this whole time? I mean that isn't unlikely of you, but trying to revive an *angel?*"

"I saved them all—"

"Maybe everyone else enjoys being a demon but I'll never forgive you for turning me into this."

"Whatever makes you feel better, Isra." Lucifer sighs. "You're the one who chose me."

"I didn't think I'd get cast out of my home!" Isra's voice quivers, and I think he's forgotten that I'm here. My fingers wrap around the hand holding the blade, but it doesn't budge. "I'm not the only one who thinks you shouldn't be in power anymore. Now, where is the portal! I won't ask again."

Lucifer tilts his head and smiles with all his teeth. His skin glows and his entire body engulfs in flames as he flicks his wrist. Death's weapon shoots out of Isra's hands and onto the floor. Right beside Lucifer. "Emotional as always."

For a second, Isra is speechless before he spins me around. His eyebrows narrow as he places his hands on my shoulders. "Okay, time to go."

The last thing I hear is a sharp, cry-like scream. Just like that, we're in a different room. Isra falls to the floor, landing with a thud and panting like he'd been choked to death. "I forgot—how scary—" He coughs and clears his throat. "—he gets."

Even in darkness, I can see the giant, circular table sitting in the center of the room with what looks like a dull map of the earth Laurel had shown me once. It never fails to stun me. What seems like a small world is far larger than I'll ever get to see. Huge bookcases stand against the walls and some crystals hang from the ceiling. "Where are we?"

"This is the war room," Isra breathes out, brushing his pants and walking over to me. "Damn," he whistles, holding a finger up. "One second." He sucks in a huge amount of air. "Okay, I'm good. Now, are you . . . okay?"

I glare at him, massaging my neck. "Why would you bring us here?"

He presses his palms against his thighs, leaning forward, still trying to recover some air. "It hasn't been used in years." He shrugs. "A lot of us are sick of this place." He wipes his head and walks toward two large doors. "Now come on, we're leaving."

I scoff. "No way."

Looking over his shoulder, he groans. "You saw him go full on fire too, didn't you? Or am I suddenly blind?"

I sigh. "I saw him."

"He's probably a phoenix right now," Isra says between huge breaths. "Which, if you don't know—"

"I know what it is!" I cut him off, walking in front of him and crossing my arms.

"I called off most of the demons but sent enough here to distract him—"

"You sent them here to *die?*"

"It's a sacrifice to get you out of here."

"I don't think Kavon is against us. I need to talk to him."

Isra sighs. "I'm going to be honest with you, Mahi—"

"—like you always are."

"—I don't care about him, and neither should you. Maybe you don't know how bad we have it right now, but Lucifer knows our entire plan. If you're not scared, you should be. And we should get out of here while we can."

I stare at him in disbelief. "You don't think I'm scared? I've been scared this entire time!" I shake my head. "You know what's at stake here. If we leave without killing him, Lucifer will destroy the city. He'll keep making those monsters. He'll hunt me down to the ends of the planet."

"And destroy hundreds of thousands of vessels and food," Isra hums, tapping his foot. "But it's just *one* city. You don't need to die over it."

"Are you—" I close my eyes and rub my temples. He's a demon. Somehow, I always forget that. "Okay. You leave, but I'm staying here. I'm not letting so many people die for me. One life for thousands is not worth it. Besides, out there wouldn't be much of a life anyway."

And my dad doesn't deserve to be tortured anymore. But Isra doesn't need to know about that. He won't understand.

"You should know by now that I'm not leaving without you." There it is. My heart skips a beat, and I hate myself for it.

"Why not?" I ask, ignoring the nauseous feeling in my stomach. I shouldn't care what his response will be. But I do, and it haunts me.

"Are you nervous?"

My mouth drops before I scowl. "You said you wouldn't do that anymore."

"And you believed me?"

I run my fingers through my hair anxiously. "Seriously, Isra. Why don't you just go?"

He scratches the back of his head, looking away. "I have my reasons."

"What was all that talk with Lucifer?" I push on, tilting my head as I lean forward. "Why do you have this weird obsession with me?"

"Mahi—"

"I don't want excuses."

Isra mutters something under his breath before clenching his jaw. "Okay, fine, you want the truth?"

"Yes!"

He sighs and rubs his horns. "You're the last, *pure* angel, Mahi."

"But I'm half human—"

"I don't care. There's nothing demonic in you. And I give a shit because thousands of years ago, when I was an angel and lived in Heaven, I rebelled against—it doesn't matter. I rebelled with Lucifer, and we, along with thousands of other angels who made the same mistake, were cast out of Heaven. It tore us apart. We lost our bodies. Lucifer gave some of us, like me, new ones with his magic, but I don't want to be like this. Some twisted version of an angel. I used to be able to control air, Mahi. You don't understand how envious I am of you. So yes, I will let a whole city die for you. I will let my entire damn army die for you. You *cannot* die."

Just like that, a painful tightness forms in the back of my throat. I think my lungs somehow grew smaller because it's harder to breathe. "So, if I wasn't an angel, then . . ."

"Then you'd be nothing." His lips curve down. "I'm sorry."

"No, you're not." I shake my head, my face turning red. I'm the biggest idiot. "Let's try to find the portal. Don't worry about Kavon. If we don't find him, he'll find me. Maybe that'll be a problem, maybe it won't."

"Through the angel bond." Isra nods his head. "I remember it. I yearn for that feeling again."

Of course, he knew about it this entire time. He just loves his mind games. "Do you have any weapons?"

Isra shakes his head. "Why not use your fire?"

"Because I can still use something else," I say through my teeth. "And all of these demons are wearing suits. I don't want to kill them if the human inside isn't fully gone."

Sighing, he fumbles through the bag. "All I have is the bracelet you made me bring and two knives." He takes out a small blade and hands it to me.

I twist it around in my hand. "Okay, so we get the scythe, and then as soon as we get to Lucifer, put the bracelet on him." I close my eyes, waiting for him to grab my arm and take us back to the room, but nothing happens. "Are you going to take us or let me look like an idiot?"

"You're already an idiot, Mahi." I roll my eyes. "But that was the last one in me. Remember how I was dying a few minutes ago? One more and I might pass out, which I won't allow to happen. I know I look all-powerful, but right now, I feel like a sloth."

I don't know what that is, but I still press my lips together, groaning. "Then what do we do now?

"Don't worry. I know where the elevator is." He smirks, heading to the door.

"Elevator?"

"Well, I was under the assumption that we'd be leaving through the portal, which is on this floor. Lucifer's room is far up."

"I meant, what's an elevator?" I lower my voice as I get close to the door. Isra places his head against it as if listening.

"You'll find out. Now stay close to me. You have to look like my prisoner."

I don't want to touch him, but I know I have to. Ignoring the urge to hide out in this room, I allow Isra to place both my hands behind my back. He opens the door, and I swallow down the lump in my throat as he pushes me out.

We walk on a detailed black carpet while glowing lamps hang above us. As we pass more circular, wooden doors, freaky-looking silver armored statues stand between each one. One of them has slanted eye slits, giving the impression that it's angry. Hopefully, it doesn't come to life.

"Shouldn't there be guards?" I whisper. Isra shushes me and, instead of continuing straight, we turn a corner, halting just as a demon almost collides into us. Flame forms in my hand.

Shoving me behind him, Isra throws his hands out. Zyanya slams against the wall at the same time, knocking over one of the armored statues. Her tail almost whips Isra in the face. "Seriously?"

"Mahi slit her throat."

I walk up beside him, getting rid of my fire. "You want to kill her?"

"It won't kill her." His arms quiver. "Hurry up, she's heavy."

"Wow, that's kind," Zyanya says through her teeth.

My palm sweats against the knife as I creep closer to her. Of course, I'm too short to reach her neck. She must be taller than Isra. Although she can't top Ozanith. "Can you lower her?"

Zyanya smirks as Isra grunts. As I raise my arm, I make the mistake of glancing at her face. I gasp when her eyes swell with darkness.

She does something I don't suspect and shoots blood out of her eyes. I drop the knife, covering my burning face with my hands just as her tail wraps around my throat.

"I can't see," I cry out, gasping for air while her tail tightens.

"It's okay, Mahi!" Isra says. "Calm down. Are you really going to do this, Zyanya?"

"Were you actually going to slit my throat? After I let you go? You know how long that takes to heal!"

"You used to do that to me whenever I pissed you off."

"Oh, so you're pissed off?"

Isra groans. "You going to turn us over to Lucifer then?"

"No, I—" She drops me onto the floor. "Screw you, Isra. Just get out of here."

I repeatedly blink. Isra helps me up, and darkness begins to fade away. The burning is still there, but subtle.

"Really?" he asks.

"I didn't take you to the cells when you told me that crap earlier. You're right, okay. Don't hold it over my head and get out of here. But if someone else sees you, I'm not doing shit."

She walks off, and Isra brings his lips to my ear. "Come on," he whispers as my vision clears. "It's just at the end of the hall."

He hands me the knife, guiding me through the rest of the hall until we reach some kind of box. Shoving me inside, I rest against the steel walls. Heavy breaths escape my mouth, and I lose my balance when the small room we're in moves.

Isra smirks. "This is an elevator. Much better than stairs."

"How is this moving?" I ask, standing upright. "Is it magic?"

He laughs. "No, it's not magic."

"Then what?"

Shaking his head, Isra leans against the side of the door. I copy him and lean against the other side. "I'll tell you later. Right now, we have to worry about what might be on the other side of that door."

"Lucifer?"

"Maybe. If he's there, we run. Don't even argue with me."

"But—"

"I took care of the knights outside his room. If there are new ones, then we take them out."

The door opens before I can ask any questions. I hold onto my knife tightly and follow Isra through the hall. One side is lined with large, circular windows. I take a second to look out at the red sky. From here, I can see the extremely heavy winds. It looks like a twisted version of Earth. Broken roads are scattered around, with hundreds of destroyed cars and buildings that fade away in a red fog.

Isra quickly distracts me by ordering me to move faster. The other side is similar to the last floor, a row of different rooms with odd-looking pieces of armored statues between each door. Occasionally, there's some kind of painting.

At the end of the hall is a large door, where two bodies are covered in armor sitting on the floor.

"These are the knights?" I whisper as Isra slowly opens the door.

"Two of four," he tells me. I'm about to shout out a question but stop myself and follow Isra into another hall. The walls are black, with a high ceiling and beautiful, shining lights.

"It's his private quarters," Isra says. "Here's his room."

I step over two more bodies, ignoring my clammy hands. We were just in here, and yet a chill runs up my spine as I step inside. Lucifer's nowhere to be seen, which only confirms my suspicion that he's out there in that crazy storm.

"Let's hurry." I flinch as Isra closes the door, a loud bang echoing in the room. "He's not going to be outside forever."

The first thing my eyes land on is Death's blade. "It's here," I tell Isra. I'm about to grab it when something cool grows around my feet. My shoes try to move past the ice, but it's as if they've turned to stone. I glance back at a frozen Isra, a block of ice over his body. Shiver's spread across my skin as Ozanith walks in front of me. I form fire and he catches my wrist. His finger trails over to my wrist.

I meet his icy eyes, but he doesn't say anything. His lips curve down slightly, black blood staining his cheek. I try to pull away, but his grip tightens, and I let out a hollow breath as ice forms on both my arms.

"Where's Lucifer?" I gulp.

"Taking care of something," Ozanith says. He tilts his head, not saying anything else.

"What was he doing to me before?" I ask, my voice quivering. "What is he going to do?"

Ozanith narrows his eyes. "Something he's been trying to do for years."

"What else could he possibly want?"

He doesn't speak. All he does is examine my face. His mistake. Quickly, I heat up my hands to break through the ice and punch him in the crotch. Ozanith grunts in pain. I melt the ice off my feet and create some distance between us. Glancing at Death's weapon, right beside him, I form two flaming whips.

A smile forms on Ozanith's face. "I'm surprised. It would've been interesting to see Lucifer mentor you."

My eyes don't leave him. For some reason, he can control ice. And I don't know what I can do against that besides using my amateur fire. I'm in over my head. My heart feels as though it's going to break from my chest when he takes a step closer, the smile gone. I resist the urge to look back. Somehow, I have to melt Isra free. That's the only way I'll be getting out of here.

Ozanith and I stare at each other for what feels like

hours, none of us making the first move. I don't know why he doesn't just break me with the centuries of training he has, unless he's actually afraid of me.

"Why did he take my dad of all people?" I ask, my voice shaking with anger.

"Your father and Lucifer. They have a history. This is personal to him," Ozanith says in the same haunting tone he's been using this whole time.

"He has history with some random human?" I question. "I find that really hard to believe."

"It's always the small things that seem to make no sense." Oh shit, he's getting closer. "You're in the lowest level of Hell. And yet, Lucifer having a relationship with a human is the thing that puzzles you?"

"What puzzles me is why you're helping him!" I raise my voice. "I've been in a containment center, and Isra is right. Soon enough, there won't be any humans left. There'll be too many demons with nothing to feed off of."

"You might be right about that," Ozanith says. "But it doesn't matter."

He sprints at me and lunges, his fist making contact with my face. I go flying into the wall and land with a thud on the floor. My head spins, but my eyes widen when Ozanith forms an ice shard and comes running toward me. Quickly, I make a whip that grabs his leg, and I pull. Ozanith trips and lands on the floor. I get up, ignoring the ringing in my ears, and form a huge fireball in my right hand. With my jaw clenched, I jump in the air. Right before I can strike him, he rolls to the side and gets up.

He grabs my arm and spins me around before

throwing me into a painting. A surge of pain comes over me. I place a hand on my stomach, sucking in a breath. I think I just broke a rib. Quickly, I heal myself.

My eyes water as shards of ice come my way. I cry out when one of them pierces my arm.

"This is pathetic," Ozanith says.

Sucking in a breath, I twirl my hands until a tornado of fire forms around me and I make my way to Isra. At least now, I can melt the ice around him, and maybe Ozanith's shards will melt before coming to me. I send a large ball of fire his way, but he is too fast. He's had hundreds of years of practice. I've only had a few months.

That last attack takes a lot out of me, and I struggle to breathe. My hands shake as the vortex around me slowly fades away, and Ozanith is getting closer by the second, barely showing any of his power.

I'm still catching my breath when Ozanith is knocked off his feet. I tilt my head in confusion.

"Let's get out of here." Isra grabs my arm with his sopping wet hands and groans when I pull away. I gulp when I taste blood and my body slouches from exhaustion. "The first fight is always tiring. You'll learn to control it."

"We can't—"

"Mahi, listen to me—"

"You should've stayed frozen," I say with slight annoyance. I glance back to see Ozanith standing as ice builds around him.

I spin toward Isra, wiping my face. "I can't beat him. I can't. But the weapon—"

Isra licks his lips, looking down at me. "We can do this."

"No. I-I can't—"

"Just like we practiced." He gives me a small smile, his eyebrows bending down. He throws his arm out. Ozanith flies into a bookcase. "Okay?"

"Maybe you can," I say.

"He's pulling off a show." Isra grabs both my shoulders. "His ice depends on how much moisture there is in the air." He grabs his knife from the floor and throws it at one of the windows. The glass shatters and a wave of heat fills the room.

A sliver of ice smashes into Isra, sending him backward. My feet start to freeze again, but this time, the ice is thinner. Weaker.

Ozanith's walking up to me quickly, his jaw clenched while a stick of ice forms in one of his hands. Up close, I'll be able to do nothing.

Forming fists, I send a barrage of fireballs his way. He dodges them, and a breath catches in my throat when he raises his blade.

With as much fire as I can conjure, I slam it into his face. Just as his blade comes down to my left wrist.

Ozanith falls to the floor, his face a crisp. At the same time, a deafening shriek releases from my mouth. Beside him is my hand, blood splurging out of it.

30

Sharp pains of anguish run up my left arm. I clutch my left wrist, warm blood trickling between my fingertips like a waterfall as I fall onto one knee.

Breathe. Holy shit. Just breathe. I try to focus on anything, but it feels as if I'm frozen in time.

"Mahi?" a muffled voice calls my name. I lose my balance and fall back. Somehow, I don't hit the ground. I feel someone's cold hands holding me up. "Mahi, heal yourself."

Tears roll down my cheeks. I groan in searing torture as I meet Isra's eyes. "H-h—"

"Here's your hand." A shot of pain goes through my arm like electricity when he places something against my open wrist. I move my head down but he grabs my chin. "Don't look. Just do it."

I whimper, short breaths coming out of my mouth as I squeeze my eyes shut. Ignoring the pressure of tears building up, I let my energy flow through my right hand. But the relief I usually feel doesn't come. As the sprinkles of pain slowly fade, I can feel my left hand, but it doesn't feel right.

I almost choke when I open my eyes. It takes a few seconds for my blurred vision to return to normal. I make a flame with my right hand, but for some reason, I can't do the same with my left.

"What?" I repeat over and over, glancing at Isra. Swaying back and forth, I grab my head to keep myself upright.

"That's interesting," Isra says, examining my arm.

"But—" I can't comprehend it. My hand feels detached from my body. "How am I supposed to—"

"It's okay," Isra says. "Right now, we need to leave."

"No. The plan—"

"Mahi, listen to me," Isra says the words slowly and helps me up. "Look around you. Look at what just happened."

There isn't much to argue with. I don't even know if we'll make it out of Hell. "Okay." I nod my head. "I'll follow you."

But not before I do this. Grabbing the scythe, I walk toward Ozanith. I'm not sure what I feel. I'm just aware that he's the one who did this to me.

"Leave him," Isra says.

I scowl at him over my shoulder. "Why?"

He sighs. "Believe me, Ozanith is loyal to anyone on the throne. And I mean anyone. He'll be useful in the future."

He deserves it. I want to scream at the top of my lungs. Instead, I place the scythe in my pocket. I can't help but hold my left wrist while I follow Isra out the door.

In the hall, he takes the mask off one of the knights,

revealing ghostly eyes and empty, bulging veins. Then he places it on his face.

"How do I look?" he asks. "I'm sure I pull this off better than them."

"What are you doing?"

"You mean we," he corrects, taking off the other demon's mask and handing it to me. "Disguises. Just enough to get to the portal."

I put the mask on. It sticks to my flesh like a new layer of skin. We quickly put on their armor, and I grab the scythe, which is now a gun. My eyes are glued to my left hand. If I can't make fire, then what about my healing?

"Don't think about it," Isra says. He sounds so emotionless. But I get it. It's not like I'm dead. As long as I'm alive, he doesn't care. This is something new for him to study. "Be careful with that and follow me."

I follow Isra back to the elevator, expecting to see a few demons after the commotion we just made, but there aren't any.

I keep a firm grip on the scythe once we step out of the elevator just to be safe. Although the halls are wide, I feel boxed in. I wonder what's in these countless rooms. Torture chambers? Bedrooms? Maybe they are empty and just here for show.

We walk among the halls for a while, sweat trailing down the side of my face. Finally, a new path forms on the carpet, growing toward an open door. Isra leans against one side of the opening while I'm on the other. After no one comes out, I risk a look inside.

I catch a glimpse of a giant circular portal beside what I think is a throne. The portal holds different swirls of blue that contrast with the room, which contains long black walls and huge windows that start from the floor all the way to the roof. They fall just behind the throne, revealing the red sky. The ceiling is higher than I can imagine and there's no one here. It looks abandoned.

Glancing at Isra, he nods his head. "It'll take us to his penthouse. Just walk to it like you belong."

Ignoring my clenching stomach from both fear and guilt of leaving Kavon, I follow his lead. It doesn't make sense why I'd feel terrible, but I do. Even though he ruined our entire plan. Then again, he believed it wouldn't work. So, he took his shot at freedom, even if it meant taking away mine.

Walking into the throne room, I realize how enormous it is. It's gigantic, and the emptiness doesn't feel right. It'll take us a while to get to the portal, but Isra doesn't stop, so I don't say anything either.

"Going somewhere?" I almost collide with Isra's back as he freezes. We both turn around, and relief floods my body when I see Zyanya, but I again turn to stone. That wasn't her voice. Slowly, I copy Isra, who's looking up ahead.

A pale-skinned demon is watching us from the ceiling, resting against one of the pillars. He jumps down, and the floor cracks underneath his feet.

Oh man, he's enormous. Those are probably the biggest muscles I've ever seen.

He grins while he walks up to us. His white horns curve back and down, almost into a circle of some kind.

"Heading back to Morningstar, prince Azazel," Isra speaks with a weird, gruff voice.

Azazel laughs, smacking his lips together. He walks

up to me with super speed. Isra pushes me to the side. But with inhuman agility, Azazel jumps through the air and lands in front of me. He grabs my right wrist, crushing my bones. The gun falls out of my grip.

I scream and try to form fire with my left hand, but nothing comes. Azazel pulls the mask off my face, hooking an arm around my throat. "That was too easy, considering you're the girl Lucifer's been looking for."

"Let me—" I cry out when he places pressure against my throat, all the hope I had of getting out of here vanishes when Zyanya knocks Isra to the ground.

Isra grunts as she twists her tail around him. For some reason, she's crying. And not just a few tears. Her cheeks are stained. "Where's Lucifer?" Isra asks.

"Outside," says Azazel. "He should be here soon."

Zyanya wipes her eyes but quiet sobs still leave her mouth. "Cut it out, Isra."

Azazel scoffs. "I can't believe you feel bad for him."

"I don't—" She sniffs, uncontrollable tears rolling down her scaly cheeks. "He's doing this."

"I'm doing this because, for some reason, that's the first emotion I sensed in you," Isra mutters.

The hopelessness fades away. For a slim second, I perk up at the twisted warmth of familiarity; a sense of safety. My eyes wander around the room as I look for Kavon. They shift to the portal where he walks out of, so casually like this is his home. He gives me a glance, no emotion on his face.

"You found them," he says.

"Because of you," Azazel says.

My jaw clenches. "You told them we were still here?"

"I rounded up all the humans in the city." Kavon

ignores me, looking past my shoulder. "They should be ready to go."

The doors at the end slam open. Now I realize why they were so huge. A gigantic flaming bird soars inside, and I'm blinded by its beauty. The bird falls onto the ground in between me and Isra, just as the phoenix slowly shrinks into a flaming person, the fire dying out to reveal Lucifer inside my dad's body.

I try to rip out of Azazel's grasp, only for the demon to tighten his grip on me. A shaking breath runs past my lips. I still have Kavon's sword in my pocket. That's the one thing they don't know.

I meet Lucifer's eyes. He tilts his head. "I'm done. No more tricks. You come with me now, or I'll tear your father's limbs off one by one."

It's not like I'm going to get out of here anyway, but he's taking away my chance of fighting back. I press my lips together.

"If I do it, they won't heal," he informs me. "I'll find a new vessel."

"Please, let him go."

Lucifer shakes his head and raises his arm. It glows as he slowly brings it down to his other one. Just as it's about to touch him, I struggle against Azazel's arms.

"Stop! Okay, stop," I cry out. "I give up."

Lucifer meets my eyes, raising his eyebrows. He nudges his head, and Azazel lets go of me. Lucifer tilts his head then, waiting for me. I ignore the feeling of bugs crawling under my skin and walk toward my father. My stomach flips with every step, and my heart skips a beat when Isra chokes behind me.

"Take Isra to the dungeon, Azazel and Zyanya,"

Lucifer says while I heal my right wrist with my face. "If he's not dead by the time I'm back, I'll take my time killing him. And Zyanya, don't let him escape this time."

Azazel, who seemed pretty smug when I first met him, scratches his head at the order, but he doesn't say anything. Both he and Zyanya grab Isra and walk out of here.

"Follow me," says Lucifer. "You too, Shadow Angel. In case she tries anything."

All of us manage to fit into the elevator despite how close the space is. Being in such proximity to Lucifer, I imagine him as someone else. Not Dad, but Gavril. Gavril wasn't so bad to be escorted by. I try to ignore Kavon and I's bond. He doesn't even look at me.

We walk past Lucifer's room, where I thought we'd be heading, and confusion replaces my fear when we enter a garden. The sky here is a clear blue and not the red I have come to expect. Lucifer wastes no time. He walks over to a flower bush, opening it like a door.

"Why the garden?" I manage to find my voice. We walk down a tunnel, the door closing behind us. Or, I should call it a hallway. The walls and floor are made of marble.

"Sometimes, I like that I can just walk into a room and enjoy the soft wind against my face and the blue sky. Reminds me of something my father made. Even if it is fake—"

"Why is this door there?" I clarify.

"Oh . . ." Lucifer trails off. "Well, no one would think to look here."

I frown. "Look for what?"

"Despite everything, I didn't expect Isra to cross me."

Lucifer ignores my question. We close in on another door. "I know he didn't like how I did things, but he was once one of my closest friends."

I freeze the second we step into the room.

I've seen so many things these past months. But *this*. This isn't real. It can't be.

There are shelves full of souls that are lined up against the walls. They are all contained in jars, glowing and pushing against the glass in an attempt to get out. I glance at Kavon. His jaw is on the floor. Even he's stunned. In front of us is a huge casket. Lucifer stares at it, sighing before motioning me to come closer.

"Finally." Lucifer strokes both my arms once I'm in front of him, pulling me into a hug. I know Kavon is watching, and I wish he'd leave.

When Lucifer pulls back, his grin turns into a frown. "What's wrong?"

I can't help but laugh. "You're actually insane. Unbelievable."

"Please, help me understand."

"You're about to kill me," I say. "And if you don't, you'll hurt my dad and destroy a city full of innocent people. How do you not understand that I fucking hate you?"

He flinches. "I have to do this."

"Do *what?*"

"Bring my brother back," he mutters. "It's my fault he's dead. And you can finally help me bring him back! I love him, and he would've loved you. I've just been planning this for too long for it to go to waste."

"You don't know what love is," I say, bringing my fingers to my back pocket. "You told me all this shit about how you'd help me learn my powers. How we could celebrate my birthdays and go to carnivals. How you'd give me everything I'd ever wanted! I always knew you meant none of that, especially since you always said that we *could* do those things. But we never were going to. I'm your daughter, and you're about to kill me. You think your brother will forgive you?"

"I—" He freezes. For a second, I don't see Lucifer, but my dad. "He won't. Oh my god, I'm doing to you what was done to me."

My eyebrows furrow, but I don't say anything. I let him ramble on while I clutch Kavon's sword. I know Kavon is watching me from behind, but he isn't doing anything.

"It doesn't matter," Lucifer says, holding my arms again. "I've waited far too long to not bring my brother back. You have to die."

"At least let my father go once I'm dead," I say.

He shakes his head. "No, I'm sorry."

"Please let me speak to him one last time then," I beg. "I can't do anything. Kavon is here, and he'll stop me if I attack you. Please let me talk freely to my father. Even for a few seconds!"

Lucifer's stare is distant. "Is that what you want?"

"Yes," I breathe out.

Lucifer caresses my cheek. I try not to cringe. "As my daughter, I'll grant you this one last wish. You have one minute." He closes his eyes, a slow breath coming out of his mouth. I whimper when there is a sweet softness to the dark brown eyes that look back at me.

"Mahi," he says, eyes glossy.

He engulfs me in a huge hug. His chest is like a

pillow, and pressure builds up against my eyelids as I think of what's going to happen.

I never want to let go, but we pull apart. "Dad, I'm so sorry," I start to ramble, blinded by the tears that bunch up in my eyes. "I never should've left the border. I'm so sorry—"

"I'm not angry," he says in Hindi. "I love you."

"I love you too." I try to control my tears, bringing out Kavon's sword.

Injure the vessel, and Lucifer will have nowhere to go.

"Wait—"

"I have to," I croak.

He grabs my right hand, and the sword falls from my grasp. He starts muttering something in a language I don't know. I groan as my veins glow yellow, and a lump begins to grow under my skin before revealing a rosy birthmark shaped like a circle. Inside it, a darker shaded sun forms.

"What is this?" I ask.

"Don't worry about it." He grabs the sword and hands it to me. I don't unsheathe it. Instead, fire erupts from the handle like a flaming sword.

"Now do it. He's itching at the back of—" Dad yells, clutching his skull. His eyes burst into flames.

"That's Michael's," his voice shakes.

My eyes widen. *Lucifer!*

He throws his arm out, and I fly to the back of the room against one of the shelves. Two jars fall but they don't break.

"Mahi!" he screams, eyes going back to normal.

"I still have time," I yell, fumbling with the sword

while Dad and Lucifer fight for his body. "My one minute isn't over."

"Kill me—*I'm going to disintegrate you*," he growls, but he's far too distracted with controlling his body to focus on me. Kavon comes up to me. His demeanor isn't threatening when he helps me up.

"Do it," he tells me.

I want to do the opposite and back off, but instead, I take quick steps toward Lucifer. My hand is in motion before I can stop myself.

I stab him. A bright orange light beams from his eyes, a piercing noise filling the air as his body burns into ashes. I choke when he leans into me, the ashes absorbing into my skin. Screeching, heavy breaths fumble out of my mouth. I drop the sword.

I had expected Lucifer to leave my dad's body and float around like some kind of essence, just like the demons, but somehow he's dead. I killed him with Kavon's sword. We had a weapon to kill Lucifer this entire time.

This whole time.

But I don't care. I feel a tightness in my chest before I burst into tears; the world spins around me.

He's gone. My dad is gone, and I killed him.

"It's okay Mahi." Kavon places his hands on my shoulder. "Thank you. I could never get that sword to work right."

As I turn around, something pierces my abdomen. A sharp pain engulfs my entire body. Slowly, I look down to see a knife inside me.

Kavon holds onto me tightly, pressing me against the

casket. He gives me a grim smile and says, "That was impressive."

"What are you do—" I scream when he twists the blade. "What are—" I struggle to breathe. "What are you doing?"

"I'm going to finish what Lucifer started."

"What?"

"You see, Mahi," he says, frowning as he grabs my hand when I try to heal myself. "You shouldn't be alive, but you are. That's what everyone's been telling you. And there really is nothing special about you. Absolutely nothing. Except you have celestial spirit and a soul, combined in one. It's strong enough to bring back a life. And finally, I can use it."

"But after everything we've been through—"

"You're so stupid, Mahi," Kavon says, shaking his head. "You think I just happened to risk my life for you . . . for what? I will thank you again, though. Finally, Lucifer can't sit on that throne."

"Kavon—"

"Don't talk." He lets go and takes a jar from one of the shelves. He quickly breaks it and absorbs the soul in one huge gulp. "Just relax."

Go to sleep—His voice echoes inside my head.

I clutch onto my skull. It's as if someone just dug their fingers in my brain. "Kavon, stop!"

You're really going to make me knock you out?

My body forcefully moves toward Kavon, and I close my eyes, preparing for a blow to the head. Instead, I'm met with the floor, gasping for air as the blade digs deeper into my body. My eyelids grow heavy with each blink, but I make out Kavon's collapsed form on the floor. His body tremors. His wings wrap around him and cover his face. A primal scream comes from his mouth.

Someone turns me over. Red eyes blind me.

"Mahi, we need to go." I can barely see Isra's face. "He's not going to be terrified for long."

"Yeah . . . yeah." Isra shakes me, and I look around one last time before the world turns dark.

31

When I open my eyes, I see the sky through the cracks of trees. The sun, covered in clouds, is almost dull as if it isn't there. A sense of relaxation, peacefulness and a steady, calm heartbeat overcomes me.

I'm dead. I should've expected death to feel better than living. Maybe I'm in Death's dimension because it's too nice to be Hell. Doesn't matter. I have no desire to be anywhere else. I don't *deserve* to be anywhere else, not after what I did.

My body goes numb. The lightness in my chest is replaced by a weighted heart, a chill running up my spine. I blink a few times, twitch my fingers, and finally sit up. A subtle breeze presses against my face, and it takes me a second to focus on Isra cooking some animal. When he meets my eyes, for a second, my breath catches in my throat as if I just saw a monster. But then he half-smiles, and I remember he saved my life.

"You're alive," he says, getting up from a log and

sitting beside me on the grass. Tensing, I back away from him, wincing at a sharp pain in my abdomen.

"What—" I clutch my stomach. "What happened?"

"Careful." Isra shuffles to be beside me. "I'm not sure your wound is fully healed. If you want to get on that."

"Where are we?"

He looks away. "We're. . . we're a country away from Morningstar. Farther than you think."

I tilt my head as I try to make sense of everything. "You took me away from everything I know?"

"I had to."

"I'm sorry—" I blurt. "That came out wrong." I exhale slowly before sucking in a sharp breath. I'm so damn *tired*. If only I could sleep for a thousand years. But by the time I wake up, the planet would probably be scorched. When I exhale, I groan at the burning pain in my stomach.

Kavon stabbed me. He *stabbed* me. That was his entire plan from the start. And he'll try again to take out my life force, soul, whatever it is. It doesn't matter how far away we go. He'll find me. No matter what, he'll always find me because of the bond. I press my hand against my face, my heart racing when I remember what happened to my left hand.

To my dad.

I pull away from Isra as the memories come rushing back. Kavon doesn't matter anymore. Nothing does.

"He's dead." Tears well up in my eyes. "Isra, he's dead."

"Mahi . . ." Isra's voice trails off. "I'm sorry. But the ferals—"

"I don't care," I scream, a waterfall of tears pouring

from my eyes. "Oh my gosh. He's dead. And I—" A shaky gasp leaves me, and I cover my lips.

"Talk to me," Isra whispers.

"No—" I squeeze my eyes shut. "I'm alone. He's dead because of me. And I'm alone. Everyone I care about is gone."

I don't know how long I sit there. Isra puts his arm around me at some point, and I don't think twice before leaning into his chest and heaving into his shirt. I don't care if he's a demon. I don't care about anything.

After everything, I'm still not free. No one is. Lucifer's dead, and yet we're not in the throne room talking about the new world. Who knows who's going to take control of things now. And I won't get to see it. Kavon will hunt me till my soul is torn from my body. The Shadow Angel, with all his support, will eventually find me.

I lick my lips, getting up and walking over to Isra's satchel. The smell of cooked squirrel makes my gut twist, but I ignore the hunger.

"Are you okay?" Isra asks from behind me. "You should rest. Or at least heal yourself."

An aggravated sigh leaves my mouth, and I roll my eyes before healing my stab wound. I rummage through Isra's bag. "I'm fine."

No, you're not. He's dead. And it was all for nothing.

I squirm, squeezing my temples. Isra takes the bag. He's about to place it down, but I speak before he can.

"Put it on," I whisper through my hiccups. I know he knows what I'm talking about. "You should've done it already. He'll find us if you don't. And he won't be alone this time."

Isra doesn't question anything. Frowning, he gently

grabs my right hand, the cold steel surrounding my wrist. My inner flame goes out, but it's nothing compared to the loss I feel.

He's dead because of you.

"No." I fall to the ground, choking on my hot tears. And I sit there, while Isra's hand gently rests on my back.

"Mahi—"

"I don't care about the ferals, Isra," I snap, rubbing my eyes. "They can eat me alive for all I care."

He tucks a strand of hair behind my ear. Usually, I'd shudder and walk away, but I don't have the energy. "Let me take the pain away."

I turn to stone and hiccup a few times. "What?"

"Let me take it away," he says again, wiping my tears with his thumb. "Give me permission, and it'll all just disappear. You won't feel a thing."

I killed my dad.

"That's crazy," I say, exhaling gently. My headache eases, but then I picture the moment all over again. The sword in my hand, the ashes, and the last time I saw my dad's face. I break into sobs once again before I nod my head. "Yes," I barely manage to speak.

Isra half-smiles, caressing my face. Slowly, my muscles ache from sudden tiredness. My eyelids droop down, and I lean back, staring at the grass.

I'm tired. Even more than I was minutes before. I could sleep endlessly for days.

Suddenly, all the worries I had are gone. Vanished into thin air as though nothing ever happened. I feel like I'm dreaming. The memory plays in my mind, but I don't feel my heartbreak.

Isra sucks in a breath, his eyes glowing and his veins fuller. He must feel as if he's on top of the world right now. I mean, I wouldn't know how much pain he took from me. I can't really remember what I felt. Right now, I just feel *nothing*.

ACKNOWLEDGMENTS

Writing a book is one of the hardest things I've ever done. I never thought I'd see the day *World of Lost Souls* would be published. It wouldn't have been possible without several amazing people.

First, thank you to my amazing brother Mandeep who read my entire novel in it's early stages. You offered amazing advice and kept up with all my annoying questions. To my cousin Raveen, who pulled me out of my imposter syndrome whenever I had doubts. To my mom and dad, who I am eternally grateful for all their support. You both are the best parents ever. As well as a thank you to all of my family, who never gave up on me.

Thank you so much to all my friends who supported me through the process and told me to keep going. From promoting my social media to helping me pick character names, I am so lucky to have all of you. I'm sorry for all the scenes I forced you to read.

And lastly, thank you to all my readers for supporting me and loving these characters as much as I do!

FOLLOW ME ON SOCIAL MEDIA

Jasmine Sidhu is a Canadian author who loves coffee and singing her heart out. She spends most of her time playing video games with her family, creating funny videos, and watching superhero movies. Anything but writing.

tiktok.com/@jaswritesbooks

instagram.com/jaswritesbooks

facebook.com/jaswritesbooks

Printed in Great Britain
by Amazon

10437694R00202